SURVIVE THE CITY

BOOK TWO OF
THE SURVIVE SERIES

ALEX TIMOTHY

FULL VOLUME
PUBLISHING

dedication

"Your visions will become clear only when you can look into your own heart. Who looks outside, dreams; who looks inside, awakes."
—C.G. Jung

other stories by alex timothy

Alien Heart

Survive Series

Survive the Streets
Survive the City
.

acknowledgements

Thank you sooooo much to Lesley-Ann Colgan for reading this book in its many, many forms. I'm sure you are relieved to see it published and not waiting in your email for the billionth time. Love you, girl!! Thank you James Daro for painstakingly going through the text with me and acting out the fight scenes. A big thanks as always to Alisha Costanzo. You give the best advice and are always so supportive and encouraging.

objective

1 Renee

As soon as she walked into the showy suburban party, Renée could pick out all the elements of her brother's planning. The spotless white of this soot-free mansion, when fire and ash covered every inch of their apocalyptic world. Those towering stacks of food—oranges, plates of imported cheese. Even bananas! *Where the hell did you find those, Gabriel?* Eight months into the worst pandemic the world had ever known, and her brother decided to host the government patrols, to serve them Camembert and fruit. *Very impressive showing, little brother.*

And then all these admiring children he surrounded himself with, their crazy dyed hair. He recruited them to his gang and named them all after himself. "What does he hope to accomplish here?" she muttered under her breath. Gabriel hadn't changed at all from the eccentric and idiotic boy she'd grown up with. "Feathertons…" she scoffed, touched her fingers to the pearls at her neck. Granny Featherton's pearls. What would that snobby old woman have thought of Gabriel labeling his criminal empire with their family name? *Daddy's name.* A flash of memory…Granny Featherton telling an eleven-year-old Renée not to talk so loud, not to throw her head back when she laughs. "It's not how a lady acts," she said and

1

touched her wrinkled fingers to the same pearl necklace. *That old bitch, I wish she could see this.*

Of course, Gabriel himself hadn't shown yet. Not to make a dramatic late arrival, like everyone here assumed. *Everyone but me.* Renée knew the truth, that her brother would need to minimize his exposure to the crowd, the noise, the influx of sensation inherent to a party. Same weak, volatile *freak.* Gabriel couldn't risk a breakdown in front of his devoted followers. He needed to impress the adults who controlled the remaining bones of infrastructure. "It won't work, little brother." These men would simply take what they want before they'd even acknowledge some suburban teenage gang and its leader. All he'd manage to do was incite their greed.

Dandridge and Lanson came up to flank her on either side. "Those hillbillies haven't shown yet," Lanson griped.

"Those hillbillies are the last hope of civilization in this mess outside the city," General Dandridge countered. "You'll do well to remember that, Lieutenant." Dandridge had been a commander on the army base before the outbreak, before the virus decimated it. Close quarters, too many men just outside of the survival range of fifteen to twenty-five… The young survivors weren't inclined to stay in place while the world around them, around their families, imploded. "Nothing here but these delinquent kids running wild. Someone should step in and take charge of this mess."

"Yes, sir." Lanson's jaw tightened. He was younger than Dandridge by at least twenty years. Twenty crucial years when it came to surviving the virus. Like Renée, Patrick Lanson had worked in a position of obscurity until all the people between him and his highest aspirations fell to Super-Flu. Renée wondered if Lanson looked forward to Dandridge catching the virus as much as she did.

Renée made a vague noise of agreement. Dandridge and Lanson and the rest of their entourage had no idea that she was the same age as these "delinquent kids." When the outbreak began, she had worked as a paid intern to the governor. Gradually, as everyone with legitimate power died, she became the last connection to the remnants of legitimate government. And she'd always looked older than her age. Men only noticed her face and body, the expensive clothing she wore. *Mother would be so proud.* The bitter words in her head made Renée wince. She followed it with a mantra of her father's, *"Whatever it takes to gain power."*

A blaring car horn and blast of music shook the windows on the back of the house—the only warning before Colton's people barreled into the back yard, driving their oversized pickup trucks.

"Is that them?" Lanson didn't hold back his disgust.

"Yes." Renée had expected this dramatic arrival. After all, she'd given that disgusting piece of work, Jaxon Colton, this idea to upstage her brother's party. She'd counted on Gabriel's complete inability to understand normal social interactions, to understand people. "Oh, he'll host an impressive party with all kinds of black-market food and booze and music…" she'd told Colton, ignoring his eyes as they roamed her breasts and legs. "But, my little brother has no understanding of fun or entertainment. Bring something for everyone to do—something they can't resist and won't forget," she'd told him.

Stupid, Rénee. She'd underestimated the psychopathic cruelty of someone like Colton. She'd meant for them to round up creatures they found on the highways, people who had ceased to be human long ago, staggering bodies with the virus fully in control. Not the feral sick that Colton's people started to throw into the empty swimming pool. Newly popped, newly infected—*these people have a chance of recovery.* But, Colton bound their arms and hands to ensure the fight stayed in the favor of anyone willing to jump down into the pool crater. "Creature Cracking"—a term used to describe anyone who went searching for the sick, to kill them for fun. The feral sick rarely attacked first.

At last, she spotted her brother.

Gabriel. His tall, thin frame outlined by the LED spotlights on the back deck. He'd dressed formally, all in black, just as she had. His height, bright red hair, and high cheekbones—inherited from their mother—made him stand out in the crowd. But, Renée saw past this glossy, superior version of her brother to a little boy with trembling lips and a snotty nose. Pauline Dufort Featherton called her son "broken," and she cringed away from Gabriel's many, many meltdowns.

Renée nodded toward where Gabriel stood, completely still, frozen in the center of unruly partygoers. *You must be barely keeping yourself together, little brother.* "That's him," she pointed Gabriel out to both Dandridge and Patrick Lanson. "My little brother," she sneered. No one would guess that she meant he was younger in minutes instead of years. "We weren't raised together," she added, a lie just to distance herself further.

As twins, they had spent their early years side-by-side, closed inside a spacious nursery with blue-and-white striped walls, a white rocking horse that neither of them played on, a string of nannies who spent more time fawning over their direct-to-video movie star mother than paying attention to her sullen twins. "I barely know him." Another lie. She knew her brother like a part of herself. She knew his frail nerves, his explosive temper. She knew his spoiled nature. Even if Pauline rejected him, Gabriel had always been their father's favorite. *Daddy's golden child.*

Kids hung off the deck railing and screeched to the brawling in the pool. Pulsing music blared around them, a wild post-apocalyptic rave. And even though Colton instigated the chaotic, frenzied atmosphere, it only highlighted the undisciplined youth of Gabriel's followers. Before the outbreak, someone would have called the police to break it all up. But this was Featherton territory now.

From her vantage point diagonal to him, Renée could see Gabriel's entire body poised in rigid control over his fight-or-flight response. How many times had she seen her brother fall apart in similar situations? He would crumple, squeeze his eyes shut, cover his ears, and shake. What would these military and government men think of him then? What would his *followers* think?

Then, something grabbed her brother's attention, the curly-haired boy she'd stopped earlier who'd looked at her with a deer-in-headlights expression. The boy had buckled over in a faint, and Gabriel swung into action to rescue him. Her brother threw his arms around the skinny kid and dragged him from the thickest part of the crowd, back into the empty kitchen. *Lucky break, little brother.* Looked like Gabriel found a perfect excuse to get out of the mob.

"This is outrageous and a waste of time," Lanson griped. "No one participating in this frenzied bloodlust and chaos deserves our respect."

Renée took another look at the people bludgeoning down the victims of the virus. "I suppose you're right," she said, hardly able to hold back her smile. "We should give up the idea of working with them." She looked one last time at the writhing, bound, sick people getting thrown into the empty pool, the candy-colored heads of the kids fighting them.

In the center of the melee, swinging a baseball bat dripping with chains and gore, she recognized Peyton Tyrone. Tall, muscular, his golden blond hair with blue-dyed tips flew back from his strong features, square jaw. *"He's beautiful,"* she almost said it aloud. *How had a freak like Gabriel managed to befriend this flawlessly masculine boy before the outbreak?* The outbreak had twisted his perfect American high-school-hero image into something vicious…dangerous. And Renée couldn't help but admire the result. *If I could have someone like that at my side…*she could take whatever she wanted. She could rule the entire city and everything surrounding it.

5

She could create an empire with someone like Peyton Tyrone at her side.

2 Gabriel

Don't fidget. You are in control. Gabriel has his hands folded in front of him on his father's desk. Willpower keeps his legs and fingers still. "It has to be you," he tells Case.

She refused the seat opposite him, so now Gabriel has the unpleasant experience of her standing over him with her folded arms and angry eyes, still blaming him for Peyton's monthslong absence. It makes his skin crawl. *You are in control.*

Case Bell does not look happy. "And you want me to tell her I'm going behind your back?"

"Yes. That's exactly what I want. Tell Renée you have side business—that you'll go behind my back to get her an extra tanker every four days. In exchange, you want meds that you plan to trade here in the territory."

Huffing disapproval. "So, not just defying you, but also betraying Feathertons."

"Correct. Those are my orders." *You are*—the fingers of one hand start drumming against the surface of the desk, rapid muted tapping. Gabriel springs up, thrusts his hands into his pants pockets. He paces to the fireplace. "Take the delivery and make the trade. Then report back to me. Shane will tail you for backup, but you won't see him."

Behind him, Case makes another frustrated noise, and the study's French doors creak open.

Finally. But, when he spins around, she's still there. Looking guilty of all things. "Why are you still here? I told you what to do. Now leave."

The round expressive eyes widen. She takes a deep breath. Gabriel knows Case Bell dislikes him, dislikes the Feathertons organization on principle, dislikes him personally because she still loves Peyton, and she suspects Gabriel sent him away. But Gabriel still values Case's honesty and bravery. He trusts her not to fumble this assignment and not to double-cross him.

That he's ordered her out, snapped at her, doesn't seem to register at all. Case catches and releases the door handle like she's thinking of leaving but can't seem to do it. "I think I should tell you... There are a lot of rumors about what really might be going on here in the compound."

Every muscle tenses. *Stay still. Don't move. Don't change expression. Don't change your breathing.* "What do people think is 'really going on here' despite the entire compound being accessible to anyone in my organization?"

"Accessible...maybe. But you're the only one who really knows what's behind every door, and you're the only one who knows every plan."

Because it would be extremely naïve to let that information be common knowledge—to guard every door that mattered, or to let Feathertons' resources and needs... He stares her down stone-faced, but even the breath inside him wants to tremble in frustration. *You are the one in charge, in control, and you don't have to tell her anything. You can say nothing at all.* He says nothing at all.

"There are rumors that you might be doing experiments on people, and trying to find a cure...or something worse."

"They suspect I'm keeping Bailey Tyrone alive, I already know this. Once he recovers, they'll be ready to hear me out on my ideas for an infirmary. We don't have to kill every person who *pops*." He can't hide the disgust in his voice at the slang term for those who reach the acute stage of the virus. "Once everyone sees that Bailey has survived, any rumors like this will end. He's young and healthy, so it can't be much longer."

Case steps closer, brow furrowed. "There's more."

Gabriel admires this about her, too. She doesn't shy away from speaking her mind if something needs to be said. "What *more*?"

"People think that you made him sick. That you tricked him into living here and then infected him on purpose. After what Colton did, turning people just to kill them for fun, use them as weapons…it isn't that hard to believe."

That people believe him capable of terrible things doesn't bother Gabriel, it's an unfortunate part of trying to keep his territory in line and protected. But that anyone would believe him capable of hurting Bailey is intolerable, excruciating. He has killed, destroyed, and suffered for Bailey. "Who is saying this?" His voice shakes. *You are in control. You are—*

Case's round dark eyes soften, and she bites at her lower lip. "Too many people, Gabriel."

"It doesn't matter. Once Bailey recovers, the rumors will stop." He turns to stare into the glowing embers of the fire. *You are in control.*

"I know you wanted to help Bailey," Case says. Gabriel can't turn around if that means facing Case's soft eyes and kind words, just the thought of her behind him with all her tender sympathy makes him want to scream out his rage.

"I know you wanted to help," she repeats. "But it's been months and—"

"Just *go* and stop wasting my time with all your gossip and…your *concern*," he spits out. He remains still, afraid to breathe, to look anywhere but into the fire. "One of the brothers will drive you home." Since Colton's attack on the mansion, Hugo and Felix Mageo both live in Gabriel's home with him. Shane, Gabriel's head of security, insisted on it. One of them, they look enough alike to be identical twins, pokes his head into the study. *Listening at the door.*

"I'll take you, Case."

"Take your brother with you, I want to be alone."

"Sure thing, boss."

Gabriel waits to hear the front door snick closed...and then he bolts from the study for the basement door. Trembling fingers key in the code on the lock.

I just need to see him. To see that he's still alive. Still here.

***

Down a flight of stairs in the dark and cool of the underground room is the barred cage. Two small plug-in nightlights near the stairs are the only illumination. Creatures abhor bright light. "Bailey?" he whispers into the shadows, clears his throat. "Bailey, it's Gabriel Featherton. Do you recognize me?"

When he comes further into the room, he can make out the vibrating sound of a person moaning. Gabriel preferred not to restrain Bailey. The abandoned quarantine camps held plenty of evidence of how that could go wrong—arms chewed off, legs twisted from their knees, hands and feet tied to a bed, but ripped free from wrists and ankles.

"I've come down here every day. I've stayed here every night with you." His voice cracks a little. *Unacceptable. Stop it.* He swallows, pulls himself under control again. "Do you remember me?"

The low keening noise stops. Inside the cage, a shadowy figure uncurls, and a pale, hollow cheeked face turns Gabriel's direction.

Bailey had ripped apart everything Gabriel shoved inside the cage with him, the floor now thick with towels torn to rags, a snowfall of cushion stuffing covering all the furniture, and slick rotting viscera of animal carcasses underlying everything. Bailey doesn't recognize food unless he kills it himself, won't drink water that isn't running in a thin stream through the cage bars.

This close, the smell becomes a fog of rot and death.

Weeks after the outbreak first began, Gabriel had awakened in this same basement cage. His father's arms scooped him up, carried his emaciated body up the stairs to suffer the fever and seizures of the virus' final stage in a comfortable bed. The memory causes his breath to catch, and sweat beads on his skin under his crisply-ironed shirt. The shadows and mess inside the cage blur, and his heart speeds up. *Stop it. This isn't helping. Don't think of him.*

Gabriel unbuttons his shirt and gulps the room's putrid air, but he can't stop the wave of crushing panic making him grip the iron bars of the cage as the room swims in front of him. *You are in control.* When the room sharpens back into focus, Gabriel lunges backward from the cage just in time.

Bailey has the telltale crouch and clawed hands of the acute phase of the virus, after the "pop" to senselessness and violence. He's bitten at or torn his lower lip, and a trail of dark blood gums his chin and neck. His loose ash-blond curls are mostly matted dreadlocks. His gray eyes focus on Gabriel, ready to charge.

Talk to him. Remind him that he's not this creature driven by the virus. He can still change back. At seventeen years old, Bailey falls perfectly into the sweet spot for recovery between ages fifteen to twenty-five. He could still recover…despite what Case thinks.

"Do you remember when we first met?" Gabriel takes slow, even steps backward until the calves of his legs scrape against the metal camp bed where he spends most nights. *I'm so tired…so, so tired.* Little by little, he lowers himself to sit on the cot. The tension in Bailey's coiled body eases just a fraction.

"My father had taken me to meet with the principal at Memorial. The school psychologist insisted on being included, along with two counselors and the school resource officer. As you can imagine, the school wasn't exactly enthusiastic about having me as a student."

That meeting had nearly broken Gabriel. He'd had to sit perfectly still, disinterested, as the entire room reviewed his history. His incarceration. The recommendations of his doctors.

Shuffling a little closer, Bailey tilts his head like a dog puzzling out words it doesn't understand. He scratches at his naked chest with the stiff clawed fingers, blood wells up into shallow marks he leaves behind.

Keep talking.

"You burst in and interrupted the whole thing, making all those demands for a student computer lab and waving your arms around, getting completely worked up about it. I'd never seen someone so willing to embarrass themselves." Gabriel's sudden laugh startles both of them, and they both seem to hold their breath for a moment. Gabriel decides to let the quiet settle for a while as he relives their first meeting again.

Bailey had interrupted the meeting, grabbed the corner of the table in front of Gabriel, expecting to be thrown out before he got to say his piece. A fat, grizzled security guard followed him inside. Gabriel had gotten a face full of wild hair. It smelled of outdoors and minty shampoo. Bailey's flailing arms and legs shook the conference table, knocking over Gabriel's untouched bottle of water and everyone else's styrofoam coffee cups, and all the official documents that labeled Gabriel as unfit for society.

"Just let Student Council have a fundraiser! Sell pizza in the cafeteria or something!"

The principal had rolled his eyes. "As I've explained to you many, many times, Mr. Tyrone, a full computer lab would take much more money than a single fundraiser, and we've already allocated funds for the year."

***

11

Gabriel speaks again into the silent basement. "Do you remember, Bailey? You threw yourself at the conference table, spilled water, made a disaster out of that meeting, and I thought you were…"

Bailey had been a blur of messy curls and energy as he made his impassioned plea for the computer lab. At first, he had reminded Gabriel of one of the more delusional hospital patients during a manic phase. After all, this curly-haired boy had a laptop bag hanging from his shoulder. It smacked Gabriel in the chest before he could scoot his chair backward. So, *he* had a computer. Did he care this much about his fellow students? Didn't he consider them competition? He should be glad to have an advantage over some of them!

"If this was about the football team or the stadium repairs, no one would make a fuss over moving funds around!" Bailey's face had flushed, his already white-knuckled grip on the table tightened. He was practically sitting in Gabriel's lap at that point. Which he must have realized, too. "Sorry about this," he'd said, so sincere, large gray eyes framed in long curling eyelashes.

The spike of attraction had jolted Gabriel from the suffocating panic, his certainty that this humiliating meeting would come to nothing. And he turned to his father. "Maybe, we can help fund this computer lab idea?"

At last, Gabriel had found the leverage he needed if he didn't want to be shipped off to some boarding school where privacy would be impossible, or stuck at home on his own, nothing to distract from his own barely manageable mind.

And this boy with his long lashes and flailing limbs and…now dimples when he smiled, somehow managed to hand it right to him. "Really?" Bailey shook loose of the angry security guard. "*That* would be so awesome." He turned his blinking-eyed eagerness on the principal. "We can't be the only high school in the district without a student computer lab!"

"I would be happy to fund a computer lab in my son's school," his father had neatly added.

"The way you looked at me. No one ever…" *looked at me like that before.* Like Gabriel was the solution, instead of the problem.

He'd liked it. More than liked it, he'd marveled at it. And he'd set about to get that look from as many people as possible, in as many ways as possible.

But, the earnest boy with the messy hair and the gray eyes always drew Gabriel's attention back.

***

Inside the cage, Bailey grips his knees, and the low crying sound starts again. He's naked and dirty and way too thin and beaten up. His bones protrude from his ribs and knees. Long scratches cover his legs. He's also shivering.

Gabriel stands and feels along the wall for the thermostat, slides the little lever until the heat kicks in with a rumble.

Bailey startles and crab crawls backward into the shadows.

"I think I became obsessed with seeing that look again…from you," says Gabriel. "I tried…so many ways to get that again from you."

Gabriel laughs, bitter and hoarse. "But everything I did to try and impress you only made you angry with me."

He waits against the wall near the thermostat for a long time, tries not to move or make noise, but Bailey stays hidden in the shadows.

mass

3 Renee

"Wait 'til you see this." The pimply teenager adjusts the belt of his ill-fitting fatigues. As far as Renée can tell, the boy scavenged his used military uniform from someone twice his size. Both Renée and Lieutenant Patrick Lanson lean over the kid's shoulders to watch security footage. "That's the guy—sliding under the barricade fence," says the teen soldier. The city barricade was intended to contain the people on the inside, keep the virus on the outside. But as the months passed, and the dead piled up, both police and soldiers struggled to guard the tall fencing and winding barbed-wire entry points.

Renée squints as she watches the screen…the tall muscular figure of the man. *You…*

In the video, he throws bricks into the windows of an abandoned church, uses his club to sweep through the shadow of a rusted car, kicks loose rubble into a doorway alcove.

"Creature Cracking—he wants to scare them out for a fight," Lanson explains.

And looks like he got his wish. Five decaying bodies emerge from their hiding spots, confused and angry. On the laptop screen, the man flashes a toothy white grin, holds his club in front of him as the creatures circle him.

The kid in fatigues raps a hand on the desk in front of him. "This is so cool," he gushes.

***

The circling feral sick crouch low, ready to attack. When two of them pounce, the man swings his club, making quick, powerful contact with the first creature's head—in the perfect spot.

"Bam! One hit, and he gets right at the junction. And, check it out, he gets *all* of them that way. *One* hit." The kid punches at the air, while, on the screen, the man spins and takes out a second creature. He leaps forward and kicks, smashing down two more. His heavy boot stomps on one of their necks as he twists to bring his club down on the other. When he swivels to confront the last creature, two more drop from a broken window of the office building behind him. They begin to close in on him, and he punches out with the club, a horizontal strike that knocks one of the newcomers to the ground before the man delivers the swift killing blow to the back of the neck—where the virus collects. That crucial juncture between spine and brain that must be destroyed to break the virus' connection to the body. To let the victim die.

"Did you see that?" The boy turns toward Renée with a wide grin.

She feels Lanson stiffen beside her. "You're watching someone fight for his life, soldier. This isn't a video game."

The pimply boy in the baggy fatigues doesn't bother to straighten up or hide his excitement. "But that's why it's so cool. This guy is a fucking animal."

Lanson gestures to the computer screen. "We picked up the man you're watching not long after this fight. Not a scratch on him."

In the video footage, Peyton Tyrone finishes off the remaining creature. He chases it down, tackles it to the ground before making a stiff two-handed plunge with his club into the creature's skull.

Renée recognized him immediately, despite his changed appearance since she last saw him. Peyton has cut off the blue ends of his shaggy hair that marked him as a Featherton. That name...*her* name. She unclenches her jaw, forces herself to relax.

Lanson acts like he disapproves of the pimply soldier's admiration, but the lieutenant also stares fixedly on the screen with something close to awe on his face. "When we picked him up, he openly admitted to sneaking into the city, even though he knows he could be shot for it." Lanson folds his arms across his chest and tips his head toward Renée. "But, instead of pleading his case, he just asked us if we'd seen the security footage. Cocky bastard." Renée understands the fascination that same skill and savagery had captivated her at the party months earlier.

Renée hums, taps a finger on the laptop screen. "So he came in through the barricade on your side? How surprising. It's usually the government side that gets breached." She grinds her teeth to keep her voice even and pleasant. "You don't guard my borders as well as you guard your own." But the military still helps itself to her resources, her carefully rationed food stores, her dwindling stores of fuel, all her medicines, and the skilled civilians.

Lanson doesn't have Dandridge's years of service to perfect his military bearing. "We can't manage all the protection, not all the time, Mayor," he shoots back. Then his lips tighten to nearly white before he releases them with a puff of air. "It's General Dandridge's call which areas need the most patrolling. Not mine. But, I didn't see any reason to tell the General about this."

Interesting. "Hmmmm... It's probably best that someone as old as Dandridge doesn't get his hands dirty. He's more vulnerable to the virus than you." Dandridge looks over fifty, has a potbelly. One scratch, one bite, a splash of blood in his eyes...

"I just didn't want to shoot him," Lanson says, matter of fact. "It seemed like a waste of talent." And *there*, the flicker of emotion she

16

is waiting for in Lanson's face. *He's not so different from the pimply teen salivating over Peyton's fighting skill...not so different from me...*

"So, why do you need me?"

Lanson's eyebrows draw together, creating a deep worry line between them. "It would be impossible to hide someone of this caliber on my end without Dandridge taking notice." For the first time she can remember, Patrick Lanson drops all pretense at his position and hers. He meets her eyes with his own. "I was wondering if you could use him?"

Yes. Renée lays a hand on his uniformed arm. "It would be my pleasure, Patrick." Lieutenant Lanson appears unaware of the contact, but Renée's hand trembles on his uniformed arm. She has a sudden flash of memory, her glamorous mother doing the same gesture as she works the room during a party. Pauline's glossy red hair piled on top of her head, her manicured nails set off by sparkling rings. *What are you doing?* Renée pulls her hand away. *You aren't like her.* She straightens her shoulders. "Take me to him," she says.

***

Peyton tips his chair back on two legs to lean against the wall. Lanson had the mystery fighter brought to an office building near the halfway point of the city. Renée finds him in a private conference room, feet propped on the table in front of him, chair balanced precariously, guards and a couple hanger-ons listening intently as he talks about the security video fight.

"It's not the first time I saw them bust out a window to get free. They're dumb as fuck, hear a noise and just run. See something they want and can't figure out how to use the stairs."

"That piston move—"

"Man, that's nothing. I could show you."

Renée has to clear her throat twice before the little clique of soldiers move aside for her to enter.

"Come on in," Peyton says, curling his fingers toward Renée. "Took you long enough." He makes the same lazy perusal of her body that he did when she encountered him in the suburbs. "Did you like my audition? I wasn't sure the camera caught the first couple takedowns." With one arm, Peyton mimics the high swing of the club that had turned Lanson's young soldier into a fist-pumping fanboy.

"It was impressive." Renée stifles the smile she wants to crack. "You do know that anyone who doesn't enter the city through a checkpoint is *typically* shot on sight."

"Yeah, but the checkpoint guys didn't like me very much." Peyton hefts his feet off the table to let the chair drop down. "So, I found some moving cameras and got myself attacked. Someone really needs to clean out that part of town, whole place is crawling with creatures."

Muscular denim clad thighs spread, thick arms rest on the table in front of him. He's the kind of powerfully built, good-looking boy who has never known a moment of self-doubt or timidity. Renée can't take her eyes off him.

"I thought it was supposed to be safe in the city." He says it like a challenge.

"The military has too much responsibility guarding the perimeter and running the checkpoints. And my side has to manage the flow of rations and services."

"And keeping the pharma labs going," Peyton adds.

He might as well have thrown a bucket of ice water over her attraction to him. "So…my brother sent you? What is he offering?"

Peyton laughs, the corners of his bright blue eyes crinkling. "Not even close. I had a friend who did some trading with you, remember?"

Months earlier, when Colton still held the refinery in Cushing, Renée had tried to open a backdoor route through Featherton territory. She'd gone to an abandoned toll station to meet with a girl named Case, but found Peyton instead.

"Anyway, I don't care about that shit." The smile drops, and he runs a hand through the thick blond hair. "Gabriel's had me doing scavenging duty for months, and I'm sick of it. You were right about him, he talks a good game...but he's not the all-knowing genius he wants everyone to think he is."

"And I'm supposed to believe you had a sudden epiphany about this?"

"I only stuck around for my brother, and now..." His chiseled features turn to a frozen mask.

Renée remembers Peyton's brother. The curly-haired boy who fainted at Gabriel's party. So, that tender-hearted boy contracted Super-Flu... "Infected... Popped?"

Peyton's eyes skitter away, and he nods. One shaking hand makes a fist. "Eight weeks and four days."

"*Eight*... You tried keeping him alive? Are you fucking stupid?"

"Yeah, I guess I am...*was*. Not anymore."

Renée sighs, looks away. She's in danger of losing control of the city because of people who made this same mistake. Who *keep* making that mistake. Even this brash boy thought he could lock up someone he loves...loved and wait out the virus. "Sorry for your loss." Her words come out flat, and Peyton rolls his eyes.

"Whatever. I just want to fight, seems like you need a fighter." Peyton does a lazy shrug, tips one hand open. "I got no reason to be loyal to Feathertons anymore." His cornflower blue eyes meet hers. "And you seem interesting."

"Interesting?" She likes that, a thrum she feels in her chest. "It's true that I could use you..." His appearance here proves that he's both reckless and disloyal. Still, someone with his charisma and talent could train and unite her struggling police force, clean out the half of the city she runs. "*If* you've completely broken with Feathertons, then yes. Come work for me."

A slow smile spreads across Peyton's face—it makes him look meaner, threatening. "You got yourself a deal...*Mayor.*"

4 Gabriel

The next morning, Gabriel drives himself to The Greens. Shane doesn't like it. Featherton Territory has grown beyond just the people who knew Gabriel, knew his parents. But, Gabriel just can't stand the company right now, even that of someone as loyal as Shane. *Not after another night in the basement...waiting.* Gabriel's grip tightens on the leather steering wheel. At least this latest round of complaints from a Neighborhood Watch will distract him. *As long as I can keep my anger in check—not lose control.* "Why the *hell* didn't I prevent those damn watch groups from getting so powerful?" His arm jerks, sudden, involuntary, frustration whiting out his common sense, and the car swerves on the empty road. Tires squeal as he wrenches the wheel back, skirting a line of cement blocks stacked like a wall against the jungle of overgrowth. "Shit!" *Get control.*

What if he had hit a runner? What if one of them *saw?* Everything Case told him about rumors has him on edge and paranoid. "I should have brought Shane," he mutters as the wide gates of The Greens open up to him. *Too late now.* A group of angry adults, two gray-faced men, a blonde woman, a handful of onlookers behind them, confront his sixteen-year-old storehouse manager. Thank God the kid shows no signs of intimidation. Rico Loeza has all the might of Feathertons at his back, and he knows it. The kid leaves the seething neighbors behind him to meet Gabriel at the car and fill him in.

"These assholes are starting to piss me off." Rico has a sour look on his face. He fishes a cigarette from his shirt pocket as he talks and lights it. Gabriel assigned Rico as the new storehouse manager for the neighborhood after a creature attack killed Rico's predecessor. Rico's older sister, his lieutenant for Quail Creek, got caught stealing from Feathertons. So, Gabriel took the three brothers from her family to live on the compound as assurance Angelica Loeza didn't suffer another lapse in her loyalty. "They need to remember who's in charge around here."

"Meaning Spencer? Why hasn't Spencer handled this?" Gabriel put the boy in charge of The Greens after Peyton left. In high school, Spencer Clarkson had worked under Bailey on the yearbook. He'd seemed competent and shrewd.

"Good question, boss." And Rico Loeza sounds like he already knows the answer. "Spencer's not much of a hands-on lieutenant, if you know what I mean. He's too busy counting up inventory and writing out request lists for the compound runners."

"That's—"

"Which, *sí*, is my job. But he keeps sending me out here to deal with these assholes." He makes an impatient wave toward the Watch leaders. "Because he's a chickenshit. Scared of his shadow." Beyond his function as a hostage, Rico has proven himself an excellent acquisition. Competent and with a backbone in him that makes him seem older than his years. He takes a deep pull of cigarette smoke and closes his eyes to release the smoke from his nose. "So here's the deal—the neighborhood wants to keep whatever they forage on the golf course. Mostly acorns and mushrooms. But I told them you want all of it turned over to the storehouses." Rico makes a disgusted snarl. "If Spencer did his job right, this shit wouldn't happen." Then he must see what Gabriel wants to say, because he jumps backward, waves his hands in front of him. "I do not want the job either. No way, boss."

21

The dramatic flailing reminds him of Bailey, and Gabriel shoves down the confusing mixture of emotions from that comparison. *Stay in control.* But his nerves start crackling under his skin.

Rico taps the cigarette out on the thigh of his jeans. "The Greens is too fucking big now, and…I'm not exactly a people person, if you know what I mean." He shakes his head. "You got Angelica, but the brothers in our family don't do good with negotiating shit."

"Peyton Tyrone is also 'not exactly a people person' and he ran The Greens for a year."

One gray-faced man breaks free of the cluster of Watch members. "We don't want Peyton back here!" he yells.

"I didn't ask for your opinion." Gabriel finds one of his hands clutched in the collar of the gray man's sweater. "I decide who runs The Greens." Every tensed muscle in Gabriel's body wants to beat this man down to a pulp, to a heap of skin and tissue that will go into the burning pit.

"I…I didn't mean to—"

"Boss. You okay?"

The clenched fist opens, and the man trips on his own feet to get back with the others. *Control. You are in control.* The Greens and Pierce Heights are the two largest and most important of his neighborhoods, and Gabriel can't allow them to destabilize.

"The golf course belongs to The Greens," he decides.

Rico throws up his hands in defeat. But then, Gabriel faces the craggy faces of the Watch. "I'm leaving it up to you to determine who can keep the foraged food on it."

Before they look too smug, he adds, "My people will be monitoring, and—if it becomes a problem—then the course and everything on it reverts back to Feathertons' holdings."

No one argues. No one would dare.

The blond woman steps forward, the Neighborhood Watch leader, Jenny Truman. "Thank you, Gabriel." Bailey and Peyton's father has lived with her since Lila Tyrone's death. And Mason Tyrone hasn't once come to ask about Bailey's survival, about Peyton's whereabouts.

Gabriel stifles the urge to sneer at her ingratiating smile. "You've been warned," he says and turns away.

He gives Rico a ride back to the day's storehouse and assures him a change will be made regarding Spencer Clarkson. But Gabriel still doesn't want to go back to the mansion, and he has a full tank of gas. He drives the cleared roads of his territory, passing runners zipping by on motorcycles, hauling trailers of goods from storehouse to customer. *I need a better system.* Too bad his thoughts and plans keep getting interrupted by the memory of Case's dark eyes and soft words. *"It's been months and—"*

Fuck her. Gabriel promised Bailey that he would recover. He *will* recover. For the second time that day, his hand moves without his permission, this time to rub at his forehead. *Control, damn it. Control.* He'll need every shred of it for what he knows is coming, for the inevitable clash with his sister. Renée orchestrated the raid on Olde Town, and because of her, Colton took Bailey. Because of her, Cecilia died. All of it, because of Renée's misplaced hatred.

As children, they slept on matching twin beds in a large nursery. Renée's polished white headboard wore a stenciled blue R, and in the same curlicue script, Gabriel's a G. They started as friends, partners. Once Nanny shut off the light and told them to sleep, they would whisper secrets back and forth. Gabriel always had the same secret. "I hate them. Nanny, too. I wish I lived here with just you, and we never had to leave the nursery."

His sister folded her hands under her chin. "Daddy is nice. I love daddy."

"I don't like Daddy either." He especially didn't like when his father made him sit beside him on the stiff leather couch in his library. His father would drink alcohol from a heavy crystal glass.

"You remind me of myself at your age," he would say, even though everyone always told Gabriel how much he looked like Pauline, his mother. *"But you're going to be so much more than me. You will be my heir and my greatest achievement."* And then his father would ramble at Gabriel about his work, about his plans, and about women he had sex with. *Disgusting.*

"You're lucky to be a girl, Renny. You don't have to be Daddy's *greatest achievement.*" But Renée didn't take that well at all. She'd reached across the ten inches between their beds and pinched Gabriel's arm with her nails. "Shut up, *Gabrielle.*"

"That's not my name!" He rubbed his arm, and a smear of blood came away from where her nails broke the skin. His breathing stuttered. "I'm bleeding." He could feel one of his fits bubbling up. His whole body tingly and vibrating. As he glared at her in the low light, he saw her clutch the white crocheted covers and roll over, putting her back to him. "Don't talk to me."

He looked over at Renée's blonde hair, the tight ball of her body turned away from his. "Why are you so mean, Renny?"

"Don't talk to me."

Gabriel hadn't understood her feelings, not until much later, when her jealousy caught fire and burned away everything good in his sister. Not until she'd become unreachable to him.

"You're better than this, Renny. You're better than either of them, and so am I."

5 Renee

After she sets Peyton free, she tells him to find a place to squat in Central Business District, in Renée's half of the city. Her people control five of the eight districts within the barricaded city, but a nearly equal square footage to the military's half. Only one important structure is on the army's side of the city, and she has to ask for a military guard to escort her to the Capitol Building. General Dandridge sends Renée's courier running back from Park Plaza District looking red-faced and teary, but the military Hummer appears at noon like she asked. Lanson waiting inside. They both remain silent for the ride, and Renée assumes the other two soldiers belong to Dandridge.

Lanson leaves them waiting outside as he follows her into the building, walks her to the governor's office. "Is there a reason the General needed to abuse my courier?" she asks him. Her heels click against the dusty marble floor. The abandoned Capitol has fallen into such disrepair that it reminds her of a haunted house she'd gone to as a child.

Lanson sighs. "I don't think he likes two sets of orders coming into the city. Your bosses, his bosses…in a state of emergency like this…" Lanson doesn't finish that thought. "And then there's the issue of fuel…"

"I'm working on that." They stop outside the heavy wooden door to the Governor's office. "Wait here."

A crisp nod, and Lanson straightens like he means to stand at attention in front of the door. Renée's lips curve into a smile, she leans into Lanson's personal space. "You aren't a guard anymore, Patrick. You're the second-in-command now."

When he flushes, she stifles a laugh. "I forget sometimes, too," she offers. A lie. Her days as a pretty intern fetching coffee and filing reports still feel too close.

Lanson's eyes flick toward her. Between the sighs and the open irritation, he's let down his guard around her. *Maybe I can thank the cocky suburban football hero for that?* Letting Peyton stay alive has become a secret from Dandridge that they both share. *That I'm open to his undermining the General.* Maybe Lanson has started to see her as a potential ally?

When the door shuts behind her, Renée closes her eyes and breathes out. Like everywhere in the city, the dropping temperature has cooled the beautifully appointed governor's office just beyond comfortable. When winter really settles in, all these chilly rooms will freeze. And, in the middle of the country, no one has reliable information on what kind of weather they will face.

We need fuel, power.

She opens her eyes and strides to the desk but doesn't sit, throwing open the heavy brocade curtains instead. *Gabriel has what we need.* That selfish prick. *He's never had to wait for what he wants, to compromise.*

Renée's earliest memory is of her mother snatching Renée's favorite toy, a plush pink bear, from her hands, "Give your brother the bear, for God's sakes!"

Gabriel had thrown himself to the floor again, screaming, clutching his hands over his ears as soon as they arrived at the Easter party.

Pauline had thrust the plush bear toward her son, and he'd grabbed at it, immediately started twisting and tugging the fuzzy toy, but the screaming continued.

Daddy plopped Renée on the ground and scooped up her writhing brother instead. "Come outside with me, son," Daddy whispered into Gabriel's bright hair.

"Oh, thank God," Pauline smoothed her shiny red hair and walked away to talk with the other parents, to smile and to soak up their attention. Renée watched all the heads turn, could hear the whispers. *That's Pauline Dufort, isn't it?*

Renée caught up with her mother when Pauline stopped to smile at someone, a tall dark-haired man. Pauline pressed a hand onto the man's arm, leaned in to whisper in his ear. Then the man caught sight of Renée standing behind her mother.

"Is this your daughter?" the dark-haired man asked Pauline. He knelt down. "Hello."

The smile dropped away from Pauline's face, as she leaned down, gripped Renée's arm, her fingernails against the skin…a threat Renée knew well. "Say hello, Renée." Then to the man, "Poor little thing takes after Maurice, not me. My son got all my looks."

The man stood again. "He must be a *very* beautiful little boy."

Renée was left alone, the other children at the party staring at her, moving away from her. She was the girl with the screaming freak of a brother.

***

When Nanny put her in the bath that night, Renée studied her reflection in the soapy water. "Mommy said Gabriel got all her looks."

Nanny sat on the narrow window sill, a cigarette between her fingers. "Well, your hair is nice. Guys always like a blonde." Nanny fanned her cigarette smoke out the window. "But, yeah. You got your dad's face. Nothing special there. When you get older, ask your parents for a nose job…" Nanny tilted her head and studied Renée's baby-fat face. "They're rich. You could get a bunch of stuff done."

Renée splashed her hands through the reflection. "I don't care. I don't want to look like Mommy, anyway. She's mean."

Nanny cracked a smile, flicked ashes into her palm. "You'll care when you're older."

***

The phone with the secured line stays silent, and she watches time tick by on the grandfather clock. The call is fifteen minutes late, then twenty. She picks up the phone and dials through the list of numbers she keeps hidden behind a drawer. All of them ring out.

27

Thirty-five minutes in the office—what could be said in that length of time?

When she comes back out to face Lanson, she's schooled her expression into something calm, but serious.

"Anything…" Lanson trails off. Orders? Direction? News?

"Not really," she says, meeting his eyes without any problem. The lies come so much easier than the truth these days. "They wanted to hear our situation and encourage us to maintain order and infrastructure as much as possible."

Lanson accepts this with his usual stoicism. "At least they're still checking in and not just abandoning us out here. That's hopeful, isn't it?"

"Definitely hopeful," she answers.

6 Gabriel

Gabriel steps out of the basement door to find Lawrence Vu chewing on a fingernail while he waits for him, clipboard tucked under one arm.

Lawrence has tried to take on his sister's duties in the months since her death, but Cecilia never seemed to think much of her brother's abilities, and because of this, Gabriel doesn't trust Lawrence with much of the workload.

Lawrence pulls his finger from his mouth and jams his hand behind him, like he expects to be chastised. His dark eyes are partly hidden by his scruffy hair. The bright red stripes have grown out some and hide inside the jet black tangles. His white shirt has a dark stain on the elbow and is untucked and wrinkled. He looks unkempt, scruffy. Gabriel can't remember if Lawrence was like this before Cecilia died or if his current sloppiness stems from grief.

Why can't I remember? I'm slipping. Unacceptable.

Absorbing Colton's territory into his own, losing Cecilia, losing Peyton... He'd thought letting Peyton go would solve most of the problems at The Greens, but it only solved those that Peyton caused. In all other ways, Peyton had held the neighborhood in check with the angry force of his personality. Without him, the rebellious underbelly of The Greens has started to show itself.

"Are you finished...down there?" Lawrence's eyes slide past Gabriel toward the heavy basement door with the keypad.

And, that's the real problem. Isn't it?

Too many nights in the basement, hoping for a change, talking to the creature version of Bailey until Gabriel is hoarse and exhausted.

"Why are you here, Lawrence? I assigned you to the Pierce Heights storehouses today. Is there an issue?" Gabriel smoothes his own wrinkled shirt, trying not to frown.

"No issue, at least I don't think there is..." His eyes keep darting from Gabriel to the basement door. "Is Bailey...is he ..."

"Bailey is none of your business." Gabriel hasn't confirmed or denied Bailey's condition to anyone. But, he might have made a mistake. Should he have let people see him? Should he have made it open knowledge that he kept Bailey alive? Should he have let them know he wanted to create a more humane version of the containment camps? Transparency would have saved all the rumors swirling through the territory about Gabriel's secret "experiments" with the virus. *No. No.* He made a lot of excuses not to be honest, when the truth is that he cannot bear to let other people see Bailey dirty, naked, feral. He can admit that much now. He can't bear to hear pronouncements like Case's... *"It's been months and—"* Gabriel knows how fucking long it's been.

All his people knew that Bailey lived at his house. And he'd had a house full of people cleaning and making repairs from the destruction left by Colton's attack when he'd brought Bailey down to the basement. No matter how loyal his people were to him, they still feared the virus. Especially after Colton weaponized the acute phase of Super Flu, turning refugees into creatures and sending them to attack Feathertons' territory.

"Hey, I don't care! I'm no fan of Bailey...not after what his brother did," Lawrence says with so much vehemence that his voice shakes with it.

"Bailey is not like his brother." The searing protective flash that always comes when people mention Bailey has Gabriel clenching his teeth and fighting not to clench his fists as well. *Calm down. This is just Lawrence Vu, his sister was your friend.*

"I'll ask again. Why are you here, Lawrence?" His voice snaps all Lawrence's attention from the door to Gabriel.

"A Pierce Heights raiding party said they ran into some rogues, like just wandering through with no..."

"Yes, I know what a rogue is, Lawrence," Gabriel sneers.

Gabriel turns down the hallway toward the study. After the raid that Colton's men had done on the house, he'd had the floor polished darker and the walls painted in glowing Rock Candy white. The effect is starker and more formal. He'd wanted to look even more untouchable after his rival's attempts to trash his home. The pristine cleanliness intimidated people used to living in the smoky, patched world since the outbreak.

The rogues said they ran across a guy who took down a whole nest of newly-popped creatures, and how they described him..."

"How?"

"Tall. Big. Wide shoulders. Leather jacket and steel toe boots like Feathertons wear, short blond hair. It sounds like Peyton. If he cut off the blue...it could be..."

Inside the study, Gabriel stops his businesslike pace to turn slowly toward Lawrence Vu.

"And if it actually is Peyton, then what would you expect me to do?"

Lawrence flushes a dark red. "He killed my sister."

Gabriel tenses. *Control.* He tries to hold himself in place. "I'm aware of what happened, Lawrence. I was there." Restless nights in the basement have blended his nightmares and his memories together until Gabriel can't tell one from the other. Colton holding a gun to Bailey's head features prominently, but so does Peyton's panicked belief that a creature had staggered out of the burning grain elevator toward his younger brother. Gabriel sees Peyton shoot Cecilia, and sometimes, he sees him shoot Bailey by mistake. Sometimes, he dreams that it isn't Cecilia, that Peyton is too slow with the gun and a creature tackles Bailey to the ground, rips into his neck. *Breathe.* Gabriel keeps his voice even, "He thought she was a creature. He didn't…"

"I don't care! He shot her, and I want you to hunt him down and—"

Gabriel's arm snaps forward, his right hand latches onto Lawrence's skinny neck. *Damn it!* Gabriel sucks in a breath, holds it, forcing himself completely still. His hand doesn't loosen, and Lawrence's eyes start to bug, face turning purple. *Lawrence is Cecilia's younger brother, of course he hates Peyton. I should have expected this. I'm slipping,* he thinks again. *Focus.* He slowly releases the grip, and Lawrence slouches down against the wall. "You do not tell me what to do, who to hunt down, who to kill. *I decide.*"

Lawrence's eyes still bulge in fear, but he nods acceptance. Cecilia would have just pursed her lips and ignored Gabriel's outburst. *She would never have approached me with suspicions like this unless she had proof and a plan.* Although he clearly wants the job, Lawrence Vu can never be a permanent replacement for his sister in Feathertons, or by Gabriel's side.

"Return to the Pierce Height's storehouses and do the job I assigned you. Your sister was my friend, so I'll let this go. But, you are not the same. You will never be what she was to me."

Lawrence's eyes fill with tears as Gabriel speaks, his lower lip trembles, but he still has a scrap of defiance left inside him. "What was she? You let the person who killed her go. You let Peyton murder her and didn't care."

"Cecilia was my friend," he says and his voice nearly cracks on the word friend. *She was my friend. A real friend, the first I'd ever had.* Consumed by Bailey's illness, by the expansion of Featherton territory, by the cold war with his sister, he hadn't realized the constant burn in his chest at losing her.

Lawrence turns away, arms folded around himself. *He's crying.* There are words people say to share their grief, to comfort, but Gabriel cannot find them in all his memories. He does not remember anyone encouraging him to share his wild emotions, only threatening him to control them. He won't seek comfort in Lawrence's shared memory of his sister. He won't offer any either.

"Well, she was my sister," Lawrence says, voice clogged with tears. "And I want justice for her death."

7 Gabriel

Gabriel decides that he has put off a confrontation with Spencer Clarkson long enough. His wayward lieutenant for The Greens works at one of the outlier storehouses that day. A shuttered two-story brick Tudor revival, hidden on a street of empty homes. He takes Shane and one of the Mageo brothers with him, just in case of trouble.

"Slow down here," he instructs Hugo Mageo. The brothers both have olive skin with Mohawk hair dyed to look like peacock feathers. Gabriel stopped insisting on the garish hair dye once he'd conquered all the suburbs. His people didn't need to identify themselves, *everyone* either worked for Feathertons or they didn't work at all. But the Mageo brothers must have liked the look and decided to keep it up. Hugo parks the Land Rover several houses down from the brick Tudor, so that Gabriel can watch the runners speed out of the garage on motorcycles with laden packs. On the edge of the driveway, Rico Loeza waves the runners away with his clipboard.

Gabriel opens the passenger door to get out, and from the back seat, Shane yawns, stretches. "Right behind you, boss." Shane also kept the Featherton dye job—his a silver tint on the stubble of his close buzzcut scalp. But, Gabriel knows that Shane keeps it as sign of loyalty, would probably welcome wearing a Featherton brand across his forehead if Gabriel demanded it. Like so many of Gabriel's people, Shane had lost everything to the virus, and Feathertons had become a reason to go on living.

When Rico catches sight of Gabriel walking toward the storehouse, the kid tucks his clipboard under one arm and shakes a cigarette out of a crumpled pack, lights it.

Gabriel will never understand the surge in popularity that cigarettes made since outbreak. None of them have breathed air completely free of the aroma of fire pit smoke since the quarantine camps fell. Maybe they want to mask the smell of burning bodies with the papery smell of tobacco smoke?

"Come to see your lieutenant?" Rico snarks.

"Why isn't he patrolling the storehouses? I checked at The Greens and Olde Town, and he hasn't gone to either in over a week."

Rico snorts. "He ain't in shape to patrol *nada*. My sis might have been doing a side hustle, but at least she showed her face to her runners and the neighborhoods. Spencer is a fucking cowardly pill-head."

"Pill-head? Drugs?" Gabriel looks harder at the cigarette smoldering between Rico's pudgy fingers. Now that Gabriel came close enough, he can catch the slight burned rubber tinge of cocaine. He whips the cigarette out of Rico's hand. "Where did you get this?" His voice like the hiss of a snake.

Rico steps back from him. "I traded it off Derek Sams for some wine my parents had stashed." As Gabriel's lieutenant for Pierce Heights, Derek Sams should turn over any drugs he has access to, and Gabriel would have remembered cocaine.

Breathe—one in, one out. Control. He crushes the still glowing cigarette in his palm, and the pain shoots up his wrist. Behind him, Shane clears his throat.

"Boss?"

The pain gives Gabriel a moment of clarity from his stuttering attention. *I need information.* And he won't get that if he gives in to the frustrated violence gathering itself like a storm inside of him.

Rico's eyes bug as he watches the smoke die in Gabriel's fist. "I'm pretty sure that Derek got them off some of the passing rogue soldiers. They got all kinds of drugs from the city, you know? But they'll give them up for fresh food." Rico can't seem to peel his eyes off Gabriel's fist.

Gabriel shakes it loose and lets the crushed mess of the cigarette drop to the ground. Inside his palm is a red pitted burn. Derek Sams doesn't use drugs, but he always recognizes an opportunity. If Derek can lay his hands on something worth trading, then he will. *Remember, this is why you picked him as lieutenant.* Derek Sams knows how to make a deal. "And Spencer? Where are his pills coming from? I haven't seen a discrepancy on any of the inventories you've turned in."

Rico draws the clipboard out from under his arm. "Now you're seeing it."

Inside the dark house, Spencer has made an office out of the tiny oval dining room area. He scribbles at a map of runner routes and schedules, a skinny and hunched figure in a soot-stained plaid jacket. Shane saunters in ahead of Gabriel, pushes all the routes and schedules aside, and parks his ass on the table. "Hey there, Spence."

Pink hair hangs limp against Spencer's face, and his eyes blink up at Shane from behind round wire frame glasses. "Wha…"

"Boss would like to have a word with you."

Gabriel grabs at the back of Spencer's jacket and kicks the chair out from under him. Spencer's glasses fly off his face. He dangles in Gabriel's grip for one stunned second, until Gabriel throws him to the ground and pins him there with a foot on Spencer's skinny neck.

"You've been stealing from me."

"What? No… I would never steal…not me," Spencer squeaks out. Shaking hands flutter near his face. He squints and then focuses on Rico's clipboard dangling from Gabriel's fingers. "It was Rico…not me."

Shane starts to laugh. "You're just making it worse for yourself, Spence."

Gabriel throws the clipboard across the room, where it slaps against the wall. It sounds just like a gunshot. "Don't lie to me. I hate being lied to." He rocks his shoe forward, pressing against each knobby bone of Spencer's neck.

"I'm not…" Spencer starts gasping and then crying.

Gabriel has fought all his life against the maelstrom of emotion trying to defeat him, and he doesn't have much pity for Spencer's drugged self-pity. "You *are*. Tell me again. Who stole from me?"

"Please…" Spencer squeezes his eyes shut. A yellow puddle forms between his splayed legs and spreads outward, soaking his pants.

***

35

That smell…

"Don't you dare embarrass me tonight, freak." Renée snapped a hair band over his arm. It didn't hurt. Her index finger flicked against a blue vein under his skin.

"Why can't I just snort it like you did?" He'd watched his sister and her boyfriend separate the white powder into long thin lines on his mother's antique writing desk. Then the two of them sucked the powder into their noses using straws they rolled from dollar bills. *Disgusting. How many hands had those bills passed through?*

"It won't be strong enough with all the other stuff the doctors have you on," his sister says. "And it's going to take a lot to make you less of a weirdo." Renée's boyfriend, Toby, guffawed like an idiot. Gabriel would wonder what she saw in the dumb-jock boyfriend, but he knew his sister didn't see anything other than Toby's popularity. Renée had an obsession with having the most people as possible liking her. *Why?* Who cared if people liked her? Gabriel had no friends at all, and it never bothered him.

"Ouch… You said this would feel good, but—" His mouth dropped open, and Toby laughed so hard that he rolled off their mother's silk couch and onto the floor. For the first time ever, Gabriel appreciated Toby's expansive sense of humor and laughed along with him.

"He's laughing *at* you, freak," his sister sneered. But the cocaine had dampened the sting of her words. Either she didn't hate him as intensely in that moment, or he just didn't mind as much. The cocaine injection had him sailing away from the turbulent conglomeration of sounds, images, sensations that made parties, like the one she planned to throw that night, so intolerable. Instead, he felt at peace with himself and the world.

"I like this. I want more."

"No. I've wasted enough on you," said Renée.

Toby raised his beer to Gabriel in salute.

Their penthouse filled with other kids the age of Gabriel and Renée, but also older and younger teens, too. Renée's ultra-elite boarding school combined grades eight through twelve on a single rolling green campus, and the school's glossy brochures advertised an "intellectual collaboration" between students of different ages. But from what Gabriel witnessed, the older students swept the younger ones up in a peer-pressure-fueled clique of drugs, alcohol, and sex. Except for Renée, of course. She passed through their parents' gilt and salmon-pink penthouse with a self-assurance that mimicked their small-time actress mother. Renée's fingers trailed across the back of a boy sitting alone. She smiled at a group of girls drinking Daddy's champagne. She laughed along with a group snorting lines from Mother's Louis XVI coffee table. Despite her official status as "a lowly freshmen" at the school, it seemed that everyone knew and loved Renée.

As the injected drugs wore off, Toby poured more whiskey into Gabriel's glass. Then, Toby waggled a tiny amber bottle in his face. "Try a couple spoons of this, kiddo. It'll wipe the scowl off your face." Toby smelled like cheap cologne.

"Did you just call me kiddo? I'm the same age as Renée. Since you're fucking her, I hope you don't also consider my sister a kid." But Toby didn't care. He tossed the whiskey bottle across the room, and it spun in the air like a football, spraying liquor over the antique rugs and the blush silk furnishings. It didn't matter. Renée had a cleaning service coming before their parents would return home from Aspen.

A doe-eyed girl slithered into the space Toby left, purple lipstick smeared on her front teeth. She blinked thick, spider-leg eyelashes at him. "You're Renée's brother?" The pink liquid in her cup sloshed over onto Gabriel's shirt. Grapefruit and vodka. He'd seen Toby stirring up a pitcher of the stuff. "That's cool," she slurred, and the glossy purple lips widened into an open mouth smile.

"I don't see why," Gabriel drawled. He held out the little vial, offered her some of the powder inside.

"Oh, that's cool." The girl leaned in close enough that Gabriel could smell her sweaty armpits. How did Renée stand these idiots at her school? Gabriel's father had decided that tutoring from home would meet all Gabriel's educational needs. "Those childish relationships are fine for your sister," Maurice told him. "But *you* don't need to bother with them." He'd resented his father's decision at the time, but Gabriel had a sudden and intense sense of relief. He couldn't imagine strolling through the penthouse filled with teenagers, the way he watched his sister do. All the shouting, the laughter, the music, the chaos…

When Gabriel unstoppered the amber vial, he found a tiny spoon attached to the inside of the cap. *Two spoons in each nostril or two spoons total?* He'd offer it to this girl first, see what she did.

"After you."

"You're such a gentleman," she said, and put a single tiny spoonful to her nose. She dug in the vial again before offering another little cup of the white powder to him. All those jangling bracelets on her wrist slid to knock against her hand as she jammed the spoon into his nostril. He sucked the powder up into his sinuses.

Oh. This burned much hotter than the cocaine had, the buzzy, electric high snapped into effect at once. *Was this how other people felt all the time?* This light and warmth sparking out toward each other? This bubbly happiness? "Give me more."

When the girl laughed, her purple smeared front tooth showed. But Gabriel decided he didn't mind it as much this time. With another spoonful of the powder, he thought that lipstick smudged tooth…while not quite appealing…it suited her. She shared her glass of lukewarm pink liquid, and the sounds and smells and sights became more than just tolerable. A ribbon of bright sensation unfurled before him like one of the red carpet events his mother attended. These people, this party…not so bad after all.

Then he found himself in his parents' bedroom, the plush vanilla carpet littered with the girl's sweaty clothing and the mismatched bracelets. He lay flat on his back, shirt untucked and pushed up his chest. Belt undone. Pants bunched to his thighs. The girl writhed on top of him, his penis sliding inside of her. "What happened to the vial?"

"What?" She fell forward over him, licked up the side of his neck. Her sticky gloss and slimy spit against his skin. Her odorous pits by his face. Her sweat pooling against his stomach. She pulled his hand from where it gripped the pillow under his head and mashed it against her chest, and his fingers sank into the clammy pulp of breast.

"Get off of me."

"What?"

"I said get off me!" He knocked her aside, and she rolled off his bed to the messy floor. His dick slipped free of the gluey wet between her legs. "What did you do to me?"

"Are you psycho? What the hell is your problem!" Her screeching must have alerted others at the party. Someone pounded at the bedroom door.

"What's going on in there?" Toby's booming voice.

Gabriel crawled to the edge of the bed, saliva filling his mouth. He couldn't get his legs underneath him. His skin crawled with all the disgusting emanations from the girl. Water…his father always kept a bottle of water on the nightstand. *The maid had the weekend off, and so it would still be there.* His fingers closed around it, and he poured it over his chest, his genitals.

"He's a fucking psycho," the girl called out to the voices beyond the door. She'd pulled back on her lacy tights, her shiny purple dress. The banging on the door intensified until a loud cracking noise split the wood. Toby's beefy arm and shoulder poked into the room

The purple girl stood over him. Tears or sweat had smeared all her makeup into a nightmare of dark smudgy anger. "Fuck you!" she screamed. She leaned in to slap or hit him, and he grabbed at her arms.

Toby and two other hulking bodies appeared. Their hands on Gabriel's throat and around his chest. A fist in his stomach and his bladder released. He fell to the ground. A kick to his back. To his head.

Renée's shrill voice, "You freak—You ruin everything. I *hate* you. *I hate you!*"

***

Gabriel squeezes his eyes against the memory. *You are in control now. You are*—he grinds his shoe down, rolls the sharp bones of Spencer's neck under the leather sole, and watches the boy's eyes water and bulge. He could keep pressing down and crush Spencer's life out for stealing, for lying, for not living up to the job that Gabriel had assigned him.

But Bailey knows Spencer, had liked him once. *I gave Spencer the job because of Bailey...*

Gabriel moves his shoe from the terrified boy's neck, and Spencer coughs and sobs into the dusty floor. "Go home," Gabriel says. "Don't come back here. I'm demoting you to salvage crew."

Spencer's eyes open again, and he gulps in air. "Thank you, Gabriel. I'm sorry. I'm so...thank you."

8 Renee

Renée leads Peyton back into the Arts District toward the police station where she'd interviewed him. "Your boyfriend, Lieutenant Lanson, blindfolded me on the way here. What a moron, like I've never seen a fucking map of the city before." Despite his harsh words, Peyton laughs, good-natured about Lanson's efforts.

"He isn't my boyfriend."

Peyton laughs again, and Renée bites at her tongue for sounding like a pissy teenager. They both dress in boots and heavy denim, both carry weapons.

Renée hasn't had to kill any creatures since the outbreak began, but she couldn't really show up in her usual dress and heels for this meeting. She needs to look like someone who understands a fight, who recognizes Peyton's merits and has confidence in his leadership over what's left of her straggling police force.

"You look good like this," Peyton had said when he first saw her.

"That's inappropriate," she'd said. But she agreed that fighting clothes fit her better than the skirt suits, the formal black dresses and pearls that had become a part of her disguise as someone older, someone who had real power even before Super Flu. Before she could stop herself, she blurted out, "I would have never been allowed to dress like this before the outbreak." *Why did you tell him that?*

Peyton just huffed a laugh, and then he baited her into the, "He's not my boyfriend" comment.

***

The nanny had guessed correctly, and she had a nose job on her thirteenth birthday. Because she'd asked for it. Then, a chin implant, a brow lift, buccal fat removal. One of the surgeon's receptionists brought Renée tea and croissants. "The after pictures are always such a happy time," she said.

"I don't want them used in any advertising—"

"No, of course not." The woman dropped her voice, "The families of celebrities are automatically given the same *elite* protocols." She poured out the tea.

"So no one can connect Pauline Dufort with an ugly daughter," Renée said.

The receptionist smiled, tried to pretend it was a joke. "The doctor will see you in a few minutes."

From across the room, Granny Featherton looked up from her magazine. "Well, you aren't ugly now." The old woman nodded to a gilt-edged mirror behind Renée. "You might not have inherited anything from that good-for-nothing mother, but my son's money more than filled in the blanks."

When Renée looked at her reflection, she saw someone new, with only her pale blue eyes the same. She still didn't look like Pauline or Gabriel, didn't have their flawless skin or glossy red hair, didn't have their tall, slender build. But she looked good enough.

"Image is everything, Renée. There's no point in having an ugly granddaughter."

Renée turned back from the mirror. "Yes, Granny Featherton."

***

Now the quiet feels heavy as they walk through abandoned streets. Broken glass, burnt automobile shells, empty sockets of darkened windows. Looting and panicking mobs have turned this once elegant section of town into a post-apocalyptic hellscape.

"Where are all the people? Everything we heard in the burbs made it sound like inside the barricade was safe." Peyton gestures with his club as he talks, points roughly into the wilds that Film Row has become.

"Not all parts are safe." If she hadn't seen the video of his fighting skills, Renée would never have come this far into the Arts District with a single guard. "As part of the first initiative to control the Super-Flu outbreak, the city put CCTV on every street within the barricade." If someone popped, authorities could catch and remove them. "Eventually, the city didn't have enough police left to watch all the video, to find and kill the feral sick." Renée can hear the frustration in her own voice. "And the more of my people who die, then the more we rely on the military to keep control."

Peyton accepts this information with a nod. No questions, no judgment. *Poor little brother, it must have really stung to lose Peyton Tyrone from your arsenal.*

They both startle at a scraping noise. "Yo!" the pimply teenager in the baggy fatigues appears from behind a burned-out Jeep Cherokee. Renée's teeth grit at the overly-familiar greeting.

"Soldier?" she questions, voice cold, dripping with contempt.

The teenager stops short, but then his eyes immediately go to Peyton's tall broad form beside her. His mouth drops open. "Oh, wow, it's *you*. Dude, that tape of you in Park Plaza—where you dropped a swarm of creatures *by yourself*—that was awesome!"

"Yeah." Peyton shrugs off the admiration, which surprises Renée. She expects boasting, conceit to match the skill, but outside of his confidence in his fighting abilities, Peyton doesn't seem to care much about getting his ego stroked. "Who are you?" He gestures with his own chained club to the heavy metal pipe the kid holds. "You patrolling here?"

The kid scoffs, "No way. Dandridge hasn't assigned anyone to this part of town in months. I'm here to join up with you." His attention slides back to Renée. The pimple-face teenager still wears oversized camo pants, and he looks to weigh less than Renée. He bounces on the balls of his feet like an excited puppy, just raring to go follow Peyton into battle. "Name's Andy," he says.

"Okay, Andy." Peyton cracks an indulgent smile. "Come with us, then. I'm joining up, too."

Renée puts a hand on Peyton's chest to hold him back. "No, not so fast."

She points a finger in Andy's face. "I don't want any problems with Dandridge or Lanson." *And I don't trust for one second that Lanson gave up a trainable soldier.* "If you're their soldier…"

"I'm not. Lanson said there really isn't any record of me with Dandridge. Also, he said it wouldn't hurt to learn some fighting moves." He gestures toward Peyton with his pipe. He'd wrapped silver duct tape around one end to make a handle and the tip of the other end looks crudely sharpened.

No, I don't think so. You're here to spy, even if you don't realize it.

This time, Peyton waits for Renée to answer. *Good.* She doesn't need him undermining her authority, no matter how much she needs his fighting skills. "Your call, boss," he says, just a hair's breadth from mocking.

Boss?

"I'm not a boss. I'm the mayor of this city. Mayor Dufort." She narrows her eyes at Peyton. "I use my mother's name, now that my little brother has perverted our family name for his criminal activities."

Andy doesn't care how Peyton addresses her. "Well, can I join up, Mayor?"

Lanson did offer her Peyton, and she doesn't want the lieutenant changing his mind. *I'll take the spy.* "Come with us," she grits out and starts walking.

***

At the station, they expect her, officers standing at attention in three straight lines. Ahead of this visit, she'd had a courier bring over the download of Peyton killing seven creatures. And she'd promised that anyone who wanted to learn to fight like him should be in attendance.

"Can you train them?" she asks Peyton.

"I've trained people, led them…I used to be—"

44

She cuts him off with a wave of her hand and rolls her eyes. "Yes, I know. Football captain. But, I don't need football players, I need fighters."

Peyton's mouth screws up, and he gives her a slit-eyed, angry look. "Yeah. I can train them."

This would take a measure of trust that she hadn't bestowed on any other living person in a very long time, since her father. *But you need him. This could be the last chance to stay in power.* Renée nods. "Fine."

Peyton faces the straight lines of Renée's police force. "Where are your weapons?" He doesn't pitch his voice overly loud, not like Renée would have to deliver that question. The entire force for the city has dwindled to thirty-six officers, and almost all of them aged in that recovery range, men and women who are in their late teens, early twenties.

They glance at each other, confused. One woman gestures toward her gun. "In our holsters... Sir?"

Peyton sneers. "Are you fucking serious? What the hell good are those?" He shakes his head. "You'd have to get an entire round of shots right at the top of the brainstem. You can't tell me fucking guns are what you carry around this place. Go get your *real* weapons."

They stare at him, some open mouthed, some ashamed, and some grinning. Andy holds out his metal pipe. "Like this?"

"Yeah." Peyton gestures to the pipe with his own chained bat. "And take off those dumbass gun holsters, and anything else that isn't tight on your body." He points at a man in front. "Like this guy's jacket. Get rid of anything the creatures can claw at. If they get you to the ground, you're as good as dead." Peyton waves a hand over the room as he berates them.

But they've seen the video. And they see him now—the classic bully that ruled every one of their schools. Peyton's bulging muscles, his good looks, his contempt...indicators of his rank in a hierarchy they all hated but understand. The lines break up as the officers scramble for the clubs, pipes, shovels they carry with them into the treacherous government-run Arts District every day.

Peyton examines them, one by one, to critique each weapon.

"That shovel looks way too heavy for you. Find one with a wooden pole, or find something else."

"Sharpen both ends of that pipe"

"A crowbar's way too short, and they get stuck too easily."

He has them all in the palm of his hand. "Wood works fine, if you add some weight." And he raises his own preferred weapon, the baseball bat with heavy chain wrapped on the end. "Until you get stronger, you need a weapon you can hold over your head, in front of you, without getting tired. You need to strike fast, without pausing. Even the half-dead creatures try to dive at you. You gotta be able to smack them away before you kill them." He looks at Renée. "They've got all these heavy desks and tables in this building."

She *knows*. She helped the governor's refurbishment committee choose the way too expensive oak wood furnishings in the remodeled police department. It was tedious grunt work when she first started as one of many state interns.

"What the hell does anyone use desks for? These are your fighters, aren't they?"

She sees where this is going…he wants to make new weapons. She also sees beyond turning overpriced heavy furniture into clubs. She sees the way each officer watches Peyton Tyrone. He proved his superiority in that video, and now he wants to train them, turn them into fighters with the skill to face seven creatures—and win.

Renée turns to the room. "Break up anything that would make decent clubs, enough for everyone to have two."

A few of the younger officers cheer, the excitement in the room palpable.

Peyton rips a fire-ax from the wall. "You got it, Mayor."

offensive

9 Gabriel

Wind beats against Gabriel's face and combs icy fingers through his hair. *I forgot to gel it. I keep forgetting things.* He ignores the gusting air to shake hands with Denny Fenton and the other kid...Beau, Colton's nephew, who spied on his barrel-chested uncle for Gabriel, lured away from his abusive relatives to a chosen family in Feathertons.

"Good to see you again," Beau says grinning. He dyed his hair the same bright red as Gabriel and looks at the Featherton leader with open adoration. "Welcome to Cushing!"

Super Flu had whipped through the small town, killing more than any tornado or hailstorm, until only a skeleton crew remained at the refinery. Under Colton, those men had lost their children and wives to Colton's experiments. They'd worked nonstop producing the fuel that Colton traded for opioids. Shortsightedness and cruelty had done Colton no favors. Now, those same men worked twice as hard for Gabriel—because they wanted to, because he treated them well and mixed in a crew of his own people to help them.

Denny punches Beau in the side to stop the younger boy's fawning. "What can I do for you, Gabriel?" Denny's eyes follow the bulky form of Gabriel's bodyguard. Shane's muscles, his towering size, his stony expression, make people nervous. Especially when they have something to hide. *Does Denny have something to hide?*

Gabriel rubs his thumb across his lower lip. "I'm going to need an extra mini tank of fuel. Case Bell will come to personally collect it every three days. You know her, don't you? You will recognize her?"

"Sure. Of course." Denny grew up on the same street, Hickory Hill, as Case…as Bailey.

No, damnit. Do not think of Bailey. Gabriel pulls a long breath through his nose. *Slowly, slowly.*

Both Denny and Beau share a quick glance. "It won't be an issue, Gabriel." Denny has started to sweat, his hairline damp. "We can fill another mini no problem." Denny had bleached and dyed his hair when Gabriel had him stationed in the burbs, but he's grown it back out to his natural dark brown. As Gabriel's silence stretches between them, Denny's hand slaps at the home-cut bowl of hair on his head. "I…there hasn't been a shipment of dye—"

"Your hair doesn't matter. But following my orders does." Gabriel points to the satellite phone in a holster at Denny's hip. "I need to know everything. Rogue soldiers." His thumb is back at his bottom lip, kneading at the skin there. "Passing refugees. All of it. I want you to contact me no matter how small the issue." Gabriel destroyed every backroad and exit that leads toward Cushing except for Highway 33, which he controls completely. But someone determined to infiltrate here could still do it. Gabriel must always reach for more. Contingency—his head aches with it.

"Yeah, I'm on it. I keep my eyes open, you know what I mean." Denny nods along for emphasis. "We're out here, but we still…we're your crew." His eyes follow the still rubbing, rubbing thumb on Gabriel's lower lip.

Gabriel balls his fist and shoves it into his coat pocket. *Pull yourself together.* "Then I expect you to do exactly what I say, when I tell you. No questions."

"I...of course..." Denny looks again at Shane, then back to Gabriel. "Did I do something wrong?"

"No. Not yet. Not ever, I hope." Denny's mother, his sister, his girlfriend all live within Gabriel's territory and depend on him, on Feathertons, for rations, for security. Every person at the refinery has family relying on Gabriel, and he needs that loyalty.

"You can count on me," Denny says, a puffed up straightening of his spine.

"Good." Gabriel throws an arm out for Denny to lead the way to the office. "Let me see your projections."

They shake off gawking, eager, Beau, and watchful, intimidating Shane. Denny takes him into the small refinery back office to show Gabriel the fuel projections. The two of them sit across from each other, charts and tanker logs spread across the gray metal desk. Gabriel leafs through training progress reports. Besides the workers spared from the virus and Colton's brutal treatment, twenty Feathertons live in Cushing. Gabriel sent them to learn how to run the refinery. They've done well.

"This is impressive, Denny. I'm very pleased. I'll send more to train with you as soon as I can." This refinery has value in their new world, but people have even more. *I can find and hold anything I want with enough people.*

"I...okay. Yeah, okay."

Gabriel hands over the letters he's carried from Denny's family. "Kelly is pregnant." Denny's girlfriend had cradled the growing bump when Gabriel retrieved the letter, her thin mouth making a thin smile. She'd asked him about vitamins and fruit rations, and Gabriel nodded along as if taking note of her requests. But, it had taken all his concentration not to lash out at the poor girl. At Denny.

What the hell were they thinking? Denny's mother had patted the girl on her back. Both Kelly's parents died from the virus.

"This is a worrisome development," Gabriel comments. "It caught me unprepared, unfortunately." Another reason for his anger—*I should have considered this.* No more pharmacies stocked with birth control. *Unacceptable, not to have considered this.* More evidence that Gabriel has failed to calculate the issues of long-term management of his territory. But, Gabriel can't put all the blame on his own poor planning. "This is a bad world to bring a baby into."

Denny turns bright red, the sweat-damp hairline now more pronounced. "Condom broke. Too late now, but I feel like a shit." He sucks his lips in and bites down.

"I could bring her to Olde Town to stay on the compound if you like." Kelly had dated Peyton before the virus spread, when they all still spent their days in high school and nights sneaking around parental rules. "She would be closer to medical care, to the clinic I'm setting up."

"No…no that's fine." The red drains from Denny's face, and his skin turns chalk white. "She'll stay with my mother and sis. She's fine." He folds his arms over his chest, obviously terrified that Gabriel will insist Kelly live in Olde Town.

This is about Bailey. About the rumors that Case told Gabriel about.

"She's fine at my mom's," Denny insists.

Gabriel turns back to the charts Denny had rolled out for him. *That extra tanker really shouldn't be any problem.* "Very well." He slides forward on his chair, one foot knocking it back as he stands. A lightning move he learned as a kid. Ben had him practice it a million times in hardback chairs just like this one. The kinds of chairs used in schools.

"One hand on the chair, ready to use it. One hand forward in a fist—quick punch." Ben mimed it for him. Ben's fist stopped just before it pounded into Gabriel's chest. *"Now, you do it."*

Denny's eyes go wide and white.

Gabriel stands over him. "You don't trust me with Kelly?"

"I…of course I trust you—"

"Bailey isn't my prisoner. I'm not doing experiments on him."

"I didn't say—"

"Knee out. Faster!" Ben sidestepped Gabriel's attack. "Defense—Hands up! Do it again."

Sweat burned in Gabriel's eyes. He hopped forward, shot his knee to Ben's groin.

"Good!" Ben's pads took the brunt of the kick, but he dropped down in the way a true opponent might. "Cross punch!"

Gabriel's body acted before his brain, and he punched out a sharp precise jab to Ben's collarbone.

"Fu—" Ben fell backward, face and body contorted in pain.

"I didn't mean—" Gabriel fell to his knees. "Ben!"

"No. Don't apologize. Good hit. Good hit."

Denny's shirt in Gabriel's fist. The chair overturned. Shane in the doorway. "All good in here, boss?"

"I have it under control." *Is that his voice?*

"I'll be right outside." The office door snicks closed again.

Damn it! "Stop denying what you've heard." That came out better, lower, steadier. "Where are the rumors coming from?"

"I…the guys from Quail Creek…Angelica, man. She hates you. She thinks you kidnapped her brothers and—"

Gabriel releases his grip on Denny's shirt and watches, impassive as he doubles over. "Thank you, Denny." The other boy looks up at him with an unmistakable and familiar fear on his face. *Psycho,* Gabriel can read the word in Denny's eyes.

***

"Your dad said you've been in some fights." Benjamin Peretz had served seven years in the Israel Defense Force before moving to Key West

and opening a gym. Mid-thirties, still built for fighting, still built for hard partying. Courtesy of the hard military life. Nearly all his clientele fit in the same demographic as Benjamin himself. And somehow, Gabriel's father decided that living in the back room of the gym, letting Peretz mold him Mister Miyagi style would solve all Gabriel's problems.

"No fights. Some other kids attacked me at a party… Because I'm a freak."

"You don't look like a freak to me. You look more like the cover of a GQ magazine."

"Yeah. Thanks," Gabriel deadpanned. In the dojo mirror, Gabriel saw his own lanky pale reflection for the anomaly it presented. He insisted on staying dressed in his gray slacks and blue Oxford. He'd never worn gym clothes before, and felt ridiculous putting them on today. Especially when he planned on quitting right off the bat. "My mother was a model and actress. I look like her." Why couldn't he take after Maurice? His father might have passed for one of these men. Maurice Featherton's well-cut designer suits hid the body of a soldier and amateur boxer. Renée had inherited more from their father than Gabriel had. Maurice's bulkier physique, his ambition, his aggression.

Ben came up to stand beside Gabriel, met Gabriel's eyes in the mirror. "Okay. Well, I'm going to teach you to defend yourself. If you get attacked again, you won't be the one going down."

Gabriel watched his own face settle into a sneer. Even if he learned to defend himself, those football player friends of his sister's would have overwhelmed him just the same. "The guys who attacked me looked more like you than…" He made a gesture like a gameshow model, waving down his thin body. But Benjamin Peretz only laughed, slapped him on the shoulder as if he and Gabriel had just shared a good joke.

"You got good height and wide shoulders. Good arm length. You just need to put on some muscle and train." At Gabriel's elaborate sigh, the bulky man laughed again, rested a hand on Gabriel's shoulder. "You'll see."

"Mr. Peretz—"

"Ben."

"Hmmm…" Gabriel's father must have paid this man a fortune to take Gabriel in and work up this ridiculous plan. "Ben, this will be a waste of time."

Gabriel had accepted his role as the family embarrassment, as the freak. He just needed his father to give up on him, leave Gabriel alone with his books and his studies. *But, that would never happen.* He knew his father would never stop trying to mold Gabriel into what Maurice wanted his son to be.

"My father must have told you something about me? I'm not…*normal.*" Gabriel's fits had lessened since childhood because he'd learned to avoid the crowds and noise that spurred them. To breathe through the hot flashes of rage and the icy panic of fear. To tense up and still himself rather than let trembling, spasming muscles control his movements. What did gym-rat Ben think he could teach Gabriel that a parade of psychiatrists hadn't already achieved?

The hand on Gabriel's shoulder tightened. But in a warm squeeze that didn't hurt like when Nanny or Mother gripped him. "Listen, I know you have doubts, Gabriel. But, I *can* help you. You just have to trust me."

Trust him? Mr. Peretz…*Ben's*…tan face split into a wide gap-tooth smile, and Gabriel stifled another annoyed sigh. What choice did he have? His father had left him here with no money and no means to leave. "I suppose…" Gabriel drawled.

Ben slapped at Gabriel's back. "Awesome. Let's get to work."

***

Gabriel leans back in the passenger seat of the Land Rover, lets Shane drive fast and reckless back to the burbs. Shane always gets a little huffy when Gabriel doesn't let him do the dirty work.

"Back to Olde Town, boss?"

"Yes. Back to the mansion." *To the basement…to Bailey…*

10 Renee

Deep Deuce, Bricktown, the Arts District, all of them lie inside her half of the barricaded city, but Renée can only keep Central Business safe enough to live inside, to walk through. In all the others, feral sick hide in the shadows, infest the abandoned shops and apartments. It won't take many more sightings and attacks before all the people under her protection demand the military take over the entire city. *Dandridge will take my place.* And once he uncovers that she's been faking her news from the crumbling national government, he will shoot her on the spot. Renée had always been on the path to leadership. At the start of the outbreak, she'd seen the irresistible opportunity opening before her. And she'd heard her father's voice in her head telling her to take it, grab the brass ring. But, Maurice had only ever given advice on how to reach for power, never what to do once she had it. *People depend on my decisions, my ability to keep them safe, fed, sheltered. The city is broken…*

But now, she has Peyton Tyrone, who promises to clean up the biggest threat.

Peyton walks beside her in the middle of a wide boulevard leading from Central Business to the Deep Deuce. Andy circles round them, trying to mimic Peyton's swagger but unable to hide bubbling excitement. "Peyton? The guys want you to check over our gear one last time before we go in." Besides the walk, Andy imitates how Peyton dresses. Instead of ill-fitting fatigues, he now wears black boots, black pants with knee pads, a black shirt. His right hand holds a lead pipe, which he taps against his thigh.

"Yep. I'll be right there."

Andy nods and bounces his way down the other direction, back toward the other members of the ragtag police force making their way to the meeting point. Only the military has enough precious fuel to patrol their half of the city. Renée's people all have to travel on foot.

"You know, I didn't expect you to hang on this long." Peyton swings the bat in rhythm with his steps, chains jingling a scratchy tune between them. He cuts his eyes at her. "You still aren't scared?"

After that first day, Renée kept coming to whatever training sessions she could. And two weeks later, she has more confidence taking up a weapon of her own to fight beside him. As long as she doesn't get jumped, or have to face more than a single creature, she can take care of herself. "I want to be there today."

"To take all the credit?" He doesn't seem bothered by the idea. Peyton Tyrone has clearly never had to fight for recognition. Not like Renée.

In response, she reaches over her shoulder, grips the long wooden spike in the sheath on her back, and pulls it out like a sword. She'd followed his advice and gotten the heaviest weapon she could wield.

Peyton scoffs and shakes his head. "Yeah, yeah. You're a real badass." The two of them stop at the mouth of Deep Deuce, waiting for the rest of the fighters. Lounging against a scorched wall, he folds his arms over his tight t-shirt, tips his head back. "You better not slow us down in there."

She raises an eyebrow at him. "I might have missed the full training, but I'd bet that I can keep my head in a fight better than puppy-dog Andy." Her irritation only makes Peyton laugh, and

Renée's skin heats in embarrassment. "You're such a cocky jerk. How did my brother stand you?"

"He really didn't." Peyton's mouth screws up, he runs a hand over his golden hair. "Maybe he was just more motivated than you because of…a *mutual interest* the two of us had."

"High school popularity? How immature."

But her dig falls flat. Peyton looks away, hiding an expression that doesn't fit their back-and-forth jibes. It throws her off. *I'm missing something.*

When the others show up, she schools her expression to something more confident. Despite the many times she came to practice with them, she gets a lot of wide eyes when the gathered police notice her standing beside Peyton. He guessed right that she wants to take credit. She wants to knock Dandridge off balance when she tells him they cleaned out another district in her part of the city. That she *personally* took up a weapon to lead the fight.

"Keep your clubs out and up." Peyton pushes against the arms of a young officer. The man adjusts his grip and lifts his metal stake higher. When Peyton nods his approval, the man's neck flushes red.

Renée holds back her eye roll.

"Keep your weapon in front of you. Sweep into and out of the dark, like a broom." He mimics taking a low hard swing of the bat. "They'll bolt into the light and come at you." In many ways, Peyton Tyrone reminds her of her first boyfriend Toby, both of them tall, blond football captains, natural leaders. But, Peyton lacks Toby's buoyant sports-hero personality. Peyton is hard, *vicious.* "Kill fast, and brace for the next one. And keep aware of your sides, your back." Encouraging words, but delivered like a taunt. "Don't count on someone else to watch it for you." In two weeks, Peyton has taken control of the staggering police force, trained them to fight, and inspired them to take pleasure in it. He makes a swirling gesture in the air. "Let's go!"

They come down the street in a wide V with Peyton pointing out the nooks and shadows worth sweeping. Two hunched and cowering men get taken down right away. *Not men…*creatures. Renée needs to remember to see the sick in the same way as Peyton. She can't afford to have sympathy for the dead and dying. She has living people who rely on her. Another three, rotting and hiding in a stoop, make easy kills.

They go another block and find the barricade in front of them. To their right, a long, red brick building untouched by fire or looting. Renée wants to move families into it, once she can assure their safety. The tent city inside the convention center has become cramped and unsanitary. With the start of winter, she worries about viruses and bacteria that could spell disaster for the surviving population.

They stop in front of the two-story brick building near the high perimeter fence. The building once had high-end apartments but has long since become overrun with creatures. "This is it," Renée says. "I need this building clean. I could fill it immediately, if I promise it's safe." And she needs people living this close to the barricade to keep watch. The less she has to rely on the military for security, the better.

Peyton waves his right hand to get the attention of their force, and with his left, points at the building. "Split into your teams. Green, enter through the west entrance. Blue, go south. Yellow takes north. Red, with me."

"Teams?"

Peyton turns at her question. "If you skip the training, then you gotta find out all the details on your own."

"What?" She refuses to jog to catch up with him. But, she does speed walk the distance to the eastern side of the building. On this side, the shadows grow longer, darker. Peyton chose the most challenging part of the building for himself—his team—Renée, Andy, Peyton, and two others, a man and woman. Only five of them, the smallest group. "Red team doesn't seem very formidable. Not enough to take this side of the building." She follows Peyton through a glass door and into a dark lobby with dusty leather furniture. "Are you listening to me? I need this building. I didn't just come here to watch you have fun."

Andy tugs on her sleeve. "We have to stay quiet and listen. Any noise could be one of them," he whispers. The gangly boy creeps toward a heavy wooden console that cuts the room in half. He crouches down, pokes underneath the console with his pipe. A screech—and the boy jumps backward, trips over the edge of the tasseled rug. He lands on his back, pipe rolling across the floor as a young girl leaps over him.

Not a girl.

Rope dangles from her arms and legs. One hand has bite marks and missing fingers like she tried to gnaw herself free. The other hand's clawed fingers scratch in the air toward Andy's face.

Peyton surges forward—bat raised, he swings at the girl with both arms extended, and sends her flying off Andy to thud against the wall. The chains rip skin from the little creature's neck, and dark thick blood slides down the tattered nightgown she wears.

"Brinda, stab her!" Peyton waves a woman forward, and Brinda rushes to his side. She spikes the creature under the chin and up, into the critical craniocervical juncture. "Good job."

When the woman yanks her spike free of the dead girl and turns, Renée can see jagged scars on the right side of Brinda's face. Four long vertical swipes from her hairline to her chin. Her black hair is pulled into a thick braid, the skin on the back of her neck scalded red. Missing fingernails on her right hand, fingers knobby, twisted. Brinda had the virus and survived. At one point, she looked like the girl she just killed. Creature…not a girl.

You're staring. "Yes. Good work, officer," Renée says. Brinda's smile drops away at Renée's praise, and she gives a tight nod. Her broad shoulders straighten.

"Thank you, ma'am."

A wide staircase leads up to two levels of spacious apartments, ten on each floor. They'll have to check each one of them, each room. At the end of the hall, the Green and Yellow teams appear. One of them calls out, "Blue team is clearing out the basement garage."

Peyton gives them some hand signal that Renée doesn't recognize. Then he turns toward her. "I'm gonna check on them. Garage is probably crawling with fucking creatures."

"You're leaving us alone?"

Peyton just smirks at her apprehension. He instructs Brinda and Andy to take the second floor and puts Renée with Nick. Renée recognizes Nick as part of the original downtown police force. Maybe even a part of the governor's security at some point. The other teams all split into pairs to search out the lofts. Renée's sweat turns the wooden spike in her hands to an oily rod, difficult to grip. *I should have roughened the stalk better. I should have worn gloves. Too late now.* She turns her attention away from her own hands to study her partner. "So, you look familiar, Nick? Have we worked together before?"

The man has a square jaw and gray sideburns, maybe around forty, but maybe younger—the apocalypse ages everyone. He twists the knob of the first door they come to. "Peyton says no talking in a hunt." But, before she can point out that Peyton works *for her,* Nick softens. "Guess it doesn't matter since we have to break these doors down anyway." He motions for Renée to step aside and bends his knees, gets into position for the kick. "I did some security work for your dad. Parties. That kind of thing." The heel of his boot smashes near the door handle and punches the lock through the frame.

"Oh, I see." The hallway fills with the same cracking noise as the other pairs breach their lofts.

"I assume he didn't make it, your dad. He was a good guy, generous with employees. Always remembered our names. I'm sorry for your loss."

"Yes… Thank you." She doesn't know this version of her father, the "good guy." In private, Maurice was ruthless, demanding. She'd felt closest to him when she took an interest in his business dealings, asked his advice on how to get noticed in her internship.

With the door breached, putrid smell rolls out of the apartment like a thick swampy fog. Rot. Death. Renée grips her weapon tighter. She pulls up the bandana around her neck, covers her nose and mouth. It helps, but just a little bit. "Is it a body?"

"Maybe…"

Whoever lived here had good taste, sculptural furniture, silk rugs, modern art. Curved glass staircase twisting up toward a second floor. Under the staircase, an immaculate steel and marble kitchen. "Well, I don't think it's food." From the decor alone, she can tell that the owner of this place didn't cook, didn't buy groceries.

"Upstairs," Nick whispers. His oily forehead above the mask shines in the sunlight pouring through the tall windows.

Renée nods. They take careful steps up the stairs, Nick leading, both of them breathing hard. The second floor has none of the pristine order of the first. Ripped cushions and scratched walls. Broken electronics and overturned lamps. They find a body, or pieces of one. Skin, bone, muscle lay in messy drag marks on the floor. Something killed and feasted here. Renée and Nick step over the bigger chunks of meat and gore.

"Do you think—" Her words cut off because they both hear it—moaning—*growling*. The reflected gleam of eye and tooth. Gray and white fur, the rush of a charge, and Renée falls back hard, spine slamming to the ground, air knocked from her lungs. A growling dog bares its teeth over her face. *Don't move. Don't scream.*

But she can't hold it in, "Nick!" *Where is Nick?* Commotion surrounds her, and it takes another beat for her to realize that it isn't just her and the dog.

Slamming, shrieking. Nick has found something to fight. A huge crash, and the dog leaps from her chest. *My spike.* Her right hand slaps at the ground where the heavy wood rolled out of her fist. Her fingers sink into wet gluey carpet. Dark, sticky blood, a string of rubbery vein sticks to her fingers.

Infected blood, infected vein… *The virus.*

Renée's mind empties of everything but the feel of that sticky Super Flu-laden blood. She scrambles to her feet.

Bathroom? *There.*

She bolts inside and locks the door. Plunges her hand under the sleek curved faucet. *Please let there be water.* A freezing stream gurgles out, rinses away the disgusting mess on her fingers. She rips the cloth from her face and takes deep gulping breaths of the fetid air. The doorknob jiggles and Nick screams on the other side of the door.

"Let me—oh, my God!" Dog barking. Creature moaning and shrieking.

Renée sinks to the bathroom floor, covers her ears.

A long time passes. When did all the screaming stop? Only the dog sniffing at the bottom of the door. *The creature sniffing?*

"Hang on, and I'll let you out." …Peyton. "One…more…second…" His words punctuated with the unmistakable sound of a club to flesh. She knows that sound. She's watched creatures killed. Seen broken bodies and puddles of blood. Everyone who has survived has.

Renée checks the mirror again. Pulls the cloth back over her nose and mouth. Refuses to check her hand and nail beds again for the infected blood. *They're clean. You already made sure, they're clean.* She unlocks the door.

"You did the right thing," Peyton sounds nonplussed. "That creature bit Nick's nose off. He'd have bled all over you." When she follows him back out into the room, he stomps over a mess of gore and destruction toward the black clad body of Nick. "Lemme show you."

She swallows back on the nausea climbing her throat. "I'm fine to take your word for it."

"Yeah, you can't really tell now, 'cause I had to crush the juncture." Peyton tosses his bat a few inches in the air and catches the handle again. He pouts, handsome face looking forlorn. "Man, it sucks I had to kill the dog, too, but for sure it caught the virus, too." Peyton reaches down, pats a furry lump curled up on the ground. He doesn't notice that the heel of one boot grinds Nick's hand into the carpet.

11 Renee

Peyton is relentless.

He fights like a man with nothing to lose, with an obsessive desperation that Renée doesn't understand. Over the next week, he takes on building after building. Renée watches on as her police force evolves from bungling peace-keepers to skilled, efficient fighters under Peyton's direction. And, while the other officers work in shifts, Peyton doesn't rest. He fights and kills with unrestrained, exhilarated, savagery. Her young officers don't just admire him, they revere him.

Because of this, Renée keeps Peyton on a very short leash. "I expect you to tell me about any developments, no matter how much training I miss."

"Sure thing, Mayor." He holds open the heavy glass door for her. All remaining city services moved their offices to the courthouse, as it lay inside the relative safety of Central Business District.

"I can never tell if you're sarcastic or not when you answer me." Peyton turns a wide-eyed look her way. He places his free hand over his heart. "I'm never sarcastic."

Curious faces watch from every door. Whispers. *The Mayor.* Pleasure fizzles up her spine until she remembers her mother. The smug twitch of her lips when people recognized her. *You aren't like her.* Peyton's bat drips a trail of water on the marble floor as he walks beside her. Just that morning, she'd declared both Deep Deuce and the Arts District safe for travel, safe for living. Now, she can start to empty out the tent city in the convention center. For the price of an oath of loyalty, Renée will move families or individuals to the once expensive city loft apartments. She'd projected photos of the interiors for the audience of refugees and city workers. "Running water. Electricity. Privacy and comfort." When she finished her presentation, she was met with open-mouth shock from the older government employees—the ones who remember the governor and his close aides, *and remember that Renée had not been among them.*

As she and Peyton pass by, a secretary from the Land Commission bursts into applause, an old woman with thick glasses and white hair. "Good work, Mayor Featherton!"

Renée's stops in her tracks. "It's Dufort. Mayor Dufort. I use my mother's name."

This flusters the Land Commission woman. "Oh, I'm so sorry. I…I didn't know. Your father was a favorite of mine." She pulls off her glasses and rubs at the lenses with a tissue. "Such a nice man. He always had a kind word to say."

A kind word? Did this old bat think her father's friendliness was sincere? The same unease creeps over her as when Nick offered condolences. *What does it matter if they remember Daddy as friendly, as a "good guy?"* But she knew that her father had used these people, their good will, to get what he wanted. He hadn't cared about them at all. *Because Daddy was a great man, not a good guy.*

Peyton stands at Renée's back, his towering, angry presence like a weapon in her hands. The nosy old woman peers up at him, owl-eyed. "I…sorry to have bothered you…Mayor Dufort."

As Mayor, Renée's first official act created a Resource Management Office to shuffle workers, supplies, and rations. They'd assigned her a single person as her staff, a trembling man who stands up from his desk as soon as he sees her.

"Mayor, you're back. You'll have an appointment coming—"

"I'm aware, Liam." The secretary flinches away when Peyton glances at him. Peyton throws his wet bat onto a leather chair and follows Renée from the reception area into her personal office.

"You could have left that in the drying rack outside, or at least— what the hell is so funny?"

"Nothing."

She'd chosen the heavy furniture, the crisp navy silk drapes, the framed portrait of the capitol building, all of it to invoke respect. Peyton takes in none of it and props a dirty boot on the edge of her desk.

Renée decides to ignore that provocation. She raises her chin. "I think it's important we present a unified team to the officers. I've added several recruits, and I'll be announcing that a period of service to the city is mandatory for living inside the barricade."

"Yeah, I don't care."

For the millionth time, Renée wonders how her squirming, volatile brother put up with someone like Peyton Tyrone. She pulls back the drapes, turns the window crank to open it. Her office gets so musty, so stifling. Or maybe that suffocating feeling comes from the weight of her position as she sits behind her desk? The brass nameplate with her title…the view of the halfway fence separating her side from the army's side. Even though the cold air smells of smoke, she sucks in a frigid breath.

Now that I have power, how do I use it?

Renée turns back from the window. "I'm asking if you can train more of them…clean out the rest of my city. Can you do that?"

Peyton cracks a smile. "Send them to me, and we'll find out."

"Damn it, Peyton. These people want to know they're safe. You can't just throw untrained conscripted civilians into a fight if they aren't—"

"You said I could run the police how I wanted." Peyton drops his foot off her desk, straightens from his slouch. "I'm not telling you how to fill up the buildings I empty, or what to say in your big shot speeches. So, stay out of my way when it comes to fighting."

"Do not take that tone with—"

Liam pokes his head around the door. "Mayor? Your appointment is here."

Renée smooths her jacket and skirt. "Thank you." The words sound perfectly normal, but frustration gnaws at her bones. She'd wanted a different tenor between Peyton and her before testing this out.

Peyton shifts to the end of his chair. "Am I done here?"

"No. I want you to stay. You'll escort my visitor back to the south gate after this meeting. Maybe you even know her?"

She braces herself to see how her test will play out. Peyton *does* know the visitor. *Will Peyton cover up his connection to the girl?* Renée has trusted him this far, but now, she'll know if he has truly belonged to Gabriel the entire time.

Andy and another young officer pull in Renée's visitor, a tall, muscular girl with mass of dark curls and round angry eyes. "Case Bell," says Renée, but her eyes stay fixed on Peyton, watching for his reaction. "Another child my brother recruited from that suburban high school he'd attended. Maybe I should have skipped private education and also gone to a state school? Gabriel obviously thinks highly of the students it produces."

Renée hoped to shock Peyton, knock the smug confidence out of him for once. Instead, he gives the girl an indolent smile. "What's up, Case?" His casual greeting makes Case's expression harden, the expressive eyes burn with repressed fury. She yanks her arm free of Andy's grip. "I agreed to meet with you, you know." The girl folds her arms across her chest and cocks her head. "You don't have to treat me like a prisoner."

"It's just a precaution…" Renée nods to Andy and the other officer, and they scramble out like they can't get out of the office, the tense meeting, fast enough. "Isn't this your high school girlfriend, Peyton?" Renée asks. "No welcoming kiss?"

"I had a lot of high school girlfriends." Peyton shrugs and looks up from where he's settled back into the leather chair. "So, you bailing on Gabriel, too, Case?" He turns to Renée. "She's a good fighter. Is she one of the new people you're giving me to train?"

"No, she isn't." Renée slits her eyes at him. "And you know it."

Peyton laughs at Renée's obvious irritation.

"I'm here to cut a deal." Case Bell's furious eyes concentrate on Renée. When she frowns, dimples form in her cheeks. "You need more fuel than Gabriel's allowing you," she says to Renée. "I run one of the fuel routes for Feathertons, so I have access you want. And I also know Colton traded with you for pharmaceuticals."

"It was a good arrangement until my brother killed him." Renée fiddles with the expensive pen on her desk, studies this girl in front of her. Case wears leggings and a fleece turtleneck in the maroon and white colors of her former high school. Her left wrist has a maroon and white hairband around it. *All those team colors, so loyal still to her former suburban high school. Just like Gabriel….*

"What about my brother?"

Case drops her arms. "I'm not a part of Feathertons. Gabriel has me working off my mother's debt by doing the fuel runs to Cushing. It's too damn dangerous, and that debt just keeps building interest with more time I owe him. And then I have to use some of that credit for food, for other things I want."

"You would trade drugs behind Gabriel's back? In his own territory?"

"Ha—I doubt he'll even notice. His territory is too sprawling, not like running a city where you can keep an eye on everything. He wouldn't even be able to stop me from bolting with my family, but where would we go? It will take years before all the feral sick die off, and there's too much I want *now*."

Want—Renée can work with someone who *wants*. And as payback for siding with Colton in the attack on Featherton territory, Gabriel has cut her fuel ration to almost nothing. All the functioning vehicles on her side of the barricaded city sit idle while Renée has to beg rides from Dandridge. Somehow, she manages to stifle the desperation clawing in her gut to feign nonchalance. "I'm willing to give this a try," she offers. "I'll even give you the same trade rates I gave Colton." She gives Case a pick-up and drop-off location just outside the city barricade. The military has their own deal with her brother. She can't trust them keeping quiet if they find out about her arrangement with Case.

Peyton watches them hammer out the details with his head tipped back to the ceiling, arms and legs sprawled out like a bored and petulant child. When she finishes the meeting, she comes around her desk to kick at his chair.

"Take Case to the gate," she orders. Again, the poor girl flushes. Peyton's ex-girlfriend did a good job of presenting her deal to Renée, but she couldn't hide that her attention drifted to Peyton in every lapse. *She still cares for him.*

"Why didn't you tell Andy to wait around?" Peyton grouses. "That dumb kid took out just two creatures the whole day. I stopped counting my own at fourteen."

"Just do it."

Peyton makes a dramatic sigh. "Yes, *Mayor*." He stands up and gives her a mocking salute. "But, then I'm off."

"Goodbye, Ms. Bell." Renée flips a hand in Case's direction, shooing her out the door. "I expect we will help each other quite a bit with our deal."

"Yeah." Case nods. The mass of wild hair undulates around her like seaweed under water. "I hope we will," Case says, voice cordial but eyes flashing resentment.

Why? Oh, of course. Case is jealous that I have Peyton's attention now. Renée knows very well the clawing, desperate anger of jealousy, just not from this side. Case Bell's lingering crush on an unattainable boy can't even compare.

"You're lucky to be a girl, Renny. You don't have to be Daddy's greatest achievement."

***

Because of Gabriel, her party had failed. After her brother's meltdown, Toby and his friends had fled, worried about getting in trouble for the beating. And once the popular seniors left, everyone else had, too. She knew that once the semester began again, no one would gush over the penthouse apartment in New York, the breathtaking views, and Renée herself. All the painful operations she'd undergone to make herself beautiful, admired…*wasted*. Instead, everyone would whisper to each other about Renée's brother, the freak.

Because of Gabriel, she would now have to face her mother's anger, and Daddy's disappointment. Professional cleaners could only do so much. Renée couldn't hide the broken door frame. The blood stained carpet and wall.

"It was Gabriel who—"

"Get out of my sight." Pauline pulled off her leather gloves finger-by-finger and plopped onto the silk couch that Renée had paid triple price to have cleaned of beer and vomit. Her mother turned to Daddy. "I want them gone."

"It can all be fixed, and you wanted to redecorate anyway." Daddy always pretended not to hear the terrible things Mother said. "Where is Gabriel?" he asked Renée.

"He's in his room."

All the snooping questions of the partygoers rang in her head.

Is your brother mentally challenged? Is he some kind of pervert?"

"Did you grow up with him?"

"He's your twin?"

***

Renée could hear Daddy's exclamation at Gabriel's black eyes, the broken nose, the broken ribs. "What happened? Who did this to you?" Renée looked inside as she passed Gabriel's room. Daddy put a hand on her brother's head, patted his hair in a comforting gesture Maurice had never used with Renée. Like a hot red sun, jealousy burned in Renée's stomach, her throat, behind her eyes.

"You're lucky to be a girl, Renny. You don't have to be Daddy's greatest achievement."

12 Gabriel

When the Land Rover turns onto Hickory Hill, Gabriel's gaze turns by habit toward the blue and white two-story home where

Bailey once lived. He'd had the house cleaned out trying to exorcize the dark memories of the unhappy family who once lived inside it. All the fragile threads holding the Tyrone family together ripped apart during the pandemic. Bailey's little sister Lucy had disappeared on the first weekend of mass outbreak. His mother died from the virus. Mason Tyrone left the family, and Peyton…

Gabriel moved another family into the house just weeks later. Both parents worked as engineers, very useful. Now, a pair of little girls chase each other in the front yard, only stopping to gawk at the gleaming black Land Rover. Their mouths drop open when they see Gabriel emerge from the car.

When the front door opens, Case ushers him inside. "You don't care if someone sees? What if it gets back to—"

"I know where all the leaks are in my territory."

She throws her hands up. "Alright, alright." Courtesy of the engineer neighbors, the Bell home has a new chimney in the living room, and Gabriel removes his long wool coat for the first time that day. Case takes a seat on the sofa, and Gabriel sits on a chair across from her. Case's face always gives away more than her words.

Right now, she looks sad. "You came to hear about what happened in the city?"

"That and more." He lets her describe the meeting with Renée. Then asks her to describe it again, more detailed… He spent all his childhood watching for clues from his sister to judge her mental state. *She tried to kill me once.* When Renée gets desperate enough, she'll try and destroy what he built with Feathertons. That's why he concocted this plan with the extra fuel tanks, to give himself time to stabilize his newly expanded territory. That, and he needs pharmaceuticals before winter sets in. While Super Flu ravaged the world, they'd ignored all other illness, but living inside, in close quarters would likely bring them all back. Thankfully, the version of his sister that Case describes sounds confident in her power. More frustrated with Peyton than with Feathertons.

"That's everything, I can't think of anything else to add." Case scoots back into the tufted green sofa, tucks her chin into her chest, and folds her arms. It disturbed her seeing Peyton, Gabriel can tell. He wants to change the subject of their conversation before she starts asking him a lot of questions that he doesn't want to answer.

Her mother brings out two cups of coffee, sets them on a small table at Gabriel's elbow. Monica Bell has aged since Gabriel last saw her. Dark hair turned gray. Steps slow and shuffling. Because of Monica trading for painkillers with one of Featherton's former rivals, she has roped her only living daughter into Gabriel's service.

"Thanks, Mom." Case doesn't look up. She pulls at one of the long coils of hair falling over her shoulders and then lets it loose to spring back into shape. "You haven't asked me about Peyton."

"I want you to take over The Greens."

"What?" Case pops up from her slouch. "I can't—what about this other thing you have me doing?"

"Now that you've made contact, I can pass it to someone else."

"No. It has to be me. You were right that it has to be me, or we'll completely lose Peyton. Gabriel, I know you're counting on Bailey to bring him back. You are, aren't you? But what if Bailey never—"

Gabriel stands, upsetting the little table and coffee sloshes from the cups. "Bailey *will*."

"But if he doesn't—"

"He will. *He has to.* Or there's no point to any of this."

"Gabriel…" Case puts a hand over her face, hides the deplorable pity in her eyes. She has no talent for disguising her emotions, and when she pulls her hand free, her huge dark eyes shine like a mirror. "I won't do it. I won't abandon Peyton, even if *he* wants me to."

Deep breaths. *Get control.* "Then, you will have to do both. Make the trades in the city, and run this neighborhood as well." He pulls the wool coat on to cover the tremors in his arms and legs. "We understand each other, Case Bell. Don't we?"

He can't bear the return of the pity in her soulful eyes…but there it is. "Yeah," she whispers. "We understand each other."

economy of force

13 Renee

"Oh—I can see them." Liam scoots forward, squints out the front windshield of the sleek, black Cadillac. Renée looks up from the notes in her lap. She and her secretary wait at a safe distance, while Peyton cleans out another building on her half of the city. Another factory built in the 1920s, remodeled into loft apartments in the 2020s. She decided to give Peyton the freedom he wants—she can't risk him getting frustrated or bored, and he wants to fight. Not train newbies. He'll take volunteers, throw them in with his crew to learn on the fly, but Peyton wants action.

"Right there!" Liam points toward the building's enormous steel frame windows, and the visible fight taking place inside. A tall figure beats a smaller hunched figure with a long heavy weapon. "I didn't realize that getting rid of the feral-infected…" Liam's nose wrinkles. Renée's skinny, nervous secretary hasn't set foot outside Central Business District since the start of the outbreak. "It's very violent."

"Yes. It is." After that first day, Renée doesn't dress for combat anymore, she prefers to wait inside her fancy car, which she ordered Liam to let idle with the heat on *because she can*. Just that morning, she traded her empty tanker for a full one that Case dropped off. Poor Case Bell—the girl can't resist staring past Renée, looking for Peyton's tall blond figure, so that he can break her heart just a little more. *But, Peyton belongs to me now.* Well…not the way Case wants

Peyton. But Renée now owns all the football hero's skill, the most valuable part of him.

"Oh no." Liam slaps his hands over his mouth. One of the feral sick must have gotten spooked or cornered. It crashes through the factory-style third-story window to escape its hunters.

"Disturbing, isn't it?" She frowns. "But they aren't people…they don't *think* like people…" Proving her point, a raving man dives out the broken window, past the iron staircase to land face first on asphalt. His limbs twitch and flail as he struggles to pull himself back up on crushed bones.

"Oh, my God!" Liam gasps. "He's stil l—" A gagging cough cuts him off.

"If you throw up in this car, I will toss you out there with them. Do not become a liability to me, Liam."

"Sorry, ma'am."

Ugh. She'd just wanted him to drive her, the look of importance that a chauffeur and the Cadillac would give her. *I need to appear powerful, untouchable.* Granny Featherton's warning vibrated through her, "Image is everything." These fighters belong to Peyton. She needs to make it clear that Peyton reports to her.

When Renée looks back from Liam's green face, she sees the woman, Brinda, chasing Peyton down the fire escape, her long black braid flying out behind her. Despite the cold temperature, she wears a black t-shirt, sinewy scarred arms on display.

Peyton levers himself over the railing one-handed and jumps to the second floor iron landing, a metal club held aloft. He'd given up the chained bat he used in the suburbs, and fashioned a streamlined metal weapon for himself. He waits until the man he chased down gets closer to the fire escape stairs, then does another lever over the edge and drops down. His club swings out while he's still in the air and makes contact with the creature's neck, drops him, before he lands.

Liam gasps. "That's…That's really…" After Peyton's dazzling athleticism, Liam must have forgotten about his earlier nausea. "He's really something, isn't he?"

"He is," Renée answers. *And he's all mine. Does Gabriel know?* Unless she's an idiot, Case wouldn't go telling tales about her trips to the city. Renée hopes her brother doesn't have any idea what happened to Peyton. That when the time comes, she will get to witness Gabriel's reaction over losing this magnificent weapon to her.

The feral woman who first threw herself from the window landed in much better shape than the man. She does that weird Tyrannosaurus Rex charge at Peyton. Renée shudders, remembering early news reports about the wrist and finger rigor that makes their hands look like claws. Peyton swings the heavy baton out one-handed, and it lands with practiced precision on the back of her skull. When she falls, Peyton turns away to motion for Brinda to return back up the iron fire escape.

"One more in the back!" He cups his hands to amplify his voice. "Go help out Tim and Jamari—meet me down here." Her fighters begin staggering outside. Red-cheeked and heaving chests, they gather around Peyton the way his football team must have done.

Liam has perked up about his driving duty. "Should I take us closer?"

"No…" Her voice trails off. One of those fighters looks familiar to her. Tight, ash-brown haircut, square jaw. *Is that…Lanson?*

"No?" Liam must sense her anger. He blinks at her.

"Damn it!" She throws open her door and marches across the wide, empty street toward the knot of celebrating police. And Lieutenant Patrick Lanson. The thin soles of her pumps crunch against broken glass, gravel, and gritty pavement. *Another thing to fix…*

When he sees her, Peyton breaks from the center of his admirers. "Mayor Dufort, we got another building for you." His metal baton drips dark blood. It splatters against his boots and black jeans. The blond hair sticks up in every direction, sweat soaks his shirt. He looks glorious. A warrior.

"I can see that." The other police, basking in his accomplishment, now turn their smiles toward her. *Their idol bows to me, so they do as well.* Again, she thinks of Toby, the swollen-headed jock she dated when she first started boarding school. "Good job…all of you." She looks at each in turn, then lands on Lanson. "And thanks for helping out, Lieutenant. How unexpected." Another five blocks and she will empty the last of the tent city. Dandridge's grimacing smiles have looked far less smug lately.

Patrick Lanson's pale skin flushes red. "I thought I could pick up some fighting techniques from Peyton." He straightens his shoulders, puffs out his chest. "My previous experience doesn't really lend itself to this type of combat."

"No, I don't suppose it would." Renée turns to Peyton. "Well, how did he do?" From the corner of her eye, she sees the flush return to Patrick Lanson's cheeks.

Peyton slaps the lieutenant on the back. "Not bad. You got that one in two hits. Not bad at all for a first time."

Lanson's pleasure at the assessment looks genuine. "Thank you, Peyton." But, he rubs at a purpling bruise on his square jaw. "And, thanks for the assist back there, that guy was right on top of me… I owe you one." Lanson clears his throat. Whatever happened in the fight has rattled him.

Renée squints at his reaction, wondering, not for the first time, about the lieutenant's age, his job, his life, before the outbreak. And then he shocks Renée further by asking Peyton if he can come along on the next building clean-out, too.

"Better ask my boss first," says Peyton, in that voice always edging on sarcasm.

"Of course, Patrick," Renée answers. Then her voice turns sharp. "Why don't you let me give you a ride back to Park Plaza?"

And Peyton must get a whiff of the politics churning underneath their casual conversation. He puts his back to them, gathers all the fighters for a debrief. Renée didn't ask, but it doesn't seem that they lost anyone this time.

"Of course, Mayor." Lanson follows her back to the Cadillac. She gets in the plush back seat, and Lanson gets in beside her, tracking dust and infected blood onto the floorboard and leather.

"We're giving the Lieutenant a ride to military headquarters."

But Lanson holds out a hand, signaling for Liam to wait. "That won't be necessary. I have my own vehicle, I just wanted this opportunity to talk in private." He turns his body toward hers, lowers his voice, but doesn't ask Liam to step out. Renée thinks he might not like the idea of impropriety with the two of them speaking alone. "We've lost too many soldiers to the feral sick. Way too many. We're running low on ammunition, setting traps, and still dying. Dandridge isn't…" A worry line appears between his eyebrows, and his bottom lip rolls out, making him look much younger than his normal military stoicism. "I've made the decision that we need to copy the methods those suburban kids use, that Peyton uses."

"You should have let me know first. How did you even… Oh, that boy, Andy, told you. *Your spy.*" Renée gives Lanson a cool stare. She learned that look from her mother, practiced it in the mirror until she could stop a conversation with the ice of her expression.

Lanson shakes his head. "No, I didn't send him as a spy. I sent him as a courier, as a means for us to communicate."

She lets his words take a moment to sink in. At last, he made the opening between them that she's hoped for. But Renée needs to

examine all the ways that this could trap her. *What does Lanson want?*
What is he after?

Liam clears his throat from the front seat. "I'm sorry, ma' am.
The young policeman…with the acne problem? That's Andy? He
did ask to speak with you several times this week. I didn't…he said
it was about uniform supplies, and I sent him to Resource
Management."

"See?" Lanson nods to Liam. "I need you to trust me, Renée."
His hand is on the door handle like he means to bolt from the car,
now that he delivered this request.

"Why?"

Lanson hesitates, depresses the door handle, but doesn't open it.
He glances at Liam, who watches the two of them from the rearview
mirror.

Renée sighs. "Whatever it is, you can tell me in front of Liam.
He's my most trusted staff." *He's my only staff.*

Lanson nods. "I think you and I need to trust each other because
we both know that national infrastructure is gone. Whatever they tell
you in your secret calls to Washington can't be any better than what
we hear from the Pentagon. All of it is gone. We're on our own
here."

When the door closes, Liam turns a panicked face toward her.
"What does that mean? What is gone? How can it be *gone*?"

"Just drive, Liam."

Once the car starts moving, Renée closes her eyes, tries to picture
her father. *What would Daddy have said? What would he have done?* She
can only remember him advising her on which favors to do, which
secrets to keep, which tasks she should take over to make other,
higher-ranking people dependent on her. *Climbing, climbing…* But
now, she sat at the top—a lone peak over the city. And she sat there
alone.

14 Gabriel

I'm dreaming. Maybe dreaming…he finds himself caught in a memory, detached from his body, unable to move, to call out, to open his eyes.

***

"Knee out. Faster!" Ben slides right, just fast enough to miss the brunt of Gabriel's leg. "Defense—Hands up! Do it again."

Sweat burns in Gabriel's eyes. Under Ben's guidance, Gabriel woke before dawn to do a six-mile run. He boxed in the mornings, then spent his afternoons sparring in not only his favorite, Krav Maga, but also karate, jujutsu, judo, wrestling. Lean muscle wrapped his bones, filled out the hollows in his ribs. Gabriel had learned to keep rigid control of the physical tics and spasms created by his constant searing anxiety. Now, his body flowed from move to move like the sinuous course of a dream. And at last, Gabriel felt the master of himself. Exhaustive training left no room for the pile up of sensation and emotion that had always plagued him. He skips forward, his knee to Ben's groin.

"Good!" Ben's pads take the kick. He drops down in the way a true opponent might. "Cross punch!"

Gabriel's body acts before his brain. He lands a solid cracking punch to Ben's collarbone.

"Fu—" Ben falls backward. His face and body contort in pain.

"I didn't mean—Ben!"

"No. Don't apologize. Good hit. Good hit." Ben's voice comes out strangled. He curls onto the mat. "Fuck. Get Freddy."

"I'm sorry—"

Freddy pushes Gabriel out of the way. "I called an ambulance." The old man already has an armful of ice packs that he stuffs around Ben's writhing body.

"*Told you, Benjamin. I told you… The kid is getting too strong for you to spar with—*"

A screech cuts through the dojo. "*Oh, my God! Benjie!*" *Elena, Ben's girlfriend, rushes between them, her pointy stilettos punching little holes into the mat. Her dark eyes meet Gabriel's.* "*What did you do to him, you freak?*"

Freddy clucks at her. "*It was a fair match,*" *Freddy's voice sounds like gravel crunching under a car's tire. He doesn't like Elena hanging out in the gym, smoking cigarettes and drinking around the fighters.* "*And, I called an ambulance.*"

Gabriel drops down beside Ben, takes his hand. "*I'm sorry. I—*"

"*Get away from him, you little homo!*" *Elena slaps Gabriel's hand away.* "*Just because your rich daddy pays our bills, doesn't mean you can do whatever you want.*"

"*It was an accident.*" *Gabriel's voice works despite his brain shorting out. Ben is on the ground, his face turning purple. The skin under his neck strains against the broken bone. It looks like an arrow tip trying to break free.* "*Ben…*"

The bone point blurs. It turns into a rough scabbed bite mark. Ben's dark head becomes Bailey's messy long curls.

Gabriel opens his eyes. He'd fallen asleep in the basement again. Not even on the cot, but right on the cold cement floor near the bars of the cage, his jacket a lumpy pillow under his head. Despite the gloomy dim light, he can see Bailey's wide gray eyes watching him. *Maybe I shouted in my sleep?*

When he sits up, Gabriel wipes a hand down his face and finds tears still damp on his cheeks. "Oh. I cried."

At the sound of Gabriel's voice, Creature-Bailey crawls back into a torn pile of mattress and straw.

"I didn't mean to scare you," Gabriel whispers. He pulls his knees to his chest and hugs them, a childish pose he would never allow himself outside the dark of this basement. "I was dreaming…or remembering… I'm not sure." Fucking Elena—he hasn't dreamed about her in a long time. *The memories I'd worked so hard to push down…*

That outburst in Cushing brought all of them boiling back to the surface. "It was Ben again."

Gabriel rubs his face against the soft wool of his trousers. "I already told you about how he was my martial arts teacher…but I left something out. Or I hadn't wanted to remember." Gabriel squeezes his eyes closed. *No that's worse.* With his eyes closed, he can see it. "Ben had a fiancé…her name was Elena, and she hung out at the dojo all the time, hung all over *him* all the time. I hated her."

"Get away from him, you little homo!" He spent a long time thinking about what Elena called him. Was it true? He liked Ben, had good feelings for him. Different from the feelings he had for Freddy? The old man lived in the dojo with Gabriel and spent more time with him. On a good training day, after a good fight, Freddy patted him on the head.

Am I gay?

Ben spent eight weeks in a sling, so Freddy took over all of Gabriel's training. The old man believed in a more rigorous system, had coached MMA competitors—winners—before opening the gym with Ben. He fine-tuned all Gabriel's training with technique and mental discipline exercises. He added meditation, cold showers, and fasting to Gabriel's regime. Then, after week eight, Ben returned to the gym. His left arm had frozen in its socket, and the shoulder sagged lower than the right. He would need another surgery, still, the prognosis didn't look good. Ben would never fight again.

A shaky hand clasped Gabriel's shoulder. "Freddy says you should compete. You could take my place." Ben's olive skin glistened with sweat, and his pupils had shrunk to pinpricks.

"No, Ben. I would never take your place." Gabriel wanted to add that he could never be as good a fighter as Ben. But they both knew the truth, Gabriel had already beaten him. Ben had underestimated Gabriel in the match that ended his career.

Elena scowled from behind Ben's still bulky chest. She'd changed, too, makeup not as fresh, nail polish chipped. "But you think you *could*?" She wrapped both her slim arms around Ben's useless one.

"Elena, come on…don't be like that. Gabriel is my student." Ben's brittle laugh ended in a groan. He hunched over like his stomach pained him.

"He's a homo, can't you see that Benjie?" Elena stepped between them, got right in Gabriel's face. She smelled like cigarettes and flowery perfume. Gabriel's stomach clenched. *Disgusting.*

"Cut it out, okay?" But, Ben had already turned away, rubbing at his midsection with his right hand. The left hung at his side, like Ben had forgotten he even had the other arm. "Freddy, I was wondering—"

The old man shook his head before Ben even finished his question. The arm might hurt, but Ben had already taken all his painkillers for that week's prescription. Worse than Elena's perfume, pity twisted Gabriel's gut.

"Are you listening to me?" Spittle flew from Elena's mouth, sprayed Gabriel's face.

"No." He retreated into the back of the dojo, to the little room with his cot, and his stack of clothing and books. Freddy had an identically spartan room beside Gabriel's. Freddy's one indulgence though was his collection of records and his beat up record player. Sometimes, the old man invited Gabriel in to listen to music with him. Gabriel didn't know any of the songs, only a few had words. Freddy called it big band or swing…it all sounded so upbeat and optimistic, but Gabriel had never seen Freddy with any expression other than a disappointed frown, sometimes a satisfied frown when Gabriel won a match.

Gabriel didn't have an impressive range of expression himself. That night, the two of them sat in metal folding chairs and listened to the high-spirited music, each lost in his own morose thoughts. Even though neither of them spoke about Ben's decline, they both noticed. Gabriel had no idea how to fix an addiction, how to even address what he saw happening to Ben. And if Freddy had any ideas, he didn't share them with Gabriel. Just as the record player's needle entered the last scratchy space between songs, a fierce knocking carried across the gym. They both sat up straighter on the uncomfortable chairs.

"Is it the side door?" Gabriel asked. That door led out to the parking lot, but Freddy always kept it locked. Only he and Gabriel had keys to it.

Freddy sighed instead of answering and pulled his keychain from its peg. Gabriel turned off the record player, picked up the disc, and slipped it back into its paper sleeve, then the cardboard album cover. Whoever Freddy let inside the dojo had a lot to say, quick demanding words that met with the old man's trademark silence. Then the scent of cigarettes and perfume trailed back into Freddy's bedroom and wrapped around Gabriel like a snake. He could hear Elena's high pitched voice, "He *needs* them, Freddy. Why are you being so stingy?"

Painkillers.

Freddy kept a stash of all kinds of drugs and medicines in a locker behind the main counter. Maybe opiates, too. Gabriel didn't know everything in there, but Elena obviously did. "Give me the key to the locker," Elena demanded.

"You'll kill him," said the old man. His voice rasped, unrecognizable when Gabriel had only ever heard the gravel bark of Freddy's orders. "Elena, you keep giving him drugs, and you'll kill him."

Then a fierce scream, and Gabriel heard the smack of blunt force against flesh. A grunt, and the unmistakable thud of a body falling to the mat.

Gabriel flew from the little room, upsetting the record player, which clattered to the floor. Elena held a gleaming trophy in one hand, blood dripped from the heavy marble base over Freddy's graying face.

"You!" Her glassy red eyes found Gabriel. "This is all your fault." One of her towering high-heeled shoes had stuck in a seam of the exercise mat and come off. She dropped to her knees to rummage through Freddy's pockets. "I'm not going to kill Benjie. That rich daddy's boy is the one who's killing him." She pulled the jangling key ring from Freddy's shirt front.

Freddy's hand reached to take it back. "No, Elena…"

"Shut up!" Elena raised the trophy again and slammed it down onto Freddy's skull. She smiled in triumph, staggered up with the key ring. And then the memories fragment.

The exit light near the back door bathing the room in red.

Freddy's warm blood welling up between his toes.

Cigarettes and perfume filling his lungs.

A scream cut off, and Elena's throat in his hand. Her fragile bones moving beneath the grip of his fingers. Chipped nails digging at his arms…

Elena dead.

***

When Gabriel looks up, Bailey has crawled from the nest of torn paper and cloth. His panting breaths gurgle from his throat. Blood coats the fingers of his clawed hands and his face, most likely the rabbit Gabriel set loose in his cage the day before. *When he recovers, Bailey will be horrified that he killed animals to stay alive.* He will blame Gabriel for making them available to him. *That won't matter.* If Bailey wants to hate Gabriel for keeping him alive…at least he will be alive.

A shuddering sigh makes Gabriel aware that he has not stopped crying. That he told the story of Ben, Freddy, and Elena with tears still coursing down his cheeks as they did during his dream.

Bailey creeps closer in jerky movements, his already raw knees scraping against the cement floor. He presses his pebbled naked skin against the iron bars of the cage to peer at Gabriel through the matted tangles of his hair. One arm uncurls slightly and reaches out toward Gabriel. A rigid, misshapen hand, broken dirty nails. They touch the tear-streaked skin on Gabriel's face.

"Bailey? Do you...are you *in there*?"

The hand pulls back against Bailey's dirty, scratched chest.

"Bailey?"

A beat of stillness, then Creature-Bailey scrambles back into the shadowed piles of debris littering his cage.

15 Renee

At first, Peyton balked at Renée's demand for late night meetings.

And she suffered through his monosyllabic answers and sarcasm until she had the idea to have Liam bring them dinner and drinks. Peyton became much more willing to report to her if she handed him a glass of bourbon when he showed up.

Tonight, he even changed out of his filthy black uniform and showered. Dark jeans and tight white sweater, golden hair brushed back from the handsome face. He looks every bit the handsome, athletic god he was before Super Flu.

He catches her checking him out. "Like what you see?" Peyton lounges back in the leather chair facing her desk, which he finally stopped planting his boots on. And, like he always does, he gives her a blatant, disrespectful once-over.

She raises an eyebrow. "Like what *you* see?"

"How come I never met you before this?" Peyton asks. "Before the fucking apocalypse?"

"Because I didn't see any point in our meeting," she keeps her voice neutral. "You were just some dumb jock my freakish brother managed to draw in."

"So, you knew about me. And remembered me." He grins.

Should she stop his clumsy flirtation in its tracks? Should she pretend to like it? *Could I control Peyton better if we became lovers?* She thinks of Case Bell, still giving him sad-eyed looks. *But, I'm not Case Bell.* Renée could never fall in love with Peyton Tyrone.

She wore her usual skirt suit today, and she peels away the jacket and combs her fingers through her blond hair. "Are you asking if I was attracted to you?" She raises an eyebrow, imitates her mother's disdainful expression, the one that rattled Lanson the other day.

Peyton just laughs. A hard, mocking, bark. "Of course you were attracted to me," he says. "I'm hot. And you must have decided I was more than just a dumb jock." The words would sound like an insecure plea in anyone else's voice, with any other expression. But, Peyton seems to find Renée's opinion of him meaningless, her assumptions amusing.

This better not be a mistake. She fights not to grit her teeth. "Clearly, you have progressed since then, and now have worth to me."

Peyton grins, revealing his straight white teeth, startling against his tan skin. "You sound just like him when you say stuff like that." He stretches an arm behind him and lets it drape across the back of his chair.

My God, he's a beautiful man. Too bad his words leave her cold. "I am nothing like my brother."

"Yeah, you are." Peyton nods at her desk. "Always with the plans and the charts." He points at her and raises slitted eyes to meet hers. "Never just doing shit for the hell of it. For *fun*."

"I know how to have fun." She slides her fingers toward her leather-bound notebook with its endless list of tasks…food distribution, electricity and water maintenance, housing, transportation, trade… To keep her half of the city from falling to ruin, she will need every single one of them accomplished. But, none of that list will happen if she can't promise security in the buildings and streets, if she can't make the city a viable center for trade, for information. Renée tips her head up, watches Peyton through her lashes. "I need your fighting skills far too much to fall for…" She flicks her fingers toward his arrogant sprawl, his flawless body, his perfect face. "I'm not some high school girl dazzled by the football captain."

"Good." The sincerity in Peyton's voice startles her. "I hate that shit. Love is for suckers. You and I know better than that."

Yes. She does.

***

Her last relationship began when she was sixteen years old. She'd escaped boarding school for a weekend home in New York. Her popularity had never recovered from the party where Gabriel had his bizarre meltdown. Rumors of her psychotic brother attacking guests, his naked fit, dogged her month after month. And then someone connected the tabloid story of actress Pauline Dufort's mentally-disturbed son murdering a woman in Florida. The link to that story had passed via text to every student and teacher at her school. And all of them watched *her*…searching for any cracks in Renée's polished image, scrutinizing her actions for any hint of familial derangement. *They're twins!* Campus had become intolerable. She needed to change schools, she needed her father to *listen* to her.

And this stuffy man, in his three-piece suit and pocket watch stood in her way. "So good to see you again, Miss Featherton. At the moment, your father has a client with him in the study. However—"

"When will they be finished? I need to talk with Daddy. It's important."

"I… His schedule is quite full. Had I known you would be coming home early, then I might have scheduled—"

"I'm his *daughter*. You can cancel some appointments for his *daughter*, can't you?"

The man pulled off his wire-rimmed glasses, studied the lenses. And, despite the fussy clothing, he suddenly looked much younger. Older than Renée, of course, but early twenties, maybe even a college intern.

She tilted her head, considered this man anew. "What's your name?"

"Oh, I'm so sorry." He replaced the glasses. "I'm Dustin Ansford, your father's assistant. I… We've met once before at your parents' Christmas party in the Hamptons. I… Your father asked me to direct you to the receiving line?"

"Yes, I remember." Not Dustin, she couldn't remember him at all. But, she did recall her father's request. Daddy had stayed at the party only to greet his guests and make a toast. Then, Maurice Featherton left the actual mingling for his wife and daughter while he caught a helicopter to Florida. To see Gabriel, of course. Even though a court had declared her brother a danger to himself and others, Daddy still loved her brother more than her.

***

"Miss Featherton?" Dustin Ansford patted down his pockets and pulled out a linen handkerchief, handed it to her. Without her realizing, Renée's stifled tears had spilled over onto the pressed white cotton of her school uniform shirt. "I'll just…" Dustin scurried toward the antique roll-top desk, booted up a laptop there, and opened a leather diary.

A frown appeared on his unremarkable face as he tapped away at the laptop. "Your father has one more meeting after this. And…" He flipped a page in the leather diary, reached for a pen and crossed something out. "There. I've canceled everything this evening. I'll get you ballet tickets and reservations at Le Tableau. That's your favorite?"

It was. With the mention of the restaurant, she had a vague memory of talking with Dustin at the Christmas party, his interest in her. *Oh, because of her looks, her expensive face.* She suddenly understood the times she saw gratification slip from her mother's face and contempt take its place. She imitated one of Pauline's benevolent smiles. "You can do that?"

"Your father won't even know that I changed things around." Dustin had worked a miracle in Renée's life, and it had only taken him minutes.

What else could he do? Could he move her to a new school? Could he get her an allowance big enough to live on her own?

"Thank you, Dustin." Renée set her hand over his, left the tears settled in her eyes because she knew they looked bluer, brighter, that way. Another trick her mother used. "You're like my knight in shining armor," her voice breathless, inviting, while nausea curled in her stomach. *Think of what Daddy would say, "Whatever it takes to gain power."*

***

Love is for suckers, she couldn't agree more. "You say I don't know how to have fun, but all I see you do is fight and kill. Is that what you think of as a good time? Beating people to death?"

"Aw, don't put it like that, now." But, he grins as if he rather enjoys how she "put it." Peyton stretches his arms over his head, and the sweater pulls tighter over the bulging muscles in his chest, rides up to show defined abs.

"Well, then tell me what else you do for fun."

"Or I could show you."

"Or you could show me…" She gives him the slow, seductive smile that always worked on Dustin.

***

They stop by her penthouse apartment in Bricktown District, so she can change clothes, and Peyton whistles at the floor-to-ceiling windows, the squishy leather couch.

"Haven't you ever been here?" she asks him. She unbuttons the top of her blouse under his eyes before disappearing into the bedroom.

He follows her in. "Why would I?"

"My father owned this apartment for entertaining. I thought my brother must have also thrown a party or two in it. I know that Gabriel used to bring people here…girls…I even walked in on him once."

"Sure. If you say so."

"You don't believe me?"

"I never came to any parties here." He leans against the doorway, arms crossed and gaze raking over her body as she shimmies into a pair of jeans, a black turtleneck. "But I went to a party at the house in Olde Town. Why didn't you live there?"

She stuffs her feet into a pair of black leather boots she hasn't worn since before the outbreak, not since she needed to look older, make people take her seriously as their superior. "I had a place of my own in Deep Deuce, but I relinquished it for housing refugees."

"How charitable…giving up a second apartment for a stronger territory."

She gives him another slow smile, this time less forced. "You understand me well."

"I guess," he says with a shrug. "Maybe, I'm just an understanding guy."

***

Peyton tosses her a black helmet but leaves his own head bare. "Saddle up," he tells her and nods to a black and white Kawasaki Ninja. The two of them go racing through the streets. Plastered to his back, first out of fear and then to shout directions, she directs him along the barricade streets. Tall fencing made of wood, cement, and razor wire separate the post-pandemic city from the wastelands of crumbling, abandoned buildings. Light from dark. The city still hums with electricity, and the jungle of vacant buildings stays dark and desolate. Once she gets a feel for Peyton's skill on the bike, Renée unsnaps her helmet and tosses it into the street. She wants to feel the sharp wind comb through her hair, to lose herself in the wild ride through the night. Peyton grins back at her. "Yeah!" Whatever shows on her face has found an answering pulse in him. She knows it. She feels it.

The Ninja jumps the curb, and Peyton steers them over a clipped grassy hill, a small park in the city that Renée placed on the refugee task list, the work for trade credits that has taken the place of currency inside the city. The bike kicks up dirt and grass, shreds a flowerbed of the carefully planted spring bulbs waiting to bloom. If Liam reported this kind of abuse to her during the day, she would have the perpetrator caught and stripped of all their belongings. She might even expel them from the city. *Territory...numbers...* No, she wouldn't expel them from the city. But she would make them pay.

Oblivious to her tally of punishments, Peyton circles a copse of trees, grinds to a stop in the tangle of roots. He twists in the seat and wraps his arms around her, the bike still purring beneath them.

"You just mangled my park."

"So what?" He threads his rough fingers through her hair. "Get someone to fix it." Smoky moonlight flits across his broad tan cheekbones, his full lips, his long Roman nose.

"Okay," she whispers, but the word is lost inside Peyton's rough kiss.

16 Gabriel

Shane's grim face pokes into the study. "Boss, we got a problem." Behind him wait Lawrence Vu and one of the younger Loeza boys.

What is that boy's name? Gabriel used to know all the names, ages, and key personal details of every member of his organization. Hundreds of refugees and the absorption of Jaxon Colton's territory have made it impossible to know everyone as intimately as before. *But this boy is Rico's younger brother, Angelica Loeza's brother. I should remember. I'm slipping.* And his lapses have nothing to do with the rapid growth of the Featherton organization and everything to do with Bailey.

Gabriel rubs at his forehead before forcing his hand down onto the desktop, folding it in with the other. "Come in."

Lawrence and the young Loeza boy both reek of sweat and smoke. The Loeza kid's eyes dart around the room as if he expects to see a cage of creatures, whips, and chains, like they found in the remains of Colton's barn. Gabriel's right leg starts to jiggle.

The younger boy's frantic gaze settles on Gabriel. "Pierce Heights is—" He must decide against speaking first. He looks between Shane and Lawrence, round dark eyes trying to judge his place in this hurried meeting.

Gabriel slams his palms against the desk, frustration bubbling beneath his skin like a boiling pot. "What is it?"

Shane pushes Lawrence Vu forward. "People are angry about the apples…and the dairy supplies…" Lawrence takes a deep breath. "A bunch of them got together and decided to raid the storehouse."

"And, where is Derek Sams?"

When the younger Loeza sees that Gabriel doesn't blame Lawrence for the bad news, he jumps back into the conversation. "Derek stayed behind to defend the storehouse with the runners. But there were a lot of people, and they started talking about getting torches and burning their way inside."

Gabriel and Shane exchange a dark look. "Sounds like trouble." Shane always sounds incensed that anyone would defy the orderliness of Gabriel's territory.

"Trouble we will end." Gabriel stands. "Pull all the guards, Shane. And, let's go."

***

Above Pierce Heights, black smoke curls into the pale winter sky, and the front entrance gapes open. Angry heat floods Gabriel's body. *What the hell has happened here?* The storehouse is a three-story designer home in a similar modern style to every other house in the twisting, hilly neighborhood. Behind the tinted windows of the Land Rover, Gabriel watches the small crowd of men and women gathered in front. "I don't recognize these people," he says to Shane.

"So, they're new." Shane's hands tighten on the steering wheel. "Refugees you rehoused, who live on your rations. They need to learn their place."

"This is their home now, Shane." *This is my fault. I should have seen this coming. Why didn't I?* He rubs his thumb against his lower lip.

A stocky woman pounds a shovel against the house's double front doors. She won't get in. Those doors have steel bars reinforcing them on the interior. But, it looks like several of the men have set fire to the wooden window sills and door frame to try and smoke out the workers inside, force them to open the doors. Since the approach of Gabriel's fleet of cars, the crowd has grown more subdued. A few men do indeed have torches, but the majority carry weapons used in defending against creatures. They drop them to their sides as Gabriel's black SUV rolls closer. Five other dark vans follow. "Wait…wait…" he directs Shane. "I want everyone to exit at the same time."

Shane whispers Gabriel's instructions into his walkie talkie. "Everyone's ready. Just say when, boss."

"When."

The van doors open and forty of his fighters climb out. Men. Women. Well, boys and girls, if Gabriel wants to be honest with himself. Their post pandemic world has nearly emptied of adults. Gabriel has a last moment of peace, then Shane opens the car door for him, and he steps into the now silent street. His dark wool coat flaps in the cold breeze. Despite his nights in the basement, Gabriel still takes pains to dress impeccably in designer suits and shoes. His height and perfect grooming set him apart from others, make him unapproachable. A necessity. He can't tolerate anything else.

The gathered neighbors look at each other, older men and women—older than the teenagers that he recruits into Feathertons.

At first, Shane hugs close to Gabriel's back, but Gabriel waves him away. He approaches the crowd with slow, even steps. "This house is my property."

A dark-haired man moves to the front of the crowd. "We just want our fair share," he says. "We heard that Olde Town got double fruit rations, and yogurt…and cheese." Emboldened by his words, the other neighbors all begin to talk.

"We want—"

"I should get—"

"You should give—"

Gabriel holds up a hand for the neighbors to quiet, his fighters close in beside him. *Stay calm. Stay in control.* "All neighborhoods receive the same rations."

The woman with the shovel elbows her way to the front. "I've got kids. I need milk and bread. I need more than what our runners give us."

Gabriel's hand twitches. He forces it still. "I understand." He doesn't really. Every person gets the same rations—children included. "I can restructure the order forms."

The woman deflates for only a second. "And I want..." Blood rushes to her face. "I want to know what else..."

The man comes to her rescue. "You told us that life here would be like before the virus. You told us if we came here we—"

"I promised you safety. Have you already forgotten what life is like outside this territory? Have you forgotten that you were starving? That you couldn't close your eyes at night for fear of a creature attack?" Gabriel's fingers have started to twitch again. He stuffs both hands into his coat pockets. Reasoning with these people won't work. He's given them the veneer of life as they remembered it, but they are still confined to their homes. Without work. Without entertainment. Without all the frivolous objects of desire and distraction. He should have considered all of this. He should have planned. *I've abandoned all my plans to wait for a miracle.* Frustration makes his jaw harden, his muscles tense.

The man in front of him takes a step back. The woman with the shovel hugs it to her chest. "We...we didn't forget..." she stutters.

A loud popping sound cuts off her words and draws all the attention from Gabriel and back to the smoldering house. A picture window on the front of the house cracks open, then shatters into a jagged open hole. Blackened and broken glass scatters over the scraggly front lawn. The fire has caught and flames burst from a wall.

Gabriel can hear screaming inside. The young Loeza boy rushes forward. "Luis!" He grabs at Gabriel's sleeve. "My brother is inside!"

"I'll get him." Gabriel pulls off his heavy coat, tosses it to the child. "Stay here," he orders. He moves without thinking. Glass catches against the pressed wool of his black suit, cuts into his palm as he vaults through the open window frame.

The smoke inside has thickened to fog, to night. Gabriel rips his suit jacket off and holds it over his face. His soldiers flank him. He can't see them, but he feels their bulky presence as they bump into his arms and legs.

"Upstairs!"

He sprints up the expansive front staircase for the safe room—a bedroom converted to hold the most precious goods he trades: medicine, drugs. Derek Sams crouches by a boarded window there. Angelica Loeza kneels beside him with two runners—both boys have fluorescent green dye streaking their hair. One of these must be Luis. *The dark-eyed one.* He looks just like the child outside, just like Rico. Gabriel pries him from Angelica's arms. "Come with me."

Derek Sams' face twists. "No way those people outside—"

Shane hauls Sams up by his elbow. "It's taken care of." The other green-haired runner locks a fist on the hem of Shane's leather jacket.

"Go," Gabriel tells him. He hoists Luis into his arms and lets Angelica follow on her own.

Outside the burning house, Featherton guards have collected the rioters, taken their weapons from them. And other neighbors have gathered to gawk. Gabriel recognizes most of them. The Vu family. The Backburns. Lizzie and Simon Duchamp. In his life before the pandemic, Gabriel and his parents had gone to dinner at the Backburn house. Thomas Backburn worked for Gabriel's father. *What is he doing now?* He looks drawn and older than the vibrant man Gabriel remembers. All these people…they are Gabriel's responsibility now. And he has ignored them for weeks. *Nine weeks.* He delivers Luis Loeza into his older brother's embrace.

What was Angelica doing here in Pierce Heights? As his Quail Creek Lieutenant, Angelica runs her own neighborhood on the other end of Gabriel's territory. *Plotting something with Sams. A takeover?*

"What should we do with them?" Shane gestures to the rioters they've captured.

"Bring them to Olde Town. Angelica and Derek, too."

While Angelica and Derek go peacefully enough, the men and women who attacked the storehouse do not. They start to scream and fight the guards. The woman who spoke up earlier, now stripped of her metal bat, throws herself to the ground. "No, please! I'll leave. I'll leave with nothing and never bother you again. Please, Gabriel!"

The dark-haired man from earlier swings at a younger, taller guard. Unlike the woman, he doesn't try to beg Gabriel, but turns toward the neighbors who have come to watch. "Are you just going to let him take us? You've all heard what he does to people in Olde Town—he'll infect and cage us. Then he'll set us on the rest of you the second you step out of line!"

That stops Gabriel in his tracks back to his car. "I've never infected anyone," his voice comes out like a growl. He bears down on the man.

Stop.

He can't. Gabriel's fist crashes against the man's face, caves his nose to pulp, and blood rushes down the front of his flannel jacket. Gabriel shakes loose his fist. Now he turns toward the assembled crowd. "I'm not infecting people. I'm not trying to weaponize the sick. I'm not Colton."

He crouches down next to the crying woman. "I promise that you will be returned to your children by nightfall. I won't hurt you."

But I just demonstrated with my fist that I will hurt them. That I can hurt them.

And, what had he told Colton? "Fear doesn't keep people loyal."

17 Renée

Renée stands at the window in a thin blue satin robe, the day's soot and smoke washed away in a hot bath, from water that she painstakingly warmed on her gas stove. Before the outbreak, her father's chef had outfitted the entire kitchen with professional appliances. If he'd lived, she would have thanked him for installing a stove big enough to heat six boiling spaghetti pots. Maurice Featherton didn't care about the kitchen. He chose the penthouse apartment for its expansive views of the city and the convenient location near the basketball arena and baseball fields. He'd picked it because it would impress other people. But, since the outbreak, the penthouse had only impressed Peyton. *It's impractical...dependent on electricity or ten flights of stairs. Drafty.*

The roar of an engine, and she spots the futuristic white and black of Peyton's motorcycle. The flash of his blond hair in the dying sun. She left all the lights off to have these moments of observation to herself. To see Peyton without him seeing her. He's hardly an inscrutable figure, but she needs to be sure. Can she trust him?

Peyton wipes a hand over his face. Then he bends over from his seat on the bike and shakes plaster dust and dirt from his hair. Another old building cleared of creatures in Renée's half of the city. *And there.* That expression Renée can't parse out, the only one. A softening of the features, eyes glassing over, lips curled in and viciously bitten—a moment of reflection where Peyton looks uncertain, vulnerable. Something eats at him, torments him. And Renée doesn't know what. That troubles her.

Is it the girl?

***

Whenever Case Bell shows up with a tanker of fuel, she makes a point to speak with Peyton, ask how he's doing. The girl looks love-starved, desperate for any attention from Renée's golden soldier, who remains nonplussed. Peyton shrugs off her questions, doesn't ask any of his own. Case never gives away information on Feathertons, on the situation in the burbs. Although Peyton ignores Case, Renée tries to engage her, but none of her efforts work on the stoic teenager.

"You should stay for dinner," Renée offered last week. "I can give you food as good as what you have in the suburbs."

"No, thanks. I just want the meds."

The place where they did the tanker switches, the shell of a burned-out factory, offered little refuge from the cold wind gusts. Stinging grit and dust rasped against their skin through the open wall frames of the impromptu garage.

"Don't you want to get warm, catch up with Peyton? You two must have so much to talk about."

"No, we don't." Peyton leaned against a soot-blackened wall. He wore head-to-toe padded black leather, arms crossed over his chest. He looked like every post-apocalyptic movie hero, right down to the hardened sneer. "Probably just the same boring shit happening out there. Gabriel still breathing down everyone's neck to stay in line." Peyton's gaze turns intense. "Nothing's changed. Am I *right?*"

Case looked pained, shook her head. "No...not...not..." But, she sucked in a breath, bit back the rest of what she wanted to say. "Anyway, Gabriel's not that bad."

Peyton kicked off the wall. "Are you fucking serious, Case? I thought you hated the guy." The usual mixture of anger and amusement rolled off of him. "You better hope he feels the same about you once he finds out you're going behind his back to give us fuel."

Us.

Renée couldn't quite hide the flutter of pleasure at his words. "Maybe she doesn't know my brother as well as we do."

Peyton's grin had nothing in common with a smile, he looked vicious—a predator toying with his prey for fun. "She doesn't."

"Y'all can stop talking over my head like I'm not here."

Renée should have been angry that Peyton ruined her chances at pulling Case over on her side. But maybe she had ruined that chance herself. Did she really want to be friends with Peyton's ex-girlfriend? It sounded like he'd had a lot of them, but something about the steady concern from Case irked Renée. She felt like she missed a lot in their conversations, despite "talking over Case's head."

Renée handed over the duffel bag stuffed with the medicine and other drugs Case had asked for. "It's all there, and a little bit more for your trouble."

Case gave her a wary look. In their new world, no one did favors without expecting something in return. "I'm not giving you anything besides the fuel. If Gabriel catches on, he might forgive theft, but spying will get me killed."

"You wouldn't be the first girl my brother murdered. He has a really bad track record with his friend's girlfriends and fiancés. You should ask him about it."

Case scowled and headed for the waiting empty tanker. Peyton sauntered behind her, smacked a hand on the truck cab as he watched her climb into the driver seat. "Not yet, Peyton. But one day…"

And there. Peyton's soft, pained expression that Renée couldn't align with anything else she knew about the hostile, swaggering killer. The partner that she'd given her police force to…and taken to her bed.

"One day what?" Renée asked.

Case turned the key, and the tanker rumbled to life. "One day things will get better," she shouted over the engine. Renée had left her just enough gas to reach the outskirts of her brother's territory, the most that the city could spare. Case would need to figure out how to get it back to Cushing from there.

Peyton shook his head, disgust and the ever-present anger fighting for dominance on his face. He made a game show flourish as Case slowly reversed the truck from its hiding place. "What do you think, Mayor Dufort? Is that attitude pathetic or just insane?"

Renée burst into laughter. But then sobered up as she watched the tanker pull away. "Things will never get better for her if she stays under my brother's thumb." She raised an eyebrow at Peyton. "He really did murder someone, you know? Before the virus. He isn't stable."

His face hard as a mask, Peyton watched the mini-tanker round a heap of broken vehicles and trash on the corner. "Nobody's stable anymore."

Renée opened her mouth to argue, to say, *"I'm stable."* But, she didn't always feel stable. She, sometimes, had the sensation of free falling, that sudden intake of breath, roll of her stomach, prickle of gooseflesh. It reminded her of looking into the mirror at the plastic surgeon's office. Her plain face replaced by the face of a doll, sculpted nose, cheeks, brow. Granny Featherton's craggy voice. *"Image is everything, Renée."*

***

When Peyton finds her at the window in her clingy blue satin, he pulls her off her feet, carries her in his arms to the bedroom and the waiting warmth of the down comforters piled there. God, she loves the way he kisses her—desperate and demanding—like he wants to steal the air from her lungs, crush her bones against the hard planes of his chest and thighs. His body presses hers into the billowy fabric. "You were watching for me?" She can't see his face buried against her neck, but his voice sounds mocking. "I'm touched."

"You were late."

"We had enough guys to clear out the rest of the block. I found the furniture store you told me about. A whole nest of creatures hunkered down in it. Some cool stuff in there, but they pissed and shit all over the place, and then there was the blood after… You should just burn it out and forget it."

"Dammit, Peyton…I told you to wait until we could scare them out."

"Did you not hear me? They'd stunk it all up. It was crazy. Everything we're fighting now, all the creatures hunkered down in the last of these buildings have been there too long. They're all goners. No fight at all." Peyton strips the thin, silky robe down her shoulders, pulls the fabric aside, not caring that it rips under her body.

"So you're bored? Work faster, and once we have people settled, then I'll give you a more challenging task."

He stops his efforts to undress her. "What kind of task?"

"We need fuel." She peers up at his shadowed face, waiting for a reaction.

"Fuel will come from Gabriel." His slitted eyes rove over her face. "You plan to make a move against him? Or do you want to trade?" She doesn't have any tells. She *knows* that she doesn't, but he acts like he sees something in her expressionless mask. "You want to move against him," he says, and a smile tics the side of his mouth.

"That doesn't bother you?"

"Are you testing me?" His smile becomes more than a tic and turns full blown and beautiful across his face. "You're so fucking easy."

"Forget it for now." The answering flare of heat across her skin infuriates her. "Tell me about the raid tonight. It was nothing but dying creatures. Did you kill them all yourself or let some of the new recruits get a try?"

He rolls his eyes. "Eh. No one else had the stomach for it once we got inside." He cuts his eyes toward her again, and the mean smirk returns. "One of them, a boy, a kid, was just letting another one gnaw on his arm while he howled like a siren. Like he couldn't even figure out that pulling himself free would—" Renée slaps a hand over Peyton's mouth.

"That's enough."

He knocks her hand away and peels the sweaty black t-shirt over his head. Then he turns his back on her to sit up and remove his boots. *Great.* She pushed him away when he needed to talk. Something upset him about cleaning out that creature nest, she'd seen it on his face when he returned.

Renée runs a hand over the muscles rippling in his shoulders. "Did I upset you? Did you need to talk?"

When Peyton turns back to her she can see that he's laughing. "Upset me? That was hilarious. You act like you're so tough, talking about being on top of the fucking shit heap of this world. But you can't even face up to the nasty sludge going on at the bottom." Now he doesn't muffle his laughter. "Man, your expression just now," he wheezes out and doubles over on the bed.

"Fuck you, Peyton. Was that even true? Did you really see them cannibalizing each other?"

Peyton raises a hand, cups the top of her head, and tugs his fingers through her hair. He forces her back to the bed and pulls her body back underneath his. "Yeah. I couldn't make that shit up. Of course, I saw it."

Renée grinds herself into his heavy strength. Peyton's mouth travels down between her breasts. His tongue carves a wet path to its goal. "They're…" her voice comes out panting, needy. How does he always do this to her? "Creatures are disgusting. I can't believe people try to hide their sick family members. Idiots!"

Peyton stops his progress down her body and props his chin on her stomach. "You don't feel sorry for them?"

"The creatures? They're already dead, so…no. And families who try and lock up the infected just endanger everyone around them. I want to fucking kill them for making my job so difficult." Then, she remembers that Peyton had also tried to lock someone up and save him…the messy-haired little brother. She bites her lip. "Maybe it would be different if… Before all this happened, I'd only ever really loved my father, and he died in the first month. So I was never faced with—"

"Your father? Kinky," he murmurs against her flesh. He bites at her waist, and she can't see his expression.

"Oh, fuck off, Peyton. That's not what I—"

Then he gets back to business, his mouth hot and searching between her legs. *Yes…right there…how does he always, always…* No wonder that doe-eyed Case Bell still moons after him.

unity of command

18 Gabriel

Gabriel paces the length of the dining room, waits for his lieutenants to take their seats at the long, polished table. Of his original five lieutenants, only three remain. Gabriel hands them the manila envelopes first.

Derek Sams and Angelica Loeza keep their faces down, reluctant to meet Gabriel's eyes, their attention focused on the content of the envelopes. Jadyn Clegg has an open expression, curious about the contents of the envelopes, upbeat about any decisions Gabriel makes. Sams and Loeza each head population-dense neighborhoods, Pierce Heights and Quail Creek. And Clegg keeps track of all the unincorporated properties scattered throughout Featherton territory. Families and individuals who refused to leave their houses, even as the rest of their neighbors died off.

The other two lieutenants are new. After Cecilia Vu died in the raid on Jaxon Colton's ranch, Gabriel allowed Lawrence Vu to sit in place of his sister for Olde Town. Lawrence pulls each piece of paper from his envelope with his fingertips, skimming it as if the words offend him. And, in place of Peyton Tyrone, Case Bell now represents The Greens. She has Rico at her side, a special allowance made because Case needs his help to take over her new role. But, just to make sure, Rico pulled Gabriel aside as soon as they arrived.

"Boss, I just want to remind you that I only want the stock manager position, not some assistant bullshit duty."

"I remember."

Rico only likes dealing with numbers and strategy. A lieutenant job means fielding questions and complaints from the people inside the territories. Once Rico shakes the papers free of the envelope with The Greens stenciled across it, he speaks up before anyone else. "What is this? Why is that dumb bitch Jenny Hutton going to be tailing me all this week? The fuck do I need her for?"

Gabriel finally slides into his own seat at the head of the table. "Jenny is going to apprentice as an onsite stock manager."

Case rears back at Gabriel's words. "She's Neighborhood Watch President. Are you sure you want her snooping around?"

"I'm dissolving the Watches."

Derek slaps a hand over his face. "Gabriel, man. Are you kidding me?" At last, he looks Gabriel in the face. "People aren't going to like this. You'll have an even bigger problem than what you saw the other day before the fire."

"The neighborhood watches threaten our stability." Gabriel sweeps his hand to indicate the envelopes with their lists and instructions. "I'm implementing an apprenticeship program and work schedule. No more rations for free. We're going back to the 'order and deliver' system we had at the start of the lockdown. You get credit for work, and you have to contribute to the community to earn what you want. We'll establish a modest credit system, but everyone over the age of twelve needs to sign up for a job to do, or to learn." Gabriel folds his hands together to keep them from trembling. "I'm not heartless, but people need goals and employment to feel…" *Happiness? Contentment?* Gabriel feels like a fool acting as if he understands either of those emotions.

***

The twitch of a smile on Angelica's face. "And school. Lessons for kids." Derek pulls his hand away from his face and stares at Angelica. She turns the smile on him. "This is good," she says. Then her expression turns stern, and she points at Rico. "You're gonna be doing these lessons, too, *chico*. Not just managing all the stock for The Greens."

"Ha, right," sarcasm drips from his words, his sneer. "Got to bring my grades up to get into college right?" When his older sister's shoulders droop, Rico scowls harder. "Just a joke. Damn." He snatches the paper outlining the lesson schedule from Case. "I could use some more math skills, I guess."

Jadyn Clegg pushes up from his chair and rounds the table. The tall black teenager worked as a photographer on the yearbook with Bailey, and even though his basketball talent and his charisma put him in Peyton and Gabriel's popularity stratosphere, he'd always stayed friendly and kind to nerdy Bailey. When Jadyn approaches Gabriel to shake his hand, Gabriel doesn't hesitate. "I'm real proud to work for you, man. Angelica is right. What you're doing here is good."

Gabriel holds up one of the sheets of paper. "A list of teachers and subjects are on the back of the schedule. They'll travel to the different neighborhoods for a week at a time. All children five to twelve must take general lessons, but they can also apprentice for one of the neighborhood jobs when they turn eleven."

The excitement of his lieutenants bodes well for the success of Gabriel's new program. Only Lawrence Vu remains silent and frowns as he leafs through the stack of papers for Olde Town—Gabriel's neighborhood.

Lawrence lets the slip of paper fall from his fingers and slaps a hand against the table. "You plan to train people in medical?" He slaps his hand again, and the rest of the room goes silent. "You'll kill us all with this plan."

Gabriel bites at the inside of his cheek. *Control. Keep in control. This is Cecilia's brother. Cecilia was your friend.* His fingers begin to tap against the table. "Carly Jackson and Rhea Han in Quail Creek were both med students." Gabriel's jittery anger has everyone at the table looking down, distancing themselves from the confrontation brewing between he and Lawrence. "Your own mother was a retired nurse... I have others—"

"But you don't just want them to take care of bumps and scrapes, right? You want them to treat the virus. It's a death sentence. Not just for them..." Lawrence balls a fist and holds it over his mouth. At the start of the outbreak, no one understood the lethality of the virus, the danger that the sick posed. Entire hospitals, medical complexes, clinics would fall within days of admitting a single patient. And while Gabriel and his lieutenants might bask in the improvements to the territory they ruled, Super Flu still threatens everyone inside that territory.

Angelica pushes back from the table, eyes fixed on Gabriel. "The virus can't be treated. No one would..." Whatever she sees in Gabriel's face eats away the rest of her sentence.

"Why this response, Angelica? I've heard your fuel runners have plenty to say about what I would or wouldn't do regarding the virus." Her blank stare answers him. She has no idea what he's talking about.

"*...Angelica, man. She hates you. She thinks you kidnapped her brothers.*" Denny lied.

Angelica hasn't spread rumors. And Gabriel left Denny—a man who lies to him—at the most vulnerable point of his territory.

"The virus can't be treated," Gabriel echoes. "I am not a fool." His mind already leaving this argument, focusing on the new problem.

Denny lied. Why? *I let someone lie to my face and then left them in charge of my refinery.* Fuel and food are his most valuable trading coins. Despite the granite in his voice, the chiseled fury on his face,

Angelica and the others sag in relief at his words. Their fear of the virus, their need to believe it won't crash down on them again, trumps every other part of survival. He sends them all away and calls for Shane.

"We need to go back to Cushing."

"Tonight?"

"Now."

***

When they get to the refinery, Denny comes out to greet the Land Rover, worry wrinkling his forehead as Shane and the Mageo brothers also hop out and surround him. Besides their blue and purple mohawks, the brothers also dress identically in black cargo pants and black hoodies. Gabriel finds them difficult to tell apart, but apparently, Denny doesn't have that problem. "Hey, Felix... Hugo." A nervous smile plays across his mouth. "What...what are you two doing out here?" Neither brother answers him, which seems to confirm to Denny that his position as refinery boss, as a Featherton, just became dangerous.

Gabriel lets that awareness sink in and then opens his own car door. He slides from the leather seat and reaches back in to grip Denny's girlfriend, Kelly, by the arm and pull her free. The girl starts screaming before she even leaves the car. "What did you do, Denny? What did you do?" Howling wind edges around the metal walls of the refinery entrance, but Kelly's shrill voice carries over it. "Denny, you stupid—"

"I didn't... Gabriel, I didn't do anything. I swear." Denny backs up a step, twists a little like he plans to run. But Felix Mageo captures him, wrenches his arms behind his back.

"You lied to me."

"I didn't!"

109

"You fucking idiot, Denny! Do you know what it's like out there?" Kelly screeches. "I'm fucking *pregnant*!" She lunges for her boyfriend, but Shane grabs Kelly, holds her to him with his beefy arms. Kelly screams, beats at the air with her fists, still trying to reach Denny. "My brother barely made it home alive, and now he can't even get through a night without waking up screaming. I'm not turning my back on Feathertons, no matter what stupid shit you got messed up in." Gabriel motions for Shane to put Kelly back into the Land Rover, but she digs her heels in the frosted gravel road. "You fucking moron, Denny!"

"I..."

Denny's eyes bug when Gabriel steps closer, wraps a hand around his neck. He feels for the pulse there but doesn't squeeze. Denny's heartbeat flutters under Gabriel's touch, and he leans in to whisper in his ear. "Angelica didn't spread the rumors about experiments and prisoners in Olde Town. She hadn't even heard them. So why did you tell me that she had?" He pulls back to look into Denny's wide eyes. "Kelly is right. You are an idiot. But I won't just let you leave, not after a betrayal like this. Now you have two truths to tell me— where did the rumors come from, and why did you lie. If you don't answer, I'll let these sociopathic brothers beat you until you do. And if you lie again, I'll let them kill you."

19 Renee

Peyton falls beside her, one arm thrown over Renée, pressing her into the mattress under its weight. He applies himself to sex like he does against the creatures, like he does during tag football, like he does in video games. But when they both are completely sated, he turns gentle. He peppers kisses along all the flesh he'd gripped as he positioned her body, and his hands smooth over her heated flesh. His eyes slide over to her. "You got anything to drink? Any booze?"

"I have a bottle of Patrón in the kitchen."

A twist of his mouth. "I guess that'll work." He doesn't bother to get dressed, but fishes a cigarette pack out of his discarded leather pants and lights it. He shakes the pack her direction.

"Sure."

When he brings back the tequila, he hands hers over and clinks their crystal glasses together. "Everything but the northwest corner is clean, and not much down there to raid. You'll have full control of this half of the city in another week."

She almost sloshes the liquor at his words. "That soon?" Before Peyton arrived, she'd wondered if she needed contingency plans on surviving under Dandridge's takeover.

"Yeah, that soon." Peyton knocks back his drink, licks his lips.

"Well…" She reaches over and runs a hand down Peyton's naked back. "That's good. I would have hated crawling to Dandridge, getting some subordinate position in his cobbled-together military."

Peyton snorts, part amusement, but part scorn, too. "You wouldn't just take off? See what else is out there?"

Renée takes a sip from her glass, the alcohol burns down her throat, feels good in the cold room. "I have no intention of ever setting off into the wilderness of a post pandemic world." She swirls the golden liquor before taking another small sip. "Maybe some other place in the country has a functioning infrastructure, but I want *this* city."

Peyton takes a drag off his cigarette. "Why?"

Renée thinks about the last time she opened up to him—he'd turned it into a joke. "I just do."

***

111

"Is Daddy running late?" At her new school, Renée applied herself to becoming valedictorian instead of queen of the social scene. She kept herself apart from her peers so that none of them could turn gossip-hungry eyes on her the way everyone had at her last school. Instead, they called her conceited, stuck-up. They didn't know that under the expensive face, she was plain. She was unimportant. The leftover child. "Oh, I see. He isn't coming, is he?"

Dustin reached out to touch her arm and delivered a socially acceptable pat instead of his usual caress. Too many people had gathered backstage, teachers, administrators. "He did ask me to send his—"

"Just forget it. I don't want to hear it." She clutched her black graduation gown and hat to her stomach. Her fingernails curled into the fabric hard enough that she thought she might rip through it. She wanted to. And she wanted to tear the mortarboard into pieces, stuff it and the robe in the trash. Turn her back on this entire pointless ceremony.

A woman on the events staff poked her head backstage. "Renée?" Her voice chirped with excitement. "We'll introduce you as soon as the seats fill." The other graduates had paraded through the school campus in their gowns and hats. Now as they began to enter the auditorium, "Pomp and Circumstance" started to play. Even over the music, Renée could hear the other students talking, laughing as they took their seats in front of the stage. From the balcony, a hum of excitement filtered down from the parents as they searched for their children. But no one searched for Renée.

Dustin took a step closer to her, but his eyes flitted around at the other people, anxious not to appear inappropriate, even though no one paid them any attention. His ability to blend into the background had worked well in their clandestine relationship. "He did arrange for your mother to come here in his stead."

Renée rolled her eyes. "I'm sure Daddy had to promise her something outrageous to get her to show up." Renée's brittle laugh sounded like a cough. She cleared her throat. "What was it? A new car? Jewelry?"

Dustin reached out again, and again, didn't touch. "She wanted to come—"

Renée cringed away from his sympathy. "Just tell me."

He sucked in a breath. "Your father promised Mrs. Featherton a spa vacation in Switzerland. She's leaving right after the reception in East Hall." Exposing ugly truths about the Featherton marriage always embarrassed Dustin, but Renée had lived all her life aware of the bartering system that was the façade of their family. Her father's assistant pulled his spotless glasses off to polish the lenses. *Such an annoying habit…*

"So, what emergency is it? Farcourt Gas and Oil again? I thought Daddy told them he wasn't interested in relocating to the middle of—" Her words cut off at the blanched face of her lover. *Something even worse than the bribe that ensured her mother's presence?* No wonder Dustin gave up that information so easily.

"Oh. No, your father actually accepted the position. He's moving his office to—"

"That's not what I asked," Renée hissed. "What was the emergency?"

The glasses needed even more vigorous polishing, and Dustin kept the whole of his attention on the task. "Your brother has experienced…difficulties."

"I thought that the freak was locked up and drugged. What could he possibly have done in that state?"

Dustin cleared his throat. "That's just it. He should be ready to integrate back into society, but so far, he's refused to cooperate with that plan."

"Gabriel has never been normal. He belongs right where he is."

"Your father doesn't believe this." Finally, Dustin gave up the ruse of polishing and put his glasses back on. "You have to understand how torn your father was by your brother's incarceration. He refuses to abandon Gabriel to that place."

"But he can abandon me?" The tears in her throat strangled her words, and blood rushed to her neck and cheeks. Humiliating, to have Dustin witness her desperate pining for her father's love. When he reached for her hand again, Dustin's touch made her skin crawl.

She turned away, walked on stage toward the podium like a robot. Gave her speech to an auditorium of strangers while Dustin's words occupied her thoughts. *Daddy had already started moving his office?* An idea bloomed behind the memorized words to her valedictorian speech. With all his quirks and instabilities, Gabriel could never rise to the ambitions Maurice Featherton had set for him.

But, Renée could. She could take a gap year. She could make herself a part of Daddy's work, she would *prove* that she had value— more value—than Gabriel.

20 Gabriel

On the drive to Cushing, Gabriel's main fear centered on his sister. If she had turned Denny into a spy, she could use him to overthrow the refinery. But, Renée had nothing to do with Denny's lies. And he hadn't technically lied. Angelica didn't spread rumors, it was Derek Sams. He'd swagger around the refinery every time he did a fuel pickup for Pierce Heights, telling everyone how he knew better than Gabriel about managing Feathertons, how much more of everything the territory would have if he ran it, how Gabriel spent all his time in the basement with his experiments and had lost touch.

Fucking braggart. But, not a real threat. Gabriel felt certain that Derek lacked the conviction and strength to run more than his own neighborhood. Really, he should thank Denny for believing an idiot like Derek Sams. Before long, Gabriel's sister would become a danger, and he couldn't trust someone as gullible as Denny Skirten.

In the dark corridor of Gabriel's home, the keypad tones sound louder than usual. He had to leave Shane behind in Cushing with the Mageo brothers. "You are the most loyal, " he'd told Shane. "I need you here, in Cushing for now." His sister *would* move against him. Gabriel could count on it. When the basement door unlocks, he trudges down the dark basement stairs, both listening and trying not to listen for any sounds from Bailey.

A shuffle.

Scratching.

A grunt.

He's alive. Still alive. Gabriel removes his wool coat and suit jacket, slips out of his shoes, and creeps closer to the cage. "I'm sorry for my lateness. A problem arose. *Another* problem…" *Where is he?* Ah, there, in the corner. Bailey's white skin, the gleam of his tousled hair. "It's going to be just the two of us in the house for a while, but we'll be safe down here. You'll be safe."

Bailey curls in on himself, moaning. He scrapes his face on the gritty damp floor, back and forth as if to rub his skin from the bone.

"Bailey, stop. Stop!" Jumping up, Gabriel reaches for the flashlight hanging on the wall. He swings it up off its peg and hammers it against the cage's iron bars. Bailey's head jerks up from the floor, and his arms and legs scrabble against the detritus of his cell in an effort to escape the loud noise. When his back hits the wall, Bailey howls in pain and anger like a wounded animal.

Gabriel can remember flashes of his own time in that cage, the rage and fear that thrummed through his blood. The agonizing pain of his rigid arms and useless clawed fingers. Light. Noise.

115

Movement. All of it an assault on his senses. Facing death from a club, a shovel, a pipe would have been a merciful release from the grip of Super Flu's acute stage. "I'm sorry, Bailey," he whispers. "But you were damaging yourself. I can't let you be hurt."

Gabriel drops the flashlight and eases himself down to the floor again. "I'm so tired, Bailey. There's so much to do, and I face opposition everywhere I look. I can't trust anyone." He rakes his hands through his hair, cracking the stiff gel until his hair hangs around his face. "I don't know why I'm doing this anymore." He waves an arm as if he's talking about the two of them, the basement, Bailey's infection. But, he doesn't mean any of those things, he will wait as long as it takes in this dank, putrid-smelling hovel for Bailey to recover. Who cares about territory if he can't have this one thing of his own? Derek Sams can have it all. *He thinks he can run things better than me? Let him try.* When he drags his hands free of his hair, his fingers tremble from his frayed nerves. Gabriel grabs at the iron bars to still them. "I *hate* people. Why am I trying to save them?" He closes his eyes to better picture the padded solitude of his cell at Wellspring. The hours spent meditating alone, unbothered, hoping that everyone in the world outside the institute had forgotten him. If they'd left him in that cell, he wouldn't have to experience this awful, gnawing anguish.

***

Maurice strolled across the scuffed linoleum floor of Wellspring's rec room, hands in the pockets of his designer pants, silk sweater under the sport jacket—his father's version of casual wear. "You drew all these?" Gabriel's sketches lined the wall. Superheroes and anime characters in chalk and oil, Gabriel traded them on commission for candy and the occasional pocketed Klonopin from the staff and other patients. Sometimes, he just gave his art away. What else was there to do in this boring place?

"They're all cartoon characters?" asked his father.

"I just draw what people ask for."

"So, you have friends here?"

"Does it look like I have friends?" Gabriel nodded toward a clutch of young men, other patients, batting a paper ball back and forth across a table. Two burly orderlies watched over them. When competition between the teams erupted into shouts or violence, the orderlies would step in to separate all the players. It had already happened twice that day.

"Son, if you only cooperated with the treatment plan…" Maurice Featherton shook his head. "Your sister already graduated. She's looking into doing an internship for her gap year. That could be you."

"I'd rather stay here."

Maurice sighed, and Gabriel could see that his father worked to steel himself against his frustration. "I've accepted the offer from Farcourt Gas and Oil."

Gabriel made a humming noise of understanding, even though he found talk of his father's business conquests tedious at best.

"Leave this place. You could attend a suburban high school where no one knows you."

"You would let me go to a real school?" Gabriel studied his father's face. He was telling the truth. "You would let me be a teenager? A normal teenager?"

"If that's what you want, Gabriel. You could have a life outside of this place."

"I'm a murderer. I belong here."

"It was temporary insanity. Your trainer, a man you admired and loved, was killed in front of you." Maurice rubbed a thumb across his bottom lip, a gesture that meant strategy and tactics jostled inside his head. "I'm not giving up on you so easily. You're my son, you have my name. I know you can be more than this."

Gabriel raised his own thumb to his mouth. At Ben's, he'd learned discipline to stifle the tics and eruptions of his nervous system on his body. But maybe, he could allow a few gestures to take the edge off that control? His father noticed Gabriel's imitation and smiled. His father enjoyed whenever Gabriel copied anything he did or said. He forced Gabriel to learn poker and billiards, like Maurice played in his downtime. His father ordered all Gabriel's clothes from the same shop and tailor he favored. Even Gabriel's training under Ben and Freddy mirrored Maurice Featherton's youth spent in amateur boxing. The two years at Wellspring, in round after round of group therapy, analysis, behavioral coaching, and cognitive awareness training had taught Gabriel a great deal about the motivations of others.

Despite the frustration of his doctors over his refusal to participate in his own so-called "recovery," Gabriel applied himself diligently to the study of the human psyche. So many puzzling actions and attitudes now made sense to him. While he didn't know his mother well enough to analyze her—it also didn't seem worth the effort to try. Even a casual observation could identify her as a vain and shallow woman. No doubt, his mother had only agreed to birth children as another tally mark in the endless transactions of her marriage to Gabriel's father. Maurice Featherton had always been the more interesting of the two. "But why aren't you giving up on me?" Gabriel asked him. "I haven't made any respectable choices. I've disappointed you. I've embarrassed you."

His father had forgotten studying Gabriel's artwork and turned his examining look on Gabriel. "Because you are my son," Maurice answered him. His voice lacked any emotion, like an impersonal fact.

"Narcissistic Enmeshment—the transferring of your own goals, desires, and identity to a protégé, or more commonly a child—"

Maurice's laughter interrupted his son's cold assessment. "Like a stage mother?" He wound an arm around Gabriel's shoulders.

"Maybe, you're right. But, it doesn't change the fact that it's time for you to leave here, to start living life again. You are my son. I will never give up on you…and I love you."

***

In the dark basement, Gabriel ends his story, and Bailey blinks at him, head tilted as if trying to understand. After a moment, he curls up on the floor again, facing away from Gabriel, the knobs of his spine protrude under his skin.

He's so thin. How much longer can his body hold out? Gabriel stretches out a hand and finds his discarded suit jacket on the ground. He rolls to his side and imitates Bailey's position. Scratched iron bars and thirteen feet of filthy cement separate them, but Gabriel tries to imagine that none of the blood, dirt, or barriers exist. "It's time to start living life again, Bailey. I'm not giving up on you…and…"

21 Renée

Why did I come here? Renée sits on the edge of a gaudy orange leather chair, tries not to breathe in the clouds of marijuana, the stale cloying smell of spilled beer and liquor. Five of her police officers have crammed themselves on an equally hideous orange leather sofa to watch a video game. They shout advice to one of the new recruits, a skinny preteen kid playing Brinda at Mario Kart. Every time Brinda laughs or smiles, a scar cutting into the right side of her mouth makes it look like a snarl. Renée can't stop staring at her. She tries to imagine what caused the four scar lines down her face. Like the swipe of a tiger…*no that's stupid.* Brinda had been feral, and someone fought her off.

"It was a rake."

Renée startles, meets Brenda's dark almond eyes staring back at her. "Sorry, I didn't mean to—"

"My grandmother tried to kill me with a steel garden rake. After I got better, I hiked my way back home, and my little sister told me the story." Brinda tips her head to one side, cracks the knuckles of her right hand, the one with the missing fingernails. "She said I killed our parents and older brother before my grandmother found me."

"Is she…?"

"I don't know. My grandmother told me to leave. I killed our family." She pulls the long braid over her shoulder. Renée had only seen the scars, but Brinda has straight white teeth, a strong jaw. She also has the broad shoulders and muscled calves of an athlete.

Maybe she was? Maybe that's why she survived? "You were sick. It wasn't your fault," Renée says.

"I still did it." Brinda shrugs, turns back to her controller and the game.

***

Peyton has turned her station into a stereotypical man cave. Renée should protest. *But, I have no grounds to complain. Do I?* Peyton brings her results. The convention center tent city has emptied, and she can walk the streets without fear of attack. Her half of the city has flourished, while rumors say the army's side has fallen apart. Regularly, they see plumes of black smoke, hear the barrage of gunshots from beyond the city divide.

A loud cheer goes up from the officers—the recruit defeated Brinda. He throws his skinny arms in the air. "Bow down, motherfuckers!" It's a favorite saying of Peyton's when he makes an impressive kill.

Where the hell is he? She catches the eye of one of the newer officers. "Where is your sergeant?"

"My what?" The boy has scabby bald spots. Missing teeth. Missing fingernails. Long scratch scars down his bare arms. Souvenirs of the virus. "You mean Peyton? Is he the sergeant?"

Then, Andy steps up near the boy and slings an arm around his shoulders. "Hey there, Ms. Mayor—lookin' for Peyton? He went out by the North Barricade to help out Lanson and some of his guys. They caught some rogue soldiers ransacking a 7-Eleven near there."

"What lies outside the barrier is none of our—"

"Yeah, Peyton thought it would be good practice instead of just patrolling. The streets are so boring now."

Renée spins and strides from the party den that her police headquarters has become. "Peyton is your sergeant. I expect you to call him that." Behind her, Andy grumbles something that makes the skinny boy beside him belly laugh.

So, Peyton chose to ignore her orders just for the excitement of fighting more challenging opponents. She should have known that his boredom would trump any order she could give. Liam brightens up when she gets back to the car.

"Are we going to watch him fight?" Even her squeamish secretary has become enamored of Peyton. Renée ignores his question.

"The northwest barricade." She has citizen crews keeping the streets paved, the grass cut, the windows and sidewalks clean, but the constant presence of smoke, the need for fire during their apocalypse always manages to leave a film of ash and soot over all her efforts to recreate normalcy. Near the northwest side of the city, closer to the military's side, the black and gray of their post pandemic world becomes more noticeable. A long rectangular pit just on the other side of the fenced barricade has burned nonstop this week. Bodies disintegrate within several hours, but the pit smolders for days.

As her Cadillac pulls up to the guarded entrance, Liam grips the steering wheel hard enough that his knuckles have gone white. "Are we going through?"

"No, we'll wait." The two of them sit inside the car, both staring at the barbed wire maze leading outside the city. She has a flicker of admiration for her brother—that he could watch over such a vast territory without fences or walls. *Well, he did close off his main compound with guards.* Compound... Ha! *Our parents' house and neighborhood.* Her admiration only lasts when she contemplates Gabriel impersonally, as another leader in their fractured new world. Then, she remembers that the leader is her brother, and all the old anger rushes back.

***

Her father disliked the idea of her following him to Farcourt Gas and Oil. "You need power first, then turn to business." Daddy smirked from behind his desk. She'd forced her way past a receptionist into his expansive office suite in the Farcourt complex.

"Power. Okay, how do I get power?"

He encouraged Renée to use her gap year interning in politics, and he'd organized a dinner party so she could make connections, even gave a contribution to one of the governor's pet projects. And he took an interest in her that he never had before, wanted to know about the people she met, her impressions of them. She'd basked in his guidance, his attention. *Why had Gabriel hated having Daddy's focus?* Renée loved it.

Her father treated her to a weekly lunch, so they could game plan connections and favors she needed to advance a career. She attended VIP boxes and galas in place of her mother. And for a year, she'd felt as close to happiness as she'd ever known. *At last... At last...* Renée even decided to extend her intern position an extra year. The governor praised her, and the state senators all liked her.

Then, her father negotiated Gabriel's release from Wellspring Mental and Correctional Institute. Maurice Featherton told Pauline in no uncertain terms that she would move into the tall Victorian house in the historic Olde Town neighborhood to act the part of a dutiful wife and mother. And he expected Renée to play her part as well...

"Don't you want to support your brother? This is an important transitional time for him." Maurice waved away the waiter from their table. "We're clearly *trying to have a conversation*. Go bother someone else." His frustration with Renée leaked out on the man trying to serve them.

Renée shook out her napkin, smoothed it onto her lap. "I can't believe you expect me to move back for Gabriel. I'm not driving forty minutes from the house in Olde Town to the city every day for my internship."

"If that's all it is, I'll hire a driver."

"No. That's *not* all it is. Gabriel ruins everything—I'm not helping him adjust to life outside his mental hospital. That freak belongs—"

"That's enough!" Maurice Featherton never cared if he made a scene, only that others gave him what he wanted. The people at the tables near them had stopped talking, pretended not to watch as he stood, looked down at Renée. She recognized the same coldly hostile expression she'd seen him use with business adversaries. "Even if you don't get along with him, I expect you to speak about your brother with respect."

"I hate Gabriel."

"Then, you hate me, too." A disappointed head shake, and he left her alone. Even the cowering waiter knew their lunch had ended. None of the staff approached her table again, but every eye in the restaurant watched her and waited to see if she would cry, rage, or grovel. *Fucking Gabriel.*

Her father never again met her for lunch—if she didn't want to play her role in welcoming Gabriel back into the world, then Maurice had no interest at all in Renée.

maneuver

22 Renee

When Peyton finally shows, he doesn't have the cocky swagger and triumphant glow that Renée expected. And neither do the soldiers who follow behind him. Lanson spots the Cadillac and gestures for his men to head the other direction, toward their own half of the city.

"Who are those women?" Liam asks, making Renée jolt in her seat. She'd forgotten his presence beside her. "They look like soldiers." Two tall women follow Peyton through the barricade. One has a camo jacket on, but Renée can't see anything else marking them as military.

Instead, she focuses on the hand shake between her police sergeant and the army's second in command. When he breaks the handshake, Lanson squeezes Peyton's shoulder. Renée tries to read the emotion between them. Lanson's cohort of beefy soldiers also take turns shaking Peyton's hand.

"Well, aren't they all chummy," Liam snarks. "Peyton knows those are the bad guys right?"

"Those are our colleagues in defending this city."

"But—"

Renée steps out of the passenger seat, she slams the car door behind her hard enough that Peyton and the others finally look her way.

"Mayor Dufort," Lanson calls. As she nears, Renée can smell the blood and sweat emanating from the group. Even through the heavy smoke. "Hope you don't mind, I thought I better take Peyton with us before we left the barricade."

Renée musters a smile and tries to imitate the straight shouldered confidence she remembers when her father greeted anyone with authority. What would Daddy have made of this situation? Of that sympathetic shoulder squeeze between the two men?

"Is everything alright?"

Lanson glances toward Peyton, as if asking his permission to answer. "We had a little trouble outside the barricade, but your sergeant handled it."

"Yes, *my* sergeant always does." *Peyton's fighting skill is my property.* Lanson should have asked her permission before inviting Peyton anywhere. "I would prefer you come to me with these requests, Lieutenant."

"Of course. I'm sorry, Mayor. I only got word of a rogue group passing through. We thought they might be soldiers, but it's just some kids." He tips his head to the side to mean the two women standing beside Peyton. They don't look like kids. They look her same age, Lanson's same age. In the new post-virus world, they are adults. The two women have heavy grooved metal weapons strapped to their hips. Both have red blood splashed on their pants and jackets, dripping from their clubs.

"Is that blood infected?"

One of the women, tall and muscular with braided cornrows, moves her body in front of the other, blocking Renée's view. "It is. We had to kill one of our own group who backed into a creature nest." She folds her arms over her chest, reminding Renée of Case Bell's usual stance. The woman has muscles as bulky as Peyton's, but she also has the worn expression of a refugee. "We'd appreciate the chance to clean up. We won't take any food or—"

Peyton holds up a hand. "I told them they could stay."

"You did?"

"You want people. They're people. I need more officers, and I saw them fight. They'll work," he says, a flat, humorless demand. It takes Peyton a few seconds to remember himself. To take stock of their audience. "But, only if it's alright with you, Mayor. I can also kick them the fuck out, if that's what you want."

Lanson and his soldiers have already moved off. The lieutenant has to pass on these fighters, just like he had to pass on absorbing Peyton into his ranks. *That must be Dandridge's orders.* Surely Lanson would take claim of these two if he could, train them as soldiers. *Dandridge will choke their side down until it dissolves.* Good. Then the entire city will belong to Renée.

"What's the call here, Mayor?" Peyton's jaw tightens. He grinds his teeth against the impatience of not having his way, but Renée feels justified in making him suffer a little longer.

"Well, ladies, what skills do you have?" Now that she gets a good look at them, she can tell they're sisters. Both with almond eyes and identical long noses, honey brown skin and freckles.

The same woman answers, "I'm Ella, and this is my sister, Angie. We were in college. Both of us on basketball scholarships in California." She tips her head back and stands straighter, ready to face rejection but not willing to grovel. "My sister was pre-nursing but hadn't taken any classes for it yet. I was elementary education. We might not have anything you could use right now, but we made it from Southern Cal to here." She tips her head to Peyton. "So, like he said, we can fight."

"Okay. What about you?" Renée cranes her neck to get a look at the other woman, and the girl's eyes skitter away. A *younger* sister, Renée decides. Quieter, with smudged tear tracks on her cheeks, two stripes through soot and dirt.

"What *about* her?" Ella fires back. "Angie and I come as a team."

Before Renée can answer, Peyton lays a heavy hand on the younger sister's shoulder. "Yeah, obviously. Nobody wants to split you up." He turns toward Renée again, scraping his heavy club into the gravel between them. "Well, we gonna stand around here, or can I take them back to headquarters? They can start on street patrol tonight."

Ella sucks in a deep breath, like she might want to argue against going right to work without resting first, but she manages to keep herself in check. "Yeah, okay."

Peyton and the women wait for Renée's decision—*as if I would ever turn away someone as capable as either of these sisters.* Of course, she will take them. "We'll house and feed you in exchange for work. My sergeant here…" She nods to Peyton. "…will assign whatever needs to be done."

***

By the time they've deposited Ella and Angie back at the station and gotten rid of Liam and the car, Renée has only calmed down a modicum from her anger toward Peyton. She wants to trust him, but she can't when he keeps meeting on his own with Lanson. "I need an explanation. Now." They walk side-by-side toward her penthouse…*their* penthouse. Peyton stays every night. Wind, cold and smoky, whips her hair and Peyton's. It carries off the edge to her words. "I don't like you helping out Lanson."

"Yeah, yeah, I already heard it a million times. They don't respect you. Blah, blah, blah…" Peyton circles his arms around her waist and pulls her against him.

"Let me down. I'm not some vapid high school girl. You aren't the quarterback who just won the game. This is about power, about *trust*. I need you to follow my orders."

"I *was* following them. You want to show up the military guys, right? I can't tell how we're doing if I don't go make nice with them."

"I asked you to clean out my half of the barricade, not act the part of double agent. Frankly, you aren't—"

Peyton's arms squeeze tighter, just past the point of comfort. "Guess you don't want to hear all the shit Lanson spilled about what's happening on their side. Huh?"

"God damn it, Peyton!" Renée elbows him, and he lets her go. He acts like he doesn't care at all about their survival, *her* survival. It's all just a joke to him, a way to stay amused between bouts of life-or-death brawling against the infected. They've stopped in front of her apartment building. "If you want me to let you inside, then you need to need to start talking."

"Basically, shit's falling apart on the army's side." One blond eyebrow raises, Peyton acts annoyed to have to retell things he doesn't care about in the first place. "Dandridge is too chickenshit to leave his tower, making Lanson run everything and report back. No word from the Pentagon or anywhere else, but Dandridge keeps talking a lot of bullshit about waiting on reinforcements. The stress finally got to him, or reality...whatever." The mean smile breaks across Peyton's beautiful chiseled features. "When their scouts caught sight of those girls, one had on fatigues. Dandridge thought this was it, that more might be coming behind them. He's fucking lost it."

"But Lanson still went to investigate?"

"Nah, Lanson knew it was just some rogue soldiers or looters. That's why he asked me along. But Dandridge? Fucking brain is scrambled." Peyton winds his arms back around her waist. "Not bad, huh?" He grins that infuriating, conceited smile that never reaches his eyes. He likes to win an argument as much as she does. "You wouldn't know any of that shit without me."

Renée grabs at him, and they kiss, bodies and mouths grinding together in an angry embrace. "You still should have sent someone to tell me. I don't like surprises."

He pulls away and points at her. "You like this one." That damn grin again. "Consider the intel a trade, I want a favor in return."

"I didn't agree to any trade…" Renée searches his expression, but only finds the usual fury and impatience written there. If he wanted to hide something from her, she doesn't think he'd have the composure for a long-con. "What do you want?"

"The girl we killed, Ella and Angie's friend…I knew her." He runs a hand through his golden hair and looks away. "We got there just in time to back up those two you met. Their friend had popped overnight. It was Via, Case's sister. I need to go back to the suburbs and tell her."

Renée pulls away with a humming sound. Should she let him do this? "Why not just wait? Case will be here in another week to trade tankers. You can tell her then."

Peyton shakes his head. "No. I need to tell Case now. I was the one who put her sister down. I'm not waiting a week to tell her, like it's some side news that doesn't matter." He reaches out and pinches Renée's cheek. "You trust me to come back, don't you?" When she squints her eyes at him, he pinches her harder. "I'll be in and out. Don't worry—probably won't even see your brother. And I doubt he's got anything new to offer or tell me." Suddenly, Peyton turns serious, no mocking laugh, no mean smile. "I'm done with Feathertons."

I'm a Featherton. I was. She remembers her father, leaning across the fine china of a restaurant. *"Let me tell you something about the governor, that you might find helpful…"* He'd seen her as a person, not just a child, an *extra* child. He respected her. At least, she'd thought so at the time…

Renée turns to key in the door code, gives herself a second to hide her expression. Oh, right. Peyton had asked her permission to deliver that bad news in person. *Don't hold him too tight, or he'll get bored.*

"I suppose I can't stop you," she says, hopes it comes out more nonchalant than she sounds to herself.

23 Gabriel

Gabriel wakes face down in grit and dust. His limbs ache from sleeping on the cement floor, his fingers are stiff with cold. In his dreams, he'd lived inside the basement cage, not Bailey. Threats surrounded him—noise and light sank into his brain like knives, hunger burned like a coal in his stomach, thirst clawed from his throat. *Just a memory. I recovered. I survived.*

He breathes through his panic and tremors the way they taught him to do in Wellspring, when images of Freddy's murder, Elena's murder, tormented him. Bailey remains curled away against the far side of the cage from him, moaning in his sleep. A buzzing ring sounds to Gabriel's right—the satellite phone—something has gone wrong. Again.

He didn't waste time changing clothes, hadn't even run a hand through his hair. He shakes it from his eyes as he steers the Land Rover toward The Greens. *Could one damn thing go right?* Once word got round the neighborhood that his black Land Rover waited outside the Bell's house on Hickory Hill, neighbors would start dropping in, gathering outside, blocking his exit with their questions and demands. Out of habit, he slows in front of the former Tyrone home first before rolling forward to Case Bell's house. He'd almost searched for Bailey's mop of hair, his wide gray eyes before remembering that he'd just left Bailey. *Damn it, focus.* Another slow, deep, calming breath, taught to him at Wellspring. *You are in control.* Gabriel bites at his cheek to keep from shouting. He stalks up the driveway of the Bell home, toward a door that creaks open as if someone watched and waited.

"Where is—" he expects Case, even a crying Case. And a dead body, maybe a mess… He hadn't expected to see Peyton Tyrone dressed in head-to-toe black leather, metal club strapped to his back, seething with his typical impotent rage.

"He found my sister," Case says, stepping between them. "She's sick…popped."

Gabriel pushes Case aside to better see Peyton. "What have you done?"

"I recognized her right off. She and some other girls teamed up to make their way back here. A bunch of them at first, but then…" Peyton makes a rolling gesture with one hand. "Via popped and took out one of them. I got there just in time to tie her down."

"And Renée just let you?"

"Hell, no. Your sister would have freaked if she knew I captured a feral, instead of killing it." Peyton's eyes harden, muscles tense, ready to fight. "She's not into bullshit miracles like you." The moment stretches with a threat of violence between them.

One mention of Bailey, and Peyton will explode with all his pent up desperation. Gabriel decides not to contradict Peyton's bitter words, to let him hang onto the rage that keeps him alive. *You are in control.* He can't allow himself any of Wellspring's breathing techniques, so he shoves his trembling hands inside his pockets and paces to shake out spasms in his legs. "Where is Via now?"

"A military officer owed me for saving his ass in a fight. He hooked me up with one of those caged trucks the patrols used to cart off the sick. It's stashed behind the weigh station on the highway exit. You'll need to give her water and…and…fuck, I don't know." His face tightens, like he doesn't want to picture whatever Gabriel does to take care of Bailey. "I think it's stupid to—" He shakes his head. "But do whatever you want. I'm gonna take my old bike to get back to the city."

Case throws her arms around him. "Peyton, thank you. That's… I'm just so…" She slaps a hand over her welling eyes and chokes against a sob.

"Um…yeah, thanks." He lets her hug him, his ears and neck bright red with whatever emotion she still brings up in him. Then he peels her arms off his body, runs his hands down from her shoulders to her wrists before letting go. Gabriel has never seen Peyton take such care with a girl.

"Are you… Did you have any trouble restraining her?" Case's eyes roam over the worn leather clothing, the skin showing through Peyton's collar and fingerless gloves.

"I can handle myself against one…" He looks down at Case. "One, um, sick person. It helped that Via was newly popped, still strong. I could knock her around some." Peyton's mouth twists, and he shrugs in apology toward his former girlfriend.

Case plucks at Peyton's stiff leather sleeve. "I need to see her. Peyton, take me to her."

"I can't. You need him to take you." Peyton makes a careless swipe of one hand toward Gabriel, but his eyes are fierce. "I just said that I would tell you and leave." Then to Gabriel, "You'll handle it from here, right?"

In his pockets, Gabriel's nails bite into his palms. He locks his muscles down to prevent himself from pacing. "I will handle it."

"Okay…good." Peyton reaches a hand out to Case like he means to pat her back, or maybe hug her. But he just lets it rest in the space between them, fingers near but not touching the skin of Case's neck. "I have to go," he tells her.

And Case looks a wreck. Her eyes red, cheeks wet. "Thank you, Peyton."

He leaves out her back door and jogs through the yard. The next street behind Hickory Hill is Merion, and Peyton must have parked somewhere along the perimeter fence there. Before Feathetons dominated the suburbs, neighbors would meet with rival gangs to trade. The highway exit nearby allowed a quick getaway. Case's own mother had gone there to trade with Colton for drugs—opiates to take away the sting of apocalypse. But, she'd ended up trading her daughter to Gabriel as the price for her disloyalty.

A transgression that Gabriel is more thankful for every passing day. "Come." He pulls Case away from the back door and Peyton's absence. "I'll take you to Via."

The scarcity of fuel has the benefit of empty highways, so no prying eyes to witness the Land Rover pulling into the abandoned truck weigh station. Peyton did a good job hiding the cage truck. Gabriel and Case have to get out and circle the squat building on foot before they spot it parked inside a tangle of pine trees and brush.

"Via?" Case pulls aside the spiky branches.

"Don't get too close." Gabriel closes his fist in the back of Case's hoodie, ready to fling her behind him if Via reaches through the bars to scratch or bite. He spots a hunched form behind the bars. "She's in the corner." The cage only has the height for someone to sit inside of it, stretch their legs. Gabriel's voice causes the senseless girl in the cage to look up. One side of her face has swollen and purpled. Peyton did indeed knock her around to get her in the cage, get the cage to the suburbs. She follows Case and Gabriel's movements, but she also turns wide eyes on the jiggling branches they knock into, a bird swooping from the shaking trees.

"Via…" Case whispers. When she steps forward, her sister growls like a furious dog. "I'm so glad you're alive. I'm going to take care of you. As long as it takes, okay?"

Via lunges at the bars with a screech. Clawed fingers scraping at the air in front of Case. One of her feet drags behind her, ankle broken or twisted. Case pries herself free of Gabriel's latch on her jacket.

"Case, your sister is young and strong. She made it all the way here from the West Coast. But she'll need you to be strong for her now. Can you do that?"

Case doesn't answer, but she turns to bury her face in his chest, wind her arms round the flapping edges of his wool coat, and sobs. He endures it until she quiets, until her arms loosen. "You can help her, can't you Gabriel? I'll feed her and…oh, God…whatever she needs. I don't care. I'll do it. I just want her to be okay. I just want her to live."

"Then I'll help you." Another promise. Another life under his control. Another responsibility. *Can I do this?* Gabriel's eyes flutter closed, then open again.

I don't have a choice.

24 Gabriel

"I'm still in high school. They won't want me at your gentleman's club, no matter how well I play cards." Gabriel stabbed at the smoked salmon on his plate, raked the tines through the soft pink flesh. Part of his father's plan to integrate his son back into society meant the two of them eating breakfast every morning together. "I can't even drink alcohol. Because I'm legally still—"

"I didn't raise you to act like a child." His father rubbed a thumb against his bottom lip, studied his son like an artist studies one of his own works. "You are not some typical teenage boy."

"That's something Wellspring Mental and Correctional Institute would agree with you about." Gabriel dropped the fork, let it clatter onto his plate. "I have school." Gabriel stood, pushed in the dining chair, but waited for his father to dismiss him.

Frustration made a muscle twitch in Maurice Featherton's jaw. "For powerful men, responsibility isn't a choice."

"I'm not powerful, I'm just a teenager…and a card game isn't a responsibility, it's recreation."

His father got to his feet so abruptly that his chair tipped back and fell. "The purpose of this card game is to make connections, foster relationships, not have fun. And you, Gabriel, will be powerful one day. I will *make you* powerful."

***

The dark brick exterior to his father's club hid between towering downtown buildings, and besides a few velvet steps leading to a carved oak door, it had no indication of the grandiose atmosphere inside. Oil money and influence bought memberships, with the stipulation that no women be invited, no one that cronies of oil and gas would feel compelled to treat with tact or courtesy.

After cards, Maurice and his buddies liked to have a last whiskey and smoke cigars. Gabriel hated the smell, hated sitting on the stiff leather chairs of the club after hours spent round a poker table. Gabriel's father took that moment to ask, "Another date with the Thompson girl?"

He could have waited to ask me at home. Or, his father could have added the question into one of the many, many texts he sent Gabriel during the school day, keeping him abreast of business decisions and dealings that Gabriel cared nothing about. "Yes. Tomorrow." He forced himself to lean back, sprawl his legs in a semblance of ease.

His father insisted on Gabriel also ordering a whiskey, despite knowing he wouldn't drink it. *"It's for image. You must let these men know that you are one of them."* Gabriel studied the men, the *gray* men, as he thought of them. They all had white or gray hair, white or gray skin, wore the same clothing in muted colors and expensive fabrics. Even the topics of their conversation blended together in boring, predictable ways.

"Ashley Thompson?" One of the gray men asked, as he swirled the liquor in his glass. "I know the Indiana Thompsons, steel business. Is she one of those?"

"I doubt it." Gabriel flashed a smile at the gray man, winked. He'd seen his father do this when he talked about women.

The man barked a laugh. "Ah, I see. Just like your old man."

Gabriel had no idea what the gray man "saw," but he nodded along. He didn't feel guilty mentioning Ashley in the same way his father talked about his women. If Gabriel wanted to get into the nitty-gritty points of his relationship with Ashley, he would point out that *he* hadn't deceived anyone. But, every time she stole away to meet with Gabriel, Ashley lied to Bailey. Gabriel brought the glass of whiskey to his lips, liked how the scent burned in his nose, the ignition of pain against his tongue when he took a sip.

"You should take her to the next basketball game, I'll give you my courtside seats," one of the gray men offered. Not as bland as the others, younger. Though, not as young as Gabriel. "I can't use them." The man shrugged. "I'll be in Italy."

Smile. Gabriel remembered to act pleased, but not grateful. His father didn't approve of gratitude. "Sure. I'd like that."

The man understood the club etiquette and raised his glass at Gabriel. "They'll be waiting for you."

"And bring her to the city loft after." When he didn't need it for throwing parties or hosting important clients, his father brought his own women to the loft in the city. Maurice's offer appeared generous on the surface, but Gabriel knew he meant to make that comparison between Ashley and his throwaway partners. "You can take my Mercedes," Maurice added.

Gabriel didn't care about the basketball game and had no desire to spend the night in the opulent loft with Ashley. But the Mercedes? Gabriel liked driving his father's Maybach GLS. "Then, I'll take you up on that, Dad." He imitated the raised-drink salute the other man had made. *Ridiculous.*

He'd left the club with his father's keys in his jacket pocket. A few thousand dollars of winnings nestled beside it. And a plan—the courtside tickets, champagne in the loft as they looked down at the city lights. He would press Ashley to leave Bailey for him. If Ashley broke things off, it would snap the long bond between her and Bailey…and then…*maybe then…*

He'd gotten so lost in his fantasy that he hadn't noticed the blonde waiting for him in the shadows. When she first stepped into a patch moonlight, the old sick feeling bubbled up inside him, the tingly vibration of one of his fits. Her teeth shone in the dark alley, bright as her hair. "Surprise, little brother."

***

Too much time to think—that's the problem with silence. Gabriel forces his mind from the past to the present. Since leaving Via, Case has her eyes closed, head leaning on the passenger side window. If she wants to sleep, too bad. "I can't afford to set you up with a Land Rover or truck of your own," he says into the quiet between them.

"What?" Case's eyes open. "Are you kidding me? Yes, you can, and you will. There are plenty of empty cars, the world is *filled* with empty cars." She holds up a finger, even though Gabriel didn't try to interrupt. "And, you can get me gas. Hell, you set it up in Cushing so that *I* can get me gas."

"Yes…" On this short trip from The Greens to the weigh station, he steers through abandoned cars like a maze of traffic cones. "But, my objection isn't about finding the right vehicle or providing fuel, Case. I can't let someone as valuable as you travel the roads on her own." Feathertons needs Case's leadership skills, her level-headed intelligence, her fighting skills, her loyalty. "I will personally drive you to Via's hiding place each day. Once Bailey recovers…" He flicks his eyes toward the fuming girl in his passenger seat. "Once he recovers, I can move Via into Olde Town, or a similar setup closer to The Greens."

At last, Case shakes herself awake. "A similar setup? You mean a cage? It isn't—"

"Safe? Yes, I agree it isn't safe to hold the feral inside a home, in a room without running water, without animals to catch and eat."

"Oh, hell." Her face scrunches, and she drops her chin to her chest, lets out a shuddering breath.

"I know you don't want to hear it, Case, but you have to. Via will need live food, mice, even bugs are fine." Enough memories survived from Gabriel's own infection that he thinks he understands the urge. "The virus drives them to replicate."

"So… Lawrence was right? When he said you want to treat them and not…"

"The structure in my basement is safe. For Bailey and for us. And once he recovers, people will see that it works."

"Once he recovers," Case repeats.

"Do not say anything, not if you wan't your sister to live. I won't tolerate it."

Case leans her head back against the passenger window and closes her eyes. "I wasn't going to."

25 Renée

Brinda shields her eyes against the white, winter sky and looks up at Renée's broken office window. "Probably someone knocked on the door, spooked him. The angle looks right." With two fingers in the air, she mimics kicking legs diving through jagged glass, arcing through the air and then landing on the sidewalk. Both she and Renée look down at Liam's body. His torn shirt and missing shoes. His clawed fingers. The empty socket where he pried an eye loose. A new kid stands behind Brinda, takes one look at the empty socket, and makes a gagging sound. The kid laces his fingers on the top of his dark spiky hair, takes panting breaths like someone about to vomit or explode.

Irritation crawls up Renée's spine. "Show some respect, officer," she snaps at the boy.

To Brinda, she says, "He didn't act sick. He drove me yesterday, and he was fine." Renée winces at her words. What does it matter how he acted, how he *seemed*? "Why didn't he say anything?"

Brinda laughs, a hard scoffing bark. "Why do you think...Mayor?"

"I would have..." *Would have what?* She has no contingency plan for infection, nothing other than death at the end of a club.

When she looks up from Liam's crumpled body, she catches Brinda and the young officer studying her. "We didn't exchange body fluids if that's what you're wondering."

"No, ma'am." Brinda elbows the man beside her. "The Mayor will need her office cleaned."

The kid backs up a step, waves both his hands. "I'm not doing it. I don't touch their blood. I don't touch their bodies."

"Shut the fuck up, Sebby." Brinda scratches at the gouge scars on her neck, and Sebby flinches. "Go find someone, and offer them an extra fruit package or something. They'll do it."

Renée watches their back-and-forth. *At least Brinda acts like an adult. Where did Peyton find this Sebby kid?* "Liam lived with his mother here in Central Business District." Renée remembers that Liam traded his milk ration to get his mother chocolates and flowers on her birthday. "Someone will need to go to his building and check on her."

"It's kinda early," Sebby says. "And there was a big party last night at the station. I don't think—"

"Where is Peyton?" Renée grinds her teeth to keep from screaming. "He should be back from... Why didn't he come?"

Both Brinda and Sebby give her blank expressions.

God damn it, they know, they just won't say. Despite the frigid morning air, sweat prickles her skin. "Tell him to meet me there, the yellow brick apartments on the edge near Deep Deuce."

Sebby scratches at the gelled spikes jutting from his pale head. "We can't exactly go get him. He's on the other side." When Brinda tries to elbow him again, he slaps her arm away.

Somehow Renée musters up her mother's cold disdain, turns the force of it on Brinda. "The other side? He went on the other side of the city?"

After a slit-eyed glance at Sebby, Brinda answers in the robotic retort of a soldier, "Yes, ma'am. He did." No one but Dandridge, Lanson, and Renée went between the city division points before Peyton arrived, and they only went when invited. Apparently, Peyton travels between them every day. *Against Renée's direct orders.* Sebby might not know this, but Brinda does. Renée can see the gears working in the other woman's dark eyes as she tries to find a cover for her sergeant. "He had some business with Lanson."

"*Lieutenant* Lanson."

Brinda's eyes flash with sudden anger, she takes a deep breath through her nose. "Yes, ma'am. Sorry, ma'am."

With Renée wearing high heels, she and Brinda are the same height. Their eyes level. Renée doesn't like the words she sees floating behind Brenda's angry glare. *She thinks I'm some stuck-up bitch. She thinks I'm fake. She thinks that all I care about is schmoozing and power...and...* Renée dips her head, gathers herself. It's Peyton who keeps defying her orders, answering all her commands with sarcasm, encouraging the officers under him to lie. "I'm sorry. You aren't the one I'm angry with, Brinda."

The other woman looks startled, wary. "I understand, ma'am."

Not ma'am…just call me Renée. But, she can't say that. Because image is everything. "If Peyton's gone on the army's side of the city, then I need you to send someone to find him. Tell him to meet me at Liam's building."

***

She leaves the Cadillac in its parking space and walks back to the penthouse to change from her skirt suit into jeans and a jacket. *Fucking Peyton—I could kill him!* But, her fighters have fallen under his spell. No fear of the virus, no fear of death… After a year of horror, Peyton's reckless abandon intoxicates everyone around him. *Time to face the truth, Peyton controls the police force, not me.*

If she wants her fighters back, she needs to stand at Peyton's side. She grabs the chained bat he keeps in the closet. And, by the time she gets to the right building, she finds Peyton waiting for her wearing his own sleeker metal club. Beside him are Lanson and the boy Andy.

Peyton shoots her that mean smile, tips his chin in greeting. "So, you're planning to fight?" Approval drips from his question. Good.

"I am."

"Mayor," Lanson interrupts. "I thought since I borrowed Peyton the other day that I could come and help you with your outbreak."

"We don't know that it's an outbreak."

Peyton huffs. "You know it fucking is. That little twerp Liam was scared of his own shadow. No way did he get up-close and personal fighting a creature. He caught it from someone who hadn't popped yet." Peyton pulls the metal club from the tight sheath on his back. "This ought to be good." He orders Andy to stay outside and ready in case a creature bolts through the door or windows. Then he, Renée, and Lanson head inside.

Liam's apartment occupies the bottom floor of a three-story converted townhouse. As soon as Peyton kicks in the main door, they can hear groaning, screeching. The meaty rotten stench of dead bodies wafts around them in the little foyer. "Called it," Peyton whispers.

Renée unlocks the door to Liam's apartment, but Peyton shoves her away to open it himself. He sweeps his club in front of him while Renée and Lanson follow him inside.

Chairs overturned. A flat screen pulled from the wall. Plants shaken loose from their pots and dumped on the carpet. The hunched figure of Liam's mother looks up at them from the destruction of her living room. When she sees them, the woman vaults over a ripped settee and down a hall. "She's fast," Lanson breathes, "…new." He sounds worried, raises his club in front of his body.

Renée raises hers, too, as she picks her way across the debris-littered floor. The chains drilled into the wooden bat jingle. "My secretary just popped a few hours ago." No lights in the hallway, but she can hear the woman panting, growling just ahead.

"Shut up. Both of you." Peyton stops short, and Renée collides with his back. "You can wait—"

The woman charges them, head down, teeth snapping. Both Renée and Lanson fall back, but Peyton leaps forward. He holds his club out to the side, handle braced against his chest. The woman plows face first into the broad side of the solid metal. Her neck folds back, and she falls.

Lanson gets his bearings before Renée. "She broke the stem, didn't she? Her neck broke right at—"

Peyton kicks the old woman over. Like Liam, his mother is small and light. Peyton stomps down on the back of her head.

Lanson gasps, but Renée forces herself to keep her cool. *Don't look away. Don't.* From now on, she'll adopt Peyton's brash callousness. *Stand at his side.* From the corner of her eye, she sees Lanson wince.

"Jesus, Peyton."

Peyton turns on him. "We had to be sure, didn't we?" A coughing laugh, and Peyton shrugs. "You always get so squeamish at the end." It doesn't sound like a dig. Except for the mean smile. The cruel laugh. Still, Peyton acts like the lieutenant's prudishness amuses him.

When his eyes meet Renée's, she keeps her face neutral. "If they both just popped, then who infected them?"

Lanson bristles from Peyton's comments, but he puts his focus on Renée. "So, now you admit, it *is* an outbreak."

When Renée doesn't react, Lanson frowns and marches back toward the hallway. "It stinks in the corridor. Someone else in the building must have popped."

Peyton flourishes a hand in front of Renée. "After you," he says and winks at her. On the second floor, they find an old couple, also newly popped. Lanson elbows past Peyton and Renée to take out the man in a series of hard hits against his back and head. Less messy and up-close than Peyton stomping Liam's mother.

Peyton leans against the old couple's piano, one finger tapping at a high sharp note. "Yeah, I don't get how one method has superiority over the other. So, whatever you're trying to prove here, Lanson doesn't mean shit. We crush the spinal juncture, and the thing dies. Doesn't matter how it happens."

Lanson's pale skin reddens. His nostrils flare. "I'm just trying to show some respect for these people." He steps back from the smashed corpse, takes a throw blanket from a nearby leather chair, and spreads it over the body.

Stand with Peyton. Renée raises an eyebrow at him. "You just wasted that blanket, you know." She'd watched Lanson fight the man while leaning on her own club like a walking cane.

"I was trying—"

"I'll thank you to not make any other decisions about the resources in my half of the city." She's not just talking about the blanket, and they both know it.

"If you two are done—I think another one scuttled into the kitchen." Peyton looks toward Renée. "Did you want a turn?"

"We aren't doing this for fun," Lanson says.

Peyton leans forward, taps Lanson on the cheek. "*You* aren't doing this for fun."

Renée can't hide her own smile at Peyton's derision. She thinks it probably looks a lot like the way Peyton grins. "Why is the lieutenant even here?"

"I asked him to come, that's why. You taking a turn or not?"

But she doesn't have time to answer—the woman must have started a charge inside the long galley kitchen. The sound of glass cracking. A moan. Peyton spins and raises his club in a single motion. He moves fast for someone with his height and muscle bulk. Behind him, Renée and Lanson skid into the kitchen, but Peyton already has the woman pinned to a thick glass window. The end of his solid club stabbing the creature's neck against the heavy pane. When he draws the metal bar back, she drops to the floor in a heap. "You smell that?" Peyton's not even winded. "Just blood, piss, and shit. These were new, too. That dead smell must be coming from the top floor." Peyton turns to face them. "Looks like you get another shot," he tells Renée.

On the top floor of the townhouse, Renée stops Peyton from kicking the door in by getting there first and trying the knob. It turns, but she doesn't open it more than a crack.

"Christ! I guess we know where the smell's coming from." Lanson punches the door with his club, and the three of them peer into the darkness. Something thumps against a wall and groans. Lanson opens the door wider, and Peyton reaches in to hit the entry wall light switch.

Balloons and a homemade *Happy Birthday Simon!* banner hang from the ceiling. A half-eaten moldy cake. Plates and glasses scattered around. Peyton has his metal club over one shoulder as he strolls into the main room. "Looks like we found ground zero."

From the darkened hallway comes another thumping sound. Peyton lowers his club, holds it in front of him, flashes his teeth at Renée. "I think you called this one, Mayor." He makes a quick squint-eye assessment of her readiness. "Go for it." He cocks one blond eyebrow, like he he thinks he's called her bluff on showing up with a weapon, acting ready to fight.

Fuck you, Peyton Tyrone. You're nothing but a dumb jock high school kid, and I've lived in the real world. I've stood toe-to-toe with ruthless businessmen and backstabbing politicians. At the hallway's mouth, they have to step over a bloated dead man.

Lanson crouches down with one hand over his mouth and nose. His voice comes out muffled, "Is this Simon?" Someone has covered the man with a green and blue striped bed sheet that Lanson peels off. "Looks like a creature attack. It took a chunk of his neck, and he bled out." Lanson drops the sheet back down and edges around the body.

Peyton takes a giant step over the man, the hardwood floor thuds under his heavy boots. "That's fucking weird. Why bother throwing a sheet on top if you're just going to leave him there?"

Another thumping noise. Then, a cough, a whimper. And they all jump at a *voice*. "Who's there?"

Peyton finds another light switch, and they all stare down at an emaciated woman hunched on the floor. She throws her arms over her head to block the light. Sweat and grime coat her bobbed hair and floral dress.

"Who's there?" she asks again and lifts her head to peer up at them. The skin on her face droops loose and gray from her cheekbones. At first, she blinks at the light, doesn't seem to see them. But as her eyes focus, she seems more lucid, tries to puzzle together the appearance of three armed fighters standing in her hallway, weapons at the ready. "Who are you? Why are you in my house?"

Lanson lowers his club. "Ma'am? Do you need some help?"

His words startle the woman out of her bleary confusion, she throws her arms wide across the door. "He didn't mean to. He's sick. He didn't mean to!"

"Who—?"

"Sounds like she's hiding one of them." Peyton reaches out and jostles Lanson's shoulder. "Take her out of here."

The woman starts to flail her arms and legs at them, but she's too weak to even make contact. She tries to scream, but her voice comes out too hoarse. "He's just a little boy. It was his birthday!"

Lanson's face drains of color, and he looks toward Peyton. "That man wasn't Simon."

"Drag her the fuck out."

The woman must not weigh much because Lanson hefts her up with one arm and throws her over his shoulder. He carries her out of the hallway while she pleads with them. "He's just a little boy—It was his birthday!"

Peyton turns the bedroom doorknob as he motions Renée forward with his chin. "Can you do this? It's a kid."

"You think I can't?" *Stand by his side. Prove you belong there.* "I'm not some tender-hearted weakling like Lanson. I can do what needs to be done."

"Lanson isn't exactly backing down. He came here with me to kill shit."

Renée raises her club in front of her face. "So did I. Now open the door."

26 Renée

Renée collapses onto her bed, blood and soot covered clothes smearing her silk duvet. *I don't care.* It can all go into the pit with that little boy's rotting corpse. In her head, the words sound strong, but she presses the heels of her palms into her eyes to hold in tears. *You didn't kill him. He was already dead.* "Children never survive the virus," she tells her empty bedroom. Their small, fragile bodies. Their greedy metabolisms. Their unfinished brains and nervous systems. *Not your fault. Not your fault.*

***

I didn't mean to kill him!

Daddy stayed true to his word, and he had nothing to do with her until she agreed to come to the suburbs, to play happy family with her mentally-disturbed twin brother. *Another injustice*—the powerful people she'd courted the past year all believed she'd taken her gap year after college, not high school, a falsehood her father encouraged. And now he wanted Renée to give up all her hard work for Gabriel. Her *own* efforts made Renée stand out among the other interns. Daddy's connections bought her way in, but the rest of the maneuvers belonged to her. *Fucking Gabriel!*

After Renée had ended their relationship, Dustin left her father's employment, and Maurice's new secretary didn't budge for a smile or sob story. "I'm his daughter—"

"I'm sorry, Miss Featherton." This assistant had more bulk and age than Dustin, acted more like a bodyguard than a secretary. He looked down his nose at her without any sympathy. "Your father left instructions that—"

"It's about my *mother*. She's ill and asked me to tell him personally about her condition. It's private, something only family knows about." A blatant lie. Pauline had gone to a hotel suite with the father of Gabriel's little school friend, Peyton Tyrone—a football player! *No doubt, Gabriel or Daddy had offered the suburban boy money in exchange for befriending my freak of a brother.*

That mention of her mother and privacy had done the trick with the guard dog assistant. "Oh…in that case…" And she'd found out about their secret boy's club. It broke her heart.

I never had a chance…

Daddy loved making deals, wielding power…he'd pushed her into politics for these very reasons. But she could never enter the most elite institutions where those high-powered deals were brokered. *Not like Gabriel.* Laughter bubbled from her chest. A defective son had more worth to Maurice Featherton than an accomplished daughter.

He only cared about Renée while Gabriel had been locked up in a mental hospital. *If…if…* She still remembered the party in New York, Toby and his buddies slapping Gabriel around for what he'd done to that girl…what was her name? It doesn't matter. Gabriel had gone into one of his fits, shaking, crying, eyes squeezed closed, hands over her ears. Her brother had vomited and peed himself. If only Daddy and the men of his exclusive club could witness her brother's meltdowns, his utter failure to maintain himself in society. *If…*

"Rough him up," she'd told the man. One of the contacts she'd made led her to him. *A useful person to know, for a certain kind of job.* "Break some bones, rob him." Their father wouldn't have sent Gabriel into a card game at the club without a wallet flush with cash. "You can keep whatever you take. I'll have plane tickets waiting when the job is finished."

And she wanted to watch. Jealous anger burned through her like a fever, sweat under her armpits, tongue chewed ragged in her mouth. She stepped out of a murky shadow like a super-villain. "Surprise, little brother."

His body jerked to a stop in the middle of the dark alley, a tremor running up and down his limbs—the shock of her sudden presence worked like an electric wand against his spine. "Wha…what—?" his voice sputtered.

"Wha? Wha?" Renée mocked. "Didn't you even know I live here in the city? Daddy never told you? He didn't. I *knew* it."

"What do you want, Renée?"

Her face turned into a mask of rage. "You should have stayed locked up in that asylum. Why didn't you? Why didn't you stay locked up where you belong?"

Gabriel's pale eyes studied her face. Behind her brother, Renée saw the man she had hired.

"You shouldn't envy me, Renée." In their years apart, Gabriel had lost the naivety she remembered. He regarded her with unfamiliar discernment. "I'm not the one you should be angry—"

The man darted forward, slipped a plastic wire around Gabriel's neck. It bit into the white flesh above his collar. Her brother's hands flew up and scratched at the garrote as it constricted, cutting off his air.

Good. Kill him. The fever built inside Renée, and her vision swam with it. The man kicked the back of Gabriel's leg and he dropped to his knees. His fingers fell away from their fight against the strangling wire. His arms fell to his side. The man choking him grunted, jerking the ends of the wire.

Gabriel fell, face to the damp alley pavement. The man's heavy body crushed Renée's brother to the ground, and he lay still, silent… Her fever broke. "No, wait… This isn't what was supposed to happen!"

Where was Daddy and the men of the club? Why hadn't Gabriel started shaking and screaming? *What have I done? What have I—?*

Underneath the man, Gabriel twitched. He ground down on his left arm and knee. Pitched both himself and his attacker over to the right. The plastic strap fell away. Gabriel knelt on the man's chest, gulped air as he began punching with both fists. And punched. And punched. The man's cheekbones shattered against Gabriel's knuckles. The man's nose crunched and gushed blood. He made a gurgling noise and fell limp, but Gabriel kept pummeling him.

"Gabriel—*stop!*"

Her brother looked up at her, pale eyes wild, deranged. He jumped off the man, blood dripping from his hands. Renée could smell it, rust and meat, dripping from her brother's torn knuckles.

His gaze focused, Gabriel shifted his eyes from the man's body to Renée. With wet panting, he said, "I'm still alive." He took a few steps away from the inert man and toward his sister. She didn't step back or run. Gabriel wouldn't hurt Renée. *He wouldn't dare.*

Behind him, the man groaned, then coughed and made a howling sound, loud enough that Gabriel turned his back on his sister to see.

The man's face no longer looked like a face, just blood and pulp with two swollen eyes inside broken sockets. Still, he somehow got to his feet, his arms curled into his body. Out of the broken-tooth mouth came a rumbling growl. His fingers froze into claws. Gabriel had knocked him out, but the man was awake. Broken and beaten, but moving. Dead, but somehow living. *I've seen this on the news, in videos. But...*

Gabriel lunged toward Renée, gripped her wrist. "Run!"

27 Gabriel

"It's only been a few days, and she's lost so much weight." Case has her neck craned back to watch the weigh station through the rear window, as if she imagines her sister watching them drive away, as if she imagines Via aware of her coming and going.

It's a compulsion Gabriel knows well. "I'll get a piglet from Colton's…from *my* ranch."

"A *piglet?*" Case makes a gagging sound that turns into a stifled sob. "I can't believe this…yeah, do it." Voice stronger, "Do it."

A tricky bit of steering down the highway takes his full concentration. Too many abandoned cars, debris, trash in the road, but it makes a good obstacle for reaching the weigh station. He can feel Case watching him, so he glances over. "You want to ask me something. Just ask."

"Did Bailey…did you have to—"

"I won't talk about Bailey."

"Alright, Gabriel. Sorry." The tenderness in her voice sets his nerves on edge, and he bites at the inside of his cheek to keep from lashing out.

When the Land Rover pulls up to her home, curious faces turn their way. "Your neighbors are out in full force, I see." Someone must have caught her leaving with Gabriel, or Case's own parents bragged about it. Gabriel can't imagine stoic Henry Bell bragging about anything. *But the mother, Monica…ah yes, there she is…*looking out the front window, then down the street to make sure the neighbors see. "Your mother must be pleased about your new position as lieutenant."

A furious glance from Case. "You can stop right there, Gabriel. I agreed to work for you, not let you make comments about my family."

"My apologies." Case hasn't opened her door yet. Gabriel turns toward her. "Was there more?"

"I want to tell my parents about Via." She has her arms wrapped around herself, still angry.

I've wounded her already, and she expects more of the same. "That's up to you."

Case's expression softens a little. She hadn't expected that answer. "But I suggest only telling your parents if you can trust them not to tell anyone else. I think you know how people react when they suspect others of concealing the sick."

Case puts her hand on the door handle. "If people find out…will you protect Via the way you're protecting Bailey?"

Gabriel's hands grip the steering wheel tighter, until his fingers go numb and the muscles of his wrists ache. He's tried not to look at the former Tyrone home next-door to the Bell house. During his year at Memorial High, he'd found every excuse he could to accompany Peyton home, he played video games he didn't care about, watched action movies he had no interest in, talked sports, parties, and girls until he thought he might go insane. It didn't take long before he realized that sociopathic Peyton Tyrone did most of the caretaking for his younger siblings. He wouldn't accept any help, but Gabriel slipped Peyton money when he could, drove Lucy to ballet a few times, tried to intervene when Peyton's efforts to toughen up his younger brother drifted toward bullying. *Case is important to Peyton, and in extension, important to Bailey.*

"Gabriel? Are you listening to me? Will you protect Via, too?"

Gabriel sighs. "I will. But, it's better if you make sure no one finds out," he says. "Keep that in mind."

She finally opens the door and climbs out. *And here come the neighbors*...strolling across the lawn to try and get his attention. Gabriel puts the car into drive and squeals away from the Bell house and from its proximity to the blue and white home where Bailey once lived.

Seeing Via earlier today only reinforced his certainty he had made the right decision to keep Bailey hidden. He would have killed anyone who injured Bailey the way Peyton hurt Via. But, how could either Gabriel or Case blame Peyton when he'd done something as dangerous and reckless to save Via's life. Capturing the feral sick would mean certain infection for anyone foolish enough to try. And only Peyton had the arrogance to attempt it without any immunity. *And he kept it a secret from Renée.*

When he gets back to Olde Town, he finds Lawrence Vu waiting for him inside the mansion study, sitting on one of the overstuffed linen couches and drinking a bottle of Gabriel's Sapporo. "Oh, hey, I was just looking for you. I've got all the latest apprentice reports if you want to see them."

"Lawrence." Gabriel freezes in the doorway. "Your access to this house is limited to the study."

"But my sister—"

"Cecilia was my friend. She was my friend first, before I started Feathertons. You were not. You are an employee, Lawrence." Gabriel shrugs off his long wool coat, holds it out. "Hang this up."

"Wha—"

Gabriel's arm stays rigid, the coat held in front of him.

Muttering to himself, Lawrence sets the beer bottle on the coffee table in front of him. He trudges forward, takes the coat, and turns to coatrack just behind Gabriel.

Gabriel takes a seat behind his desk, flips through the stack of apprentice jobs and applicants. He can feel Lawrence still standing over him, watching. "Say whatever it is you want to say, Lawrence. Then, go home."

"You say that my sister was your friend, but you let Peyton Tyrone kill her and then you just…let him leave."

"Peyton was only trying to—"

"Oh, *I know*. You don't care because he was trying to save Bailey. And you don't care if my mom or everyone else gets infected *because of Bailey*. My sister wasn't your friend, she was in love with you, and you treated her like crap because—"

Gabriel slams his hand on the desk. "That's enough! Do not ever, *ever* say Bailey's name to me again, Lawrence." At some point, Gabriel must have stood up, must have come out from behind the desk. Lawrence stands in the doorway like he'd been prepared to run. *Don't hurt him. This is Cecilia's younger brother.* Gabriel turns away, walks back to his desk, and lowers himself into his chair again. *You are in control.*

Lawrence stays in the study doorway, his whole body trembling. "I…*Gabriel*—"

Then, Derek Sams pushes open the front door and saunters into the entry vestibule. "How's it going? Gabriel, Little Vu. Hey, did you get those apprentice reports, Gabriel? Big improvement in morale around Pierce Heights, I can tell you that much. People are much more pleasant to be around, you know?" Derek shifts his attention from Gabriel to Lawrence. "Did I interrupt you, Little Vu?" When Lawrence glares at him, Derek laughs.

"Lawrence was just leaving." Gabriel leans back in his chair.

Derek smirks. "Yeah, run along, kid. I got to talk some neighborhood business with the big boss."

Lawrence's face has turned red, and his eyes fill with tears. When he rushes from the mansion, Derek shows his hands up, feigns getting knocked back.

"Can't stand that kid, he's not even half as smart as his older sis was. But, your call on who gets to be a lieutenant, Gabriel, and I get the whole sentimental factor there. Derek strolls into the study, sits in the same spot Lawrence had, leans back, and crosses his leg. "Oh, Sapporo, nice." He points at the bottle. "Won't be able to find any more of that in another year or two. You think Japan still exists? All those unmanned reactors…" A whistle. "Probably all melted down like on the East Coast."

Gabriel folds his hands together in front of him, resisting the urge to clench his fists and scream. *You are in control.* "How can I help you, Derek?"

"I'm here because I want to know what's going on. Why are you making special trips to The Greens every morning, driving off with just Case Bell for company? Pierce Heights deserves the same side hustle you've got going with Bell's neighborhood. I should get the same—"

"But you want more than that, don't you? You want everything."

Derek freezes. Then, he slowly uncrosses his legs and sits up. "What do you mean?"

"In Cushing. You've been telling everyone what a better job you'd do than me as the head of Feathertons. So, you don't just want the same as Case Bell—you want more." Gabriel watches fear drain the color from Derek's face, but a beat later, some unexpected resolve has the Pierce Heights lieutenant raising his chin.

"Yeah. I said that. You've made a lot of weak-ass decisions since…" Something in Gabriel's face warns Derek off from saying the words, *"Since Bailey got sick."* Derek rubs a hand over his face.

When Gabriel had his people dye their hair as markers, Derek chose jet black, but his natural ash brown color has started growing back in since then. He looks like a punk kid. *He is just a punk kid. Not like me, I keep forgetting.*

"I just don't think it's right that you took Angelica's brothers. She only started trading on the side to get extra food and clothes for them. And they needed bikes, too." Derek stands up, stiff, shoulders back. He reminds Gabriel of a man facing a firing squad. "I get that you needed to make an example out of her, Gabriel, and you *did*. But it's time for them to go back home."

Gabriel's hands twitch, and Derek's eyes go right to them. *You are in control.* He reaches for a pen to give his fingers something to do, a plastic fountain pen with a mangled cap. Teeth marks, like someone chewed on it. *Bailey.* Messy hair, gray pleading eyes.

"Gabriel, you can't break up her family like that."

Happy families mystify Gabriel. He'd seen the dysfunction in Peyton's household right away, could recognize Peyton's hatred for his parents long before the push-pull of his love for his younger brother. Gabriel rubs his thumb along the mutilated pen cap. "I'll return the Loeza boys, the two younger ones. Rico stays in The Greens as stock manager." When he lifts his eyes back up to Derek, the Pierce Height's lieutenant nods, sweat dampening his temples. "I doubt Rico wants to go back to living under Angelica, not now that he's lived alone. As an adult."

A moment for it to sink in, and Derek relaxes, wipes his palms on his pants legs. "Yeah. Okay. That works."

Gabriel's eyes flick to the study doorway, and Derek gets the hint. *No more questions about Case, that's good.* He slides open the top drawer of his father's desk—*my desk*— meaning to tuck the fountain pen away. But, he changes his mind and slips it into the inside suit pocket instead.

28 Gabriel

"I try to be a good person." Gabriel ticks the pen against the cage bars, a light and steady tap like rain. Bailey cocks his head at the noise but doesn't shriek or cover his ears. Gabriel reaches between the bars, holds the pen out to him. "Do you recognize this? I think this was yours when we worked on the rehousing project for Pierce Heights."

Bailey cringes away from Gabriel's outstretched hand. Gabriel drops the pen. "Today marks thirteen weeks since you popped." *Over three months.* Gabriel had only spent three weeks feral, not months. "That's alright," he tells Bailey, as he strips off his suit jacket, starts unbuttoning his shirt. "The virus affects everyone differently. And I might have had a different strain."

***

"I might not have it at all," he'd told his father. The scabs on his knuckles itched and bled for days after, caught between healing and Gabriel tearing them open every time he worked out with the bag. Even now, he could feel them ripping inside his training gloves, so he hopped back a step to work on his kicking instead.

Beside him, his father made a frustrated noise and grabbed hold of Gabriel's sweat slick arm. "But the man who attacked you…he looked like what we've seen on television? On the internet?"

Gabriel dropped his leg and turned toward Maurice. "Yes. I *told* you." But, he hadn't told him everything. Not the part about Renée hiring that man to beat him up. If Maurice knew that part… Gabriel thought if his father knew about Renée's part in what had happened that he might hire someone just like Renée had. *What would be the point?*

"We won't tell anyone. I'm not sending you one of those hospital camps they're setting up. You'll stay here. I'll take care of you."

"On the news they said that's too dangerous." In the face of his father's panic, Gabriel had buried his own horror deep enough to leave himself numb. *Easy enough*…childhood had trained him to put Maurice's feelings first. Gabriel lined up with the bag again, readied himself for a roundhouse kick. "You should just send me to the camps." Gabriel's foot struck the bag with a sharp thump.

"Absolutely not! Which is why you will tell no one about what happened. Just live your life as normal, and I'll take care of everything."

"Live as normal?" Gabriel looked down at the sweat dripping off his body, puddling on the mat of his home gym.

"The chances of passing it with sweat, with normal human contact is minimal, Gabriel. You just need to be careful. And tell no one." His father smacked the side of his head. "No one, Gabriel."

"Yes. I understand."

***

He canceled the date with Ashley, couldn't even think up an excuse beyond just "not in the mood" for sitting courtside at a Thunder game, let alone catered dinner and drinks in the penthouse. She looked devastated.

"Is it something I did? Are you mad that I haven't broken up with Bailey yet?" Her bottom lip trembled like she might cry, right there in front of her locker and a hallway full of ogling students. *All because of a stupid date.*

"Well, you haven't, have you?" he snarled, a response so different from the princely charm he'd used on her before that her mouth dropped open in shock. "Everything with you has been a mistake. I'd rather just go see the game by myself than spend another second with a lying cheat like you, *Ashley Thompson*." He'd spun round to see

Bailey at the end of the hall juggling a stack of books, his backpack, and a coffee. Peyton elbowed his younger brother in the back, and two of the books slipped free. Bailey fought to grab them without spilling his drink.

"Dork, why did you need so many books?"

"Gee, I don't know, Pey. Maybe because I actually care about my grades? Maybe because this is a *school*, and not just a place for dumb jocks to hang out between football games?" He'd gotten worked up, and his cheeks had turned pink. His dark blond curls bounced in time with his lecture.

Gabriel couldn't hide his grin at Bailey's explosion. No one else would dare talk to Peyton like that, not unless they wanted his fist in their face. As Peyton moved to elbow his younger brother again, Gabriel called out to him. "Don't pick on the lowerclassmen, Peyton. You never know who's watching." *Like me. I'm always watching.*

Bailey didn't act grateful for the help and shot Gabriel a nasty glare—*because of Ashley.* Because of Gabriel's idiotic plan to break them up. That glare plunged into the well of things Gabriel tried to keep from feeling. The plastic wire over his throat. The scraped open skin on his knuckles. The feral man's blood mixing with Gabriel's blood.

***

He did go to the penthouse, just not to the basketball game, poured himself a drink from his father's liquor cabinet. Once he'd downed it, he grabbed the Glenfiddich and took a swig right from the bottle. He'd buried too much inside, and willpower alone wouldn't keep it down. The dark night sky turned the wall of windows into a mirror. "How much of this stuff do I have to drink to feel better?" he asked his reflection. He held the bottle to his mouth and took another long drink.

A loud ringing signaled a visitor's arrival. *Dear Old Dad.* "God, can't you just give me a single night alone? A few hours where I don't have to be your son?" The reflection had no answers. "Fine, fine." He buzzed up the elevator. Not until the doors slid open did he remember that his father wouldn't have needed Gabriel to buzz him up.

Ashley stepped out, looking nervous and shy. She'd curled her long brown hair into ringlets and put on a shimmery pink slip dress, pink shoes, pink dangling earrings...*pink, pink, pink.*

"What are you doing here?" Gabriel turned his back on her and stumbled to the leather sofa. "How did you even know about this place?" Then he held up the bottle of scotch. "Want a drink?"

Ashley took a seat beside him. "Carly Mayton's dad came to a party here. She bragged to everyone about it. You didn't hear?"

"Mayton...Arnold Mayton from New Plains Energy Corp?" Now he sounded like one of the gray men from his father's club. Gabriel dropped the Glenfiddich to cover his eyes. Scotch permeated the air. "Fuck, fuck, fuck everything!" Tears leaked between his fingers.

"Gabriel?" Ashley's soft hands covered his own, then the press of her lips. "Is this because of me? Because I wouldn't break up with Bailey?" She pulled at his hands to lower them, and he let her. *What does it matter if this girl sees me crying?* Ashley pressed a kiss onto his mouth, her lips sticky with gloss. The warmth felt good though, comforting. No one had ever comforted Gabriel this way before, with a kiss or hug, with affection.

Ashley slid onto his lap, her silky pink dress riding up her thighs, and Gabriel pressed himself into her, rubbed his face into the skin of her neck. "I'm not a good person," he told her. "Not like Bailey. He's always helping people, always believing in a cause. Always so clear on what's right and what's wrong."

161

"Forget about Bailey," Ashley whispered in Gabriel's ear and then bit down on the lobe. That felt good, too. The small spark of pain distracting him. "Bailey doesn't matter right now." Ashley lifted Gabriel's limp hand, set it over one breast. She'd peeled away the top of the dress, didn't have a bra on underneath the slinky material.

Forget about Bailey? Impossible. After their first meeting, Gabriel had become obsessed with the boy. "I never know what's right, what's wrong. I only know what my father expects, what Freddy or Ben, what the…" Ashley's mouth covered his. …*what the doctor's at Wellspring expected of him.* And now, he'd gone back to his father, to the first set of expectations, the familiar parameters of Maurice Featherton's "greatest achievement."

Ashley unbuttoned his shirt, his pants. He wanted to stop her, tell her to leave, but he craved the relief from his grief. The warmth of her skin, the wet touch of her mouth, the slick sweat of her body, all of it gave him the solace he'd craved from the liquor.

Losing himself inside the warmth of another body—in sweat and intimacy—worked until the scotch wore off, until his head cleared. He woke with his skin plastered to the pale leather of the penthouse sectional, his chest sticky against Ashley's naked breasts, his stomach rolling from the Glenfiddich.

And the shushing sound of the elevator doors opening to the penthouse living room.

Renée stood over him. "Did Daddy say you could bring girls here?" From the back of the couch, Renée's fingers plucked up Ashley's slip dress. "Cheap girls."

Ashley opened her eyes and sat up. She hugged her arms over her chest. "Wha…who are you?"

Gabriel's sister threw the slinky pink fabric at her. "Did you tell him about that night?"

"Not all of it. Not the part with you… Obviously."

Ashley had pulled the dress over her nakedness. "Gabriel, who is this? What's going on?"

Renée said nothing about Gabriel keeping secret that she'd hired someone to attack him, but she turned on Ashley with a sneer. "You better hope *nothing* is going on. Right, Gabriel?"

Fear froze his breath, froze his heart. He looked down at his knuckles. The scabs had cracked again, red blood smeared across the back of his hands.

What have I done?

surprise

29 Renée

Peyton aims a spray nozzle at his discarded club and boots, blasts them both with a jet of water. "Fucking Simon and his fucking superspreader birthday." When Renée first arrived at the rectangular burning pit, she watched Peyton toss his shirt and pants into the fire along with the limp body of his latest kill. "We lost Cori, fucking creature bit her right in the face."

Renée scans the group of fighters, all of them in various states of undress as they take turns hosing off infected blood. *Which one was Cori? The gap-toothed girl? The one with the neck tattoo?*

After they'd found the ruins of the birthday party inside Liam's building, Renée counted up the plates of molding cake and realized their problem had leaked beyond the tenants of a single converted townhouse. She and Peyton spent the next three days tracking down everyone invited. Turns out, when the slobbery birthday boy blew out the candles on his cake, he'd infected every slice. Central Business District began to crawl with new creatures, all of them pumped with adrenaline, savage when provoked. They fought back against her police like rabid animals.

"Most of this is Cori's blood, but whatever." Peyton turns to address the remaining six officers under him. "Burn anything that got more than just a splatter. And wash off your fucking hands and face before you leave here." The cool weather had turned bitter in

164

the last couple days, and the water from the hose must feel glacial. But, her officers don't act like they mind the cold, all of them sweating and flushed from fighting, killing, dragging bodies to the pit. Brinda and another officer also had to burn their blood-soaked clothes.

Despite the meaty smell and heavy smoke, Renée luxuriates in the heat emanating from the burning pit. She plants her boots on the cinderblock edge and lets the fire's red glow sink into her. Without the ability to run consistent heat into any of the city buildings, the cold never quite leaves her bones. And even though she'd worn skirt suits all during the sweltering summer and fall, with the frost, she adopted Peyton's leather and wool combinations in black, all black. *Look the part,* something Maurice had once advised her, during their lunch meetings.

Her father's wide, thick hands holding his knife, his fork. Maurice had been a boxer in his youth, and he still had the powerful build, the rough, heavy hands of a strong man. "If you look like someone important…" Daddy gestured with his steak knife to mean his Armani suit, his Hublot watch. "…people will treat you like someone important."

He didn't know—or didn't care—about all she'd done already to "look the part." The many surgeries to perfect her face, her body. Granny Featherton had died the week Renée began her internship and gifted her pearls to Renée. They hung around her neck as a reminder of everything else the old woman paid for. She'd bought herself a granddaughter who would look worthy of the Featherton name. "Yes," she dutifully answered her father. "I understand."

***

Right now, "looking the part" means presenting herself as half of a unified team with Peyton—*if you follow him, you follow me.* Renée steps down off the cinderblock and turns, catches Brinda watching her with curious eyes. Then the other woman looks away.

"Spray off your skin before you get dressed again, Terrance," Brinda orders. Terrance, a gangly boy with knobby elbows and knees, follows her orders with trembling lips. He looks new, green, and freaked out.

"I...I will."

Sebby, the officer Renée met over Liam's body, laughs. *"I...I will,"* Sebby mocks in a high-pitched voice. "Damn, you act more scared of washing up than you did when that crazy bitch in the robe dropped down on you."

Brinda unhooks her bra and tosses it next to her boots. Her dark nipples erect from the cold. "Fuck off, Sebby, you were whining like a little bitch about scraping creature guts out of the mayor's office."

Renée glances at Peyton, but he ignores Brinda's breasts and cracks up at the dig against Sebby. "Yeah, dumbass, I had to finish off that kid you chased down, and Terrance cracked that robe-woman's head with one swing." Peyton slaps Terrance on the back as he bends over to vomit. "Don't get all sensitive about it. That takedown was pure legend."

Andy appears around the barricade, his arms filled with a stack of black cloth. He stares at Brinda's naked chest until she barks out directions for him to pass out everyone's replacement clothing. No more blue uniforms, just black t-shirts and black denim. All of it an imitation of Peyton's gear.

Peyton tugs on a pair of tight black cargo pants, buttons them up. "I got one more building to check, and then we just have to wait."

Renée takes a step closer, despite the spray of freezing water, despite the thick scent of infected blood. "You think people are hiding creatures?"

Peyton raises an eyebrow, "No shit. Someone always does." He combs his fingers through his wet hair and looks away.

There it is again. That vulnerable sadness that he keeps secret from Renée. He snatches a long-sleeved black t-shirt from Andy and tugs it over his head. It fits him like a second skin. He bends to retrieve his wet boots and club. Once he's turned away, he asks, "Any sign of the tanker and Case?" Something about the forced casualness of his tone bothers Renée.

That look he gets…it can't be the hometown girl. When they do the tanker switches, Peyton doesn't flirt, doesn't go out of his way to touch Case. But, Renée can feel something there, some unasked question that she can't parse out. "It's a little early still for the switch. Why do you ask?"

Evasive doesn't suit him, and Peyton must know it. He turns back and meets her eyes. Stands a little too close so that he looks down at her. "What's with the suspicious tone? I just want to know how she's doing. Her sister died."

"Because you killed her."

Peyton's nostrils flare. Sculpted arms tense. A palpable threat of violence hung in the air between them, thick and suffocating as the burning pit's smoke. His voice like a growl, "She was sick."

Both Brinda and Andy go silent. And Renée can feel herself on the knife edge. Brinda hurriedly pulls on black t-shirt of her own, dark eyes flicking back and forth between Peyton and Renée.

Renée takes a deep breath. Forces herself to relax. She raises a hand and strokes Peyton's cheek. "I'm saying that Case might not want to see you right away." A lie. But, two years spent with politicians had taught Renée to lie well. She doesn't want Peyton meeting with Case because she doesn't trust either of them not to unite against her. She adopts a gentle, consoling tone, "It's better if I meet with her alone this time."

Brinda struggles into a pair of tight black jeans. As she bends over, the tips of her dark wet hair dangle in the mud. "Come on,

Sarg. Let's get the rest of Simon's buddies before it gets dark out." The straight white teeth appear again. "I call dibs on the next one."

***

Waiting in the shadows of the burnt factory, Renée sees Case before the other woman spots her. Peyton's ex-girlfriend used to pull into the factory truck stall one nervous inch at a time, but after months of twice weekly deliveries, Case now swings into the space with ease, and the mini-tanker's brakes emit an echoing whine. The driver side door opens and Case hops down from the truck's running board. "Well, aren't you in a hurry today, Case Bell. What has you so eager?"

Case flips her head toward Renée, long wild curls swirling like smoke. When she pushes them back, her expression goes rigid, except for her angry burning eyes. She cranes her neck to see behind Renée. "Where's Peyton?"

Interesting. "Hmmm…he was awful eager to see you today as well. Mind telling me what that's about?" Renée closes the space between them. She hasn't changed out of her boots and jeans, even though she considered putting on a suit for this specific meeting. She didn't have time to change and also make certain that Peyton and the other police stayed occupied searching out creatures in the newly filled residential buildings. At least no one under Renée has candy-colored hair or school hoodies. Case still dresses like a suburban high school girl in her baggy maroon Bulldogs sweatshirts and athletic leggings. And the act she tries to pull off now, taking forever to lock up the truck and hand over the key, is fucking obvious. "Stop dawdling. He isn't going to suddenly show, I have him busy doing a job. This pathetic crush of yours is really starting to annoy me." *I can't have you luring him away—I can't take the chance that Peyton's melancholy expressions are about you.*

Folding her arms over her chest, Case faces Renée with narrowed eyes and stiff posture. "I want to talk to him," Case says. She looks unmovable.

That Gabriel found this girl before she did elicits a stab of jealousy in Renée's gut. *I should have tried harder to recruit her...* But, no, that wouldn't have worked. This girl would have ideas of her own, opinions about all Renée's decisions. "I told you, he's busy. He doesn't have time for you, or anyone else from the suburbs." She hopes for a reaction, but Case gives her none. *You're good, Case Bell, but I've cracked shells tougher than yours.* "I'm just surprised you even *want* to see to him, after how he had to put your sister to rest." Renée pouts at her. "She made it all the way here from...I think Peyton said USC? And then she gets infected." Renée's lips curl into a smile. "How heartbreaking."

And...*there!* Renée broke the stoic facade. Though what she finds underneath isn't what she expected. No tears. No rage. Fear widens Case Bell's eyes and causes a quick gasp of air. "Right." She tosses the truck keys to Renée, and they hit the ground between them. "I'm going."

"I thought you wanted to wait for Peyton. You looked like you were about to fight me for the chance." Case ignores her words, doesn't even look Renée's way, just steps around her toward the empty tanker.

"Giving up?"

"I'm not giving up anything." Case opens the passenger side door and collects the waiting black duffle on the seat. "You spend a lot of time thinking 'bout me and Peyton. Maybe you should be playing nice instead—so I keep making drops for you." Case unzips the duffle to check the contents.

"Oh, don't think for a moment that I believe you are driving two tankers a week from the refinery in Cushing, cruising right through the heart of Featherton territory and Gabriel *still* doesn't know a thing about it."

Case looks up from the duffle. "Girl, I don't care what you think you know."

"You shouldn't let Gabriel use you like this, Case."

"Yeah. Thanks for the life advice, but I'm good." Case steps up into the empty truck and starts the engine. She adjusts the mirrors, dawdling to drag the time out even longer.

Renée shouts over the engine's roar, "I could give him a message for you. He won't care, but I can tell him."

Case drops an arm out the driver side window. "Sure. You can tell him that I think his new boss is a bitch."

Laughing, Renée shakes her head. "That's seriously your message? Don't you trust that I'll pass one to him? Give me a real message."

Case tosses her puffy hair back over the seat rest and bites her lip. "You think you're his handler or something, don't you? But, I'll give you some advice, *Mayor*," Case sneers at the title. "You don't really know Peyton, not at all. And that's why you'll never understand how to deal with him." Then Case guns the tanker in reverse, making certain she got the last word.

30 Gabriel

With the new apprenticeship program and credit system in place, the streets inside Olde Town have both emptied and grown busier. Everyone occupied, moving, involved. Gabriel takes meeting after meeting to iron out the requirements and qualifications of each new position. Not until evening can he run some errands of his own. Before her death, Cecilia would come with him, asking questions and helping organize priorities. Gabriel misses her companionship. He misses his friend. Because of this, he invites Lawrence Vu along with him.

As they cross Elm Street headed for Maple, Lawrence makes a noise behind him. "Are you listening to me? I thought we were getting the runners new jackets."

"We are." Gabriel unlocks the deadbolts on the unassuming yellow brick bungalow. One of four storehouses inside the Olde Town compound walls.

"Well, I thought that meant the Elm storehouse, not this one."

Derek Sams had called Lawrence Vu's appointment a "sentimental" choice, and Gabriel agrees. *I couldn't return the feelings Cecilia had for me, but I can at least help her brother.* Despite the boy's shortcomings, his annoying impatience, Gabriel resolves to train Lawrence, guide him, until he becomes a good lieutenant.

"Then, why aren't we at the house on Elm? That's the best stuff."

"Because, I want to look here, Lawrence."

Inside the yellow bungalow, stacks of canned goods line the entry foyer. The shuttered front room has aisles of shelving stacked with camping equipment. Gabriel has to turn sideways to make his way though them. "You know, Cecilia organized this storehouse," Gabriel says. A tic of a smile. "Which is why all the passageways only fit her." When he turns around, Gabriel sees Lawrence snag a protein bar from a bin near the edge of the room.

"That's coming out of your credit tally, Lawrence. I don't tolerate stealing."

"I thought we were going to the house on Elm. It has better coats, leather jackets even." Lawrence tosses the protein bar back. "I saw them when you took Bailey there."

Gabriel pauses with his hand on a package of hooded windbreakers. He'd taken Bailey to the house on Elm to impress him, to show off the best of what he'd gathered from the suburban shopping malls. It hadn't worked at all. Bailey didn't care about clothes or luxuries. Not until Gabriel explained his plans for a hospital, for housing the refugees streaming through his territory, did Gabriel finally earn Bailey's respect. Gabriel stayed away from the storehouse on Elm since then. *Because you're avoiding it.* He hangs his head, sighs. "Fine. Let's get the runners the leather jackets."

As chatty as Lawrence had been on the walk to the yellow bungalow, he now marches silent, head down, toward Elm street. Maybe he has the very same reason for avoiding the bungalow storehouse that Gabriel has for not wanting to return to the house on Elm. The narrow, Cecilia-sized aisles, the low shelves. To Lawrence, the yellow bungalow probably feels haunted with his sister's presence.

The front door to the storehouse on Elm is set in an alcove with a small porch step, and Lawrence stands behind Gabriel, waiting for him to unlock a string of deadbolts on the door. Snow swirls through the cold wind, but so far, nothing has gathered on the ground.

The last deadbolt snicks open. "I'll turn on the heat—"

Lawrence falls into Gabriel's back, a full-body thump that knocks the air from his lungs. At first he thinks Lawrence fainted, so Gabriel turns to grab him, to keep Cecilia's younger brother from hitting the floor. A quick spin with arms stretched forward to catch. But other bodies converge onto the storehouse porch and shove Gabriel backward. *Three against one.* In his peripheral vision, he sees the club, a long metal pole swing toward him—but the press of bodies holds him in place. The pole thuds against Gabriel's temple, drops him to the ground.

Don't pass out.

A kick to his ribs, which he fights not to curl into. *A terrible defensive move.* He swallows against the pain, his vision spotty and warped. One of the men throws his full weight on Gabriel's right arm, while another kneels on the left.

172

Gabriel sucks air in through his nose. *Don't pass out.* Lawrence stands over them all. "Let us into the basement."

Cold rage surges through Gabriel's veins. "Why should I do that?" Gabriel can feel the blood trickling down toward the side of his face.

"Because we told you to," says the man on his left. "And we're the ones giving the orders now."

Another punch to the face, and Gabriel's upper lip splits against his teeth. *Damn it. Concentrate.* He recognizes that voice… *How? Who?* Gabriel twists his neck and blinks up at a familiar puffy face. Only familiar though. *Who are you?*

The man punches him again, and Gabriel's left eye fills with blood that he tries to blink away.

The man on Gabriel's right reaches out and pushes back on the violent one. "Cut it out, Craig. You're going to kill him."

Craig…Craig…Oh, of course. "You're Josh Spooner's brother."

"That's right, fucker." In the early days of Feathertons, Gabriel assigned Craig Spooner as Peyton's stock manager. Then Craig's younger brother caught the virus, popped right in Olde Town. Craig twists the arm he pins. "You let your boy Peyton kill my little brother, so I'm going to kill *his* brother. Eye for an eye, got it?"

Lawrence makes a loud frustrated groan. "Shut up, Craig, this isn't about revenge. We have to keep the virus out of the burbs. His stupid restructuring plan is going to kill us all."

Gabriel's stomach heaves. *Fuck. A concussion.* He turns his head and vomits on the man at his right. Another familiar face, Keon Han, Rhea Han's younger brother. In the lieutenants meeting, Gabriel had mentioned Rhea by name as a med student with some minimal experience in treating illness and injuries.

"Can't we just—?" Keon's arms and legs tremble as he grounds Gabriel's right arm down. "We don't want trouble. We just don't

173

want our family taking care of creatures. We don't want you making a quarantine camp here in—"

"We're already in trouble, Keon." Lawrence's voice has gone high and reedy. He throws himself forward and cinches his hands around Gabriel's throat. "You're just watching Bailey rot away and putting all of us in danger. Let us into the basement, and we'll kill him fast."

"No." Blood from his split lip fills Gabriel's mouth. "You aren't trying to save anyone, Lawrence. You just want Bailey dead—"

"Fuck yes, I want him dead, but here's the thing…he already died. It's been months. Everyone knows it but you. Bailey's dead."

"Plant your foot. Drive with the hips." Freddy holds the pad over Gabriel's head. *"Front kick!"* Bucking off the floor, Gabriel kicks Lawrence in the jaw.

No amount of sitting at his father's desk and configuring trade and territory can erase those two years of training—living—in a dojo. Of two more years practicing every day while locked inside Wellspring. Gabriel twists and knees Craig in the face. When Craig lets go of his arm, Gabriel screws his body in the other direction and punches forward into Keon's throat.

"On your feet!" Freddy slaps his hand against the mat. *"On your feet, arms out, knees bent."* Gabriel follows Freddy's voice in his head with the body memory that the old man ingrained in him. Up. Ready. Gabriel spins and launches himself on top of Craig Spooner just in time to knock him back down. Gabriel slams Craig's head against the floor.

"On your toes—hands up." Freddy holds both fists in front of this face.

Lawrence lies unconscious. Keon stays low on the ground, doesn't move, doesn't breathe. Gabriel nudges Craig with his foot then crouches down to check for a pulse. Nothing.

"Is he dead?" Keon asks.

"Yes."

"Ah…" Keon wipes a hand over his face. "Shit."

A hoarse moan, and Lawrence lifts himself up, blood pours from his mouth, and one cheek bulges with crooked teeth. Both hands flap against his head. The moans come faster and faster until he sounds like a wounded dog. Or one of the creatures. Lawrence bicycles his legs, twists and untwists against the pain.

"You made this happen." Gabriel tells him, but Lawrence can only writhe on the floor. So Gabriel turns to Keon. "Tell me why. Why did you do this?"

Despite Gabriel's soft tone, Keon jumps. "Yeah. He… His sister died because of Bailey and…" Keon swipes at his cheek. "I just don't want my mom working at a camp."

"There won't be camps." *But that's not true, is it?* Gabriel *does* want to cage the sick. Let them wait out the virus. Just like the camps tried to do. And it didn't work.

"Then what was Lawrence talking about? Did he make it up?"

"He…" Gabriel clamps his mouth tight. *It didn't work. It didn't work. You walked through one of the those camps, and you saw. You saw…*

Keon looks up at Gabriel, waits for him to answer.

"There won't be camps," Gabriel says.

31 Gabriel

Gabriel sends a runner to Pierce Heights to collect Mrs. Vu. *Time to put her old nursing skills back into use, starting with her son's broken jaw.* Gabriel has Craig Spooner's body thrown in a burning pit.

His attack creates a stir in Olde Town that wakes up the entire compound. Tomorrow, Gabriel planned to send tillers into the neighborhoods, create gardens where houses once had useless lawns. Instead, he'll need to stem the flow of gossip, bring more guards into the mansion. And his head *throbs*, a definite concussion. He almost considers asking Lawrence's mother to check him over as he watches her shaking hands twist a bloody stained cloth between her hands. After she'd patched up her son, Gabriel had her brought to the study. *What did she know?* He has half a mind to kick the entire family out of their home in Pierce Heights and send them on the road.

"I am very sorry for my son's actions." Mrs. Vu keeps her eyes focused on the ornate wool rug in front of Gabriel's desk. "Lawrence hasn't been the same since Cecilia's death, or he would have never done something to offend you."

"Offend me?" He sits ramrod straight, stares her down, and tries to ignore the background ringing in his ears. "Your son tried to stage a coup. Not a very good one, either. Your son is a fool."

"Please, Gabriel, don't judge our family for what Lawrence has done." She balls up the stained cloth and tucks it into her coat pocket. Gabriel probably left Lawrence disfigured and in constant pain. A relative certainty without a surgeon to reattach the bones in his jaw. "I have two other children, and my husband's heart is not good." Gabriel has his hands on the desk in front of him, fingers folded neatly. He feels like a mafia don again, after so many months aspiring for something more noble—the leader who addressed weary refugees on his front lawn. Bailey had admired that version of Gabriel. He grinds his teeth against the sound of this woman's grating appeal for mercy.

"Please, Gabriel, we like it here in Featherton territory. If you forced us to leave, it would be a death sentence for us. I can promise you that Lawrence will not bother you again."

"I am certain he won't bother me again. I have him locked him up with the rioters from Pierce Heights. I've got quite the little prison growing inside my hospital cages."

Mrs. Vu's eyes finally move from the floor to Gabriel's face. "You intend to…keep infected here?" Fear shakes her voice. "In Olde Town?"

He manages not to flinch as the memory of the quarantine camp surfaces again.

He'd discovered it at the end of an unmarked gravel road off I-35. His boots crunched across broken glass, sticky with dark, infected blood. All the staff had died, ripped to pieces by their patients, body parts scattered across the medical tents. Tied in their beds, feral infected people chewed on their own arms and hands trying to break free.

He'd followed one of the caged military Humvees from his neighborhood, hanging back just enough not to get arrested or shot. When he saw the Hummer turn off on the unmarked road, Gabriel parked his stolen truck in a ditch and made his way on foot. The soldiers didn't go far, they just pulled to the side, dragged a man and woman from the cage, forced them to their knees, and shot them execution style. They didn't even burn the bodies, they just threw them out along the side of the road, sprayed them with bullets, and laughed as they sped away.

"I saw the camps myself. I've seen how easily they fall apart." Gabriel's words sound robotic, but they twist through his body like poison, like a knife, like a bullet.

"Your daughter Cecilia was my most trusted lieutenant and my friend. Make sure your other children are like her and not Lawrence."

"Yes. I will. Thank you, Gabriel."

**

Jadyn Clegg takes her place on the study's rug. "I could stay here tonight," he offers. Gabriel forgot he'd sent for Jadyn. *Fucking concussion!*

"That won't be necessary, but I do want you taking over Olde Town starting tonight. There will be no more unincorporated housing. I don't want any more outliers. It's too difficult to deliver to houses scattered in dead neighborhoods. And we use too much manpower trying to protect them."

"You want those people to move? They won't like it, boss. These people stayed in their homes while everyone on their streets popped or got eaten. A bunch of damn attitude problems, every last one of them."

He can't keep himself rigid and calm a moment longer—the organizing of security and retrieval of Craig Spooner's body, the cleanup had taken up most of the night. Gabriel rubs a hand across his sweat damp forehead.

"You okay, boss?"

"I'm fine. Just…" Deep breath. *You are in control.* He folds his hands again. "Tell them they either agree to move into one of the neighborhoods, or they're out. I'm going to demolish the empty streets…most of them are infested with creatures anyway." Gabriel has never had problems with Jadyn throwing up a lot of arguments, like Derek Sams, or acting secretive like Angelica Loeza. "I should have given you the position as soon as Cecilia died."

"Well, I appreciate it now, man." A wide smile breaks across Jadyn's face. He must consider the move a promotion from the wilds of looted buildings and darkened houses. "Thanks, Gabriel." Jadyn takes a step closer and holds his hand out to shake.

Good God, when will this day end? "Yes. You're welcome." Jadyn and Gabriel shake hands, even though the touch of another person's skin makes him want to vomit again.

***

He stands for a long time on the terrace. A storm has started coming in, maybe the first heavy snow. "New jackets for the runners," he says to no one. Another deep pang for Cecilia's loss. Why does he feel her absence so intensely now—months after her death? "I've been too focused on…" Gabriel scrubs his palms over his face. He'd promised Bailey that he wouldn't give up, but all around him the stability he created crumbles into fear and back-stabbing. Bailey had worried more about hurting others while feral than he'd worried for his own fate. What would he say about Gabriel letting down all the people depending on him? *If I really have lost him for good, I should honor his wishes.* And Bailey didn't want to live a half life inside a fetid cage. He wouldn't want Gabriel to abandon his territory, to not do his best to assure the safety and wellbeing of his people.

It's been months. Gabriel pinches the bridge of his nose, presses his fingers into the corners of his eyes. "What am I even thinking? I can't do it." *But, if not me then who else?* The encroaching cold burns his eyes, his sinuses. His throat aches. He forgot his wool coat somewhere and just now notices that he's shivering. If not him, then who else? It has to be him.

Gabriel turns back to the house. Inside the study, behind the desk, is a metal pipe. The heft and grip both instantly familiar to him. In the early days, he'd matched Peyton kill for kill. They'd fought side by side as if they'd synchronized each move. But Gabriel never enjoyed it like Peyton.

He enters the code on the basement keypad with ice-cold fingers, the electronic tones bounce around his concussed skull like a siren. Each step down the narrow staircase reverberates up through the bones of his body. He grits his teeth against pain in his gut. Bailey lies on the far side of the room, facing the wall. His mottled, dirty skin. His grimy, tangled hair. "If not me, then who else?" Gabriel asks the boy in the cage. *It has to be me.*

Bailey—the creature—thrashes his legs and moans. Gabriel left him—*it*—in that same position this morning. The creature hasn't moved all day. *It's dying.*

"I didn't mean for you to suffer like this. I'm sorry for that."

179

Gabriel can remember that suffering, every moment full of agony…physical, mental. *And I've made him live like that for months.* He closes his eyes, leans his forehead against the cold iron bars. "After I recovered, entered the final stage, my father brought me from this cage back to my bedroom upstairs. He was a strong man, had been a boxer and wrestler when he was younger. But, it still couldn't have been easy to carry me up from the basement, then two more flights of stairs to my bedroom." Gabriel remembers opening his eyes, his father's face hovering over his own. For the first time since Gabriel could remember, his father had a beard. An unkempt scraggy beard. *"Can you hear me, Gabriel? Son, do you understand what I'm saying?"*

"I was so weak, so thin and helpless. But, I'd survived. My father was so happy I survived." Gabriel unlatches the cage door, pushes it across the cement in jerking stops and starts. "My father stayed by my side the entire time. He wiped me down when I sweated out my fevers. Spooned water in my mouth until I could drink on my own." Inside the cage, Gabriel takes whispering steps toward Bailey's curled body. Closer…closer. His leather dress shoes track across smears of blood and gore from the animals Bailey killed, sticky puddles where he pissed, smears of shit. *It isn't Bailey—not anymore.*

***

"Then, something happened…"

"Just a little more, son. Another spoonful, and I'll let you rest."

"I…I can't…" Inside him, that tingling pressure of a seizure had built, that underwater numbness. The light filtering through his curtains started to waver and shine. His legs stiffened. His arms shot out from his sides and beat at the air. He clipped the spoon from his father's hand. The glass cracked against the bedside table.

***

Gabriel studies the metal pipe in his hands, holds it out in front of him, ready. "Something happened…" *The glass cracked against the bedside table.*

Gabriel crouches down at Bailey's back, can hear his quick wheezing breaths, can see the shivering tremors in his dying body. "A glass broke, and my father cut his hand, and…" Gabriel's heavy breathing mirrors Bailey's wet panting. For a frozen moment, their labored respirations sync up. Gabriel continues, "My sweat and saliva and tears, they were all over him. He knew he caught it, but he still didn't leave me." Gabriel swipes at his nose. Fuck. He's crying. When did that happen?

"By the time I could leave my bed and walk, he had started feeling stuffy and sick. I knew he didn't have long, but I thought I could take care of him, keep him in the same cage he'd made for me and wait for him to get better." A laugh breaks free. "I'm such a fucking idiot."

***

"You want me to get you a doctor?"

"Yes. They have doctors at the camps. You were sick for weeks, you don't know. They have treatments to…ease the feral stage. I'll have a chance if you get me those drugs. Just ask for the treatment pack, and they'll give it to you."

"A treatment pack?"

"Find a doctor."

***

The tears come faster. Gabriel tightens his grip on the pipe and snivels back the snot and tears clogging his throat. "My father just wanted me out of the house. He sent me on a stupid errand—to get a doctor. He made up a story about a drug that could… Fuck, it doesn't matter. There was no miracle drug. He just wanted me out

181

of the house. I followed one of the military Hummers back to a camp and…" He swipes his face against his shoulder, chokes back a sob. "When I came home, I found him dead. He'd hung himself in the back yard. That giant elm. I had it torn out." What a waste of time and effort to have a tree removed as the world slipped into dystopia, but he couldn't stand to see it again. He couldn't shake the image of his father's broken neck, the sound of his belt creaking against the bottom branch.

I can't do it. I can't. Fuck the territory. Fuck what Bailey would want. And fuck his father for saving Gabriel in the first place. He can't do it. He won't. Gabriel throws the pipe out behind him, and it hits against the cage bars in a thunderous clanging, rolls across the cement. "He wasn't a good father. He was selfish, right to the very end. But he saved me, and I killed him." He doesn't hide the watery sob that follows. "Why bother saving me if—" The loud hiccuping sound of trying to catch his breath.

"It…wasn't…your fault." The croaky words come from the creature…from Bailey.

Gabriel grabs at his shoulder and turns the shivering boy on his back. Bailey's teeth are clenched, cords in his neck bulging taut, but his gray eyes meet Gabriel's, and they see him.

Bailey sees him.

"He saved you because…" Bailey breaks off panting. "Because…he loved you. That's love."

Gabriel's tears drip down and stripe through the dust and grime on Bailey's face. "Yes. It is." Gabriel hoists Bailey into his arms. He's not that heavy, not really. Gabriel thinks he can bear the weight for three flights of stairs.

32 Renee

No matter how many times she insists Peyton follow her commands, no matter how often he agrees to just that, situations like *this* keep happening. "Peyton, do you copy?" Still nothing. "God damn it!"

When she gets to the headquarters, Renée finds Andy sitting on a folding chair out front, club across his knees, a half-empty bottle of gin near one boot. The boy murmurs something into a chunky black walkie-talkie. Renée snatches the hardware out of his hand. "Who gave you this?"

"What?" Andy glances around them, raps his knuckles on the glass door behind him.

"Are you stupid? I asked you who gave you this walkie-talkie."

"Um... I don't remember."

The door behind him opens to reveal Brinda with her dark searching eyes. "He's not here," she says. "Most everyone is on patrol." She's holding the door open like she expects Renée to still come inside even though, with Peyton gone, there's no reason to.

Renée follows her in anyway. "I guess I could get warm while I wait."

The corner of Brenda's mouth tics up. "Okay. Sure."

Another video game is playing on the massive screen, and a handful of teenagers watch from the orange leather couches. One boy spoons pineapple from a can and calls out moves for the girl holding the game controller. The room stinks of body odor.

"Do you want some water or something?" Brinda asks. "Sebby and Pedro found a crate of Dr. Pepper. We're keeping it outside, so it's cold and everything." Brinda folds her scared arms over her chest, leans back against a ping pong table covered in beer bottles and candy wrappers.

"You should have turned that in to the resource manager. We'll just continue to have food shortages if people keep whatever they find."

"Resource manager got the virus. Gay dude who Liam hooked up with, I guess. That's what Peyton said."

Renée's nails bite into the skin of her palms. "Why wasn't I told?" They both hear the roar of Peyton's bike outside. Andy holds the door open, and Peyton drives right through it, parks the black and white Kawasaki Ninja on the industrial carpet. He shoots Renée a cocky grin that she doesn't return.

"Yo, Brinda." Peyton kills the engine. "Take whoever's here and do a patrol across Central Business. Fucking kids running around in the streets, and who knows which of them have a connection to the little birthday bastard."

Brinda doesn't need to say a word. Once their sergeant entered, he'd captured the attention of the room, they'd even paused the full-decimal video game. Still, Brinda makes a circle motion in the air. "Grab your clubs, and let's go."

This is what you wanted, Renée reminds herself. She'd needed Peyton to galvanize the struggling police force underneath her, and he'd done exactly that. She tries not to sound shrill, "What happened to my resource manager?"

Peyton circles his arms around her waist. "I was going to tell you tonight, babe."

"Don't call me babe. I'm not your babe, I'm your boss."

He doesn't let go of her. "Okay, then I was going to tell you tonight, *Mayor.* I had a feeling we'd find a mess in that Resource Office. Half the time I'd go in there Liam would be hanging all over that Martinez dude. Didn't you ever notice?"

She hadn't. "I only discussed work with Liam." Renée breaks out of Peyton's hold, or he just let go, she isn't sure.

He strides over to a small square window, cranks it open. "Well, dude never missed the chance to check out my ass, I can tell you that much." A six-pack of Heineken sits on the outside windowsill. Apparently, her band of officers found more than just a crate of Dr. Pepper. Peyton holds a bottle in the air. "Want one? Might be the last German beer in the whole US of A."

"Heineken is Dutch, you moron. And I doubt that's the last one."

"Well, it's the last one I've seen around here." Peyton cracks the bottle open and takes a long thirsty pull. "You're going to need a whole new Resource staff in there pronto. I locked up the doors, but...you should run things how Gabriel does and—"

"Don't tell me how to run things." Renée forces her lips closed, air into her lungs. Then, "I guarantee that my brother didn't think up how to run anything in his territory. His little girlfriend did all that."

Peyton chokes on a swallow of his beer. With his free hand he thumps his chest and coughs. "What *girlfriend*? You mean Cecilia?"

"I don't know her name. The Asian girl with the white hair."

He lifts the beer bottle back to his mouth and squints at her while he drinks. Then, "She died."

"Ha—she did? Too bad she didn't take out my brother when she popped."

"She didn't pop... I killed her. It was an accident."

"Oh. Then, no wonder my brother let you go. He's such a weakling when it comes to his emotions. What happened? Why did you—"

"Look, I don't really want to talk about Gabriel, or Cecilia or...any of that. Fuck—I just thought Gabriel did a good job of using runners to deliver shit instead of having people come pick it up themselves."

"So, you're offering to make deliveries now?"

"No. Just fucking forget it."

Renée strolls past him, examining the disaster he's made of her police station. Bags of chips, popcorn, cookies, and candy litter every surface of the expansive room. Beer cans and bottles of liquor, too. "It smells like a locker room in here." They took out the front desk, all the desks, every last bit of office equipment and turned the place into a lounge. She turns to find him watching her. "So, where were you? Andy got really cagey when I showed up."

"Ha, if you're done being a bitch, maybe I'll tell you…I was over on the army's side, talking to Lanson."

For a hot moment, she sees red. Somehow, she manages to grit out, "About what?"

Peyton drinks the last of his beer and lobs it across the room into a trash barrel. "Dandridge finally kicked the bucket. Lanson says he offed himself."

"Jesus—Okay, so Lanson is in charge?"

"So far… But, he's been losing people for months now. Not enough food. Not enough to do. That half of the city has gone wild again." Peyton stalks toward her, reminding her of a tiger stalking prey. He wraps his arms back around her, hands cupping her ass. "Anyway…" he draws the word out. "I was thinking…you should take the city."

"What do you mean?"

"I mean, let's move in on their half and take over. Tell them to work for us."

"And if they won't?"

Peyton makes the smile that never reaches his eyes. "They will. I already told them—work for us or get the fuck out."

"You did what—!"

"Hey, it's what you wanted. You should be fucking thanking me."

security

33 Gabriel

"Drink your milk." Gabriel points toward the kitchen doorway. "And go back to bed. You've only just recovered." He takes a sip of coffee and studies Bailey's progress. His fever broke two days ago and he already looks better than he did in the cage, color in his skin, movements less stiff. Healing scabs and bruises. Gabriel's baggy red tracksuit hides Bailey's weight loss, just his wrists look a little bonier, his cheekbones more pronounced. All in all, Bailey has none of the usual aftereffects of the illness. He had spent a long time in the feral stage, but he'd spent that time protected, cared for.

Bailey scratches at his floppy curls and pouts. "I'm not a child, you know. Jeez." But, he swallows down the milk and pulls out the chair nearest Gabriel at the kitchen table. "Wait...are you laughing at me?"

"I'm not. Not, really." Gabriel touches a finger against where Bailey's hand rests near his own. "But you should go back upstairs, if you aren't ready to see anyone, that is. My lieutenants will all be here soon."

"Lieutenants? Will Peyton be here?"

"He doesn't know you've recovered."

Bailey spins the milk glass between his palms. "Well… he probably wouldn't care anyway. He didn't exactly stick around to see whether I made it or not."

"He's not as strong as you think he is, Bailey. When he left it was because he couldn't bear to stay. He left because he couldn't handle it if you didn't survive."

Slumping back in his chair, Bailey crosses his arms over his chest. He might not have Case's expressive wet doe eyes, but Gabriel has studied Bailey's expressions for a long, long time. "If he knew you were alive, I don't believe your brother would be anywhere but here, by your side."

"I guess. Unlike my dad, huh?" Bailey makes an attempt at a laugh.

Gabriel pushes a plate of fruit and pastries toward Bailey. "Eat something."

"Can I at least ask Case about my brother?" He glares up at Gabriel through his long lashes. "Or is that the real reason you want me to go back to bed? So I—"

Setting the coffee mug down a little too hard, Gabriel grabs the seat of Bailey's chair and drags him forward, tips his forehead to touch Bailey's. "You can do anything you want. *Anything.* I'm not keeping you prisoner here."

"Yeah. I know that. I don't feel like a prisoner. Not even close, Gabriel. Okay? I want to be here. With you." Bailey closes his eyes, lets their heads rest together a moment longer. They stay like that a long moment, breathe each other's air. Bailey's hands fold over Gabriel's where he grasps the seat of the chair.

"Oh, my God. *Bailey?*" Angelica Loeza stands at the kitchen entry, one foot forward and one pointing the other way, ready to bolt from the house. She looks like she's waiting to see if Bailey crouches into a charge. "Are you…Are you…"

"Better? Yep." Bailey's eyes open, and he pulls away from Gabriel, shoves his hands in the pockets of the bilious red track pants. "No longer interested in ripping your face off and snacking on it. Talking, bathing... using the toilet like a big boy and everything."

Jadyn appears behind Angelica with a wide smile that contrasts with her shock. "Hey, up and about, I see." Jadyn bounds forward and play punches Bailey's arm. "Lookin' good. Gabriel wouldn't let anyone in to see you while you had the seizure part of Super Flu. Or the uh—"

Bailey curls his fingers into an imitation of the stiff claws characteristic of the virus' feral stage. Jadyn laughs. Then, Bailey cuts his eyes to Gabriel with a look so warm and grateful that the Feathertons' leader can feel a blush heat his face and neck.

Jadyn doesn't notice Gabriel's discomfort, still marveling at Bailey. "You even got all your teeth, son. You look good."

And finally, Angelica steps forward, but with her hands clasped behind her back. Still not willing to chance physical contact like Jadyn. "You do look real well, Bailey. The best I've ever seen from someone who came back."

By the time they've moved out of the kitchen and headed for the austere dining room where Gabriel holds meetings, Case and Derek Sams arrive. Derek gasps and falls back like Bailey just popped in front of him. Then he darts forward and grasps Angelica's arm.

"Let go, *pendejo*. Can't you see he's recovered?"

"Jesus—Bailey? Can you see me? Are you there?" Derek waves a hand in front of him.

"Dude, I had fucking Super Flu. I'm not a ghost."

Gabriel takes a not so subtle step between Sams and Bailey, blocking Derek's view with his own cold stare. "Derek."

Derek Sams throws up his hands. "Well, good to a...have you back." His eyes flick nervously from Bailey to Gabriel.

"Yeah. Thanks," Bailey deadpans.

That's enough pleasantries. Gabriel smooths a hand over his suit jacket. "Everyone go on and take your seats. Bailey needs to speak alone with Case. And we have a lot to discuss. Lawrence Vu is no longer a part of Feathertons."

Angelica's forehead creases. "No shit. We are already aware, Gabriel." When he raises an eyebrow at her tone, Angelica shakes her head. "Don't look at me to be sad for Lawrence. My brothers tell me, all the time, that he's crazy. Since the first they been here in Olde Town, they hate his *estupido* ass."

"Well, yes. Good to know." Gabriel ushers Jadyn, Derek, and Angelica into the dining room. But he pauses with his hand on the double doors. As much as he would like to give Case and Bailey privacy, he can't make himself leave. A pause and he closes the dining room doors in front of him and returns to Bailey's side. This conversation has the potential to hurt Bailey, and Gabriel needs to take control if that happens. He turns to give his iciest look to Case. "Bailey has some questions for you."

Can she even hear him? Her dark round eyes scan Bailey's face and body, searching out the cuts and bruises, the still-dark circles around Bailey's eyes, the missing fingernail on Bailey's left hand. A sob escapes, and Case puts a hand over her heart. "Can I hug you?"

Bailey twists at the bottom of his sweat jacket. "Uh. Sure?" He makes an oof sound as Case's arms close around him and squeeze. His eyes widen in alarm when she buries her face into his neck and takes a wet, tremulous breath.

"Bailey. I'm so glad you're alive. I'm so, so glad." Another sob. "Peyton has been lost without you. He… He needs you to save him."

"What? Me save Peyton? Ha!" Bailey cranes his face away from Case's teary one. "When has Peyton ever listened to a thing I say. And he left me here! He didn't care that I was—"

The slap takes all three of them by surprise. Bailey grabs his smarting cheek, and Case looks at her hand as if it acted on its own to strike him. Gabriel lunges forward and pulls Case off her feet, tackles her to the white leather chair, holds her there, pinning her arms behind her.

"I…I didn't mean to—"

"Gabriel, let her up!"

He releases her, but stands over her, one hand clutched in the front of her shirt.

"The fuck, Case? You hit me!" Bailey makes a snorting huff. "Just let go of her. Gabriel, I'm fine."

She drags her arms back around, palms open, and Gabriel releases her shirt. "I didn't mean to hurt him." When she gets to her feet, she looks away from Gabriel and focuses on Bailey again. "Listen, Bailey, I am sick and tired of your bullshit with your brother. I know Peyton sheltered you from your mom's issues, so it isn't totally your fault, but he's the only one who took care of you and Lucy when your good-for-nothing parents didn't give a shit."

Gabriel doesn't know if he should come between them again or not. Should he make her leave? He doesn't know how to defend Bailey against this—the truth.

"Who made sure you got to school and made you dinner all the times when Lila was sleeping off her pills and booze? It sure as hell wasn't your dad. He just left the three of you and headed for the club to play afternoon golf or have drinks with other women. My mom would come back from tennis or swimming and would have seen your dad in the dining room eating a steak. Meanwhile, Peyton would be back home burning mac and cheese for you and Lucy."

Bailey's lower lip trembles. "Then, where is he? Didn't he even care if I survived or not?" He wipes at his nose with his sleeve. "Sorry. I'm so fucking emotional ever since…"

"It's alright, Bailey." Gabriel clenches and unclenches a hand. He has no experience in comforting another person. Instead, he flicks an angry look at Case.

"She won't let me talk to him." Case sits back down on the leather chair where Gabriel had pinned her. She grasps the edge of the seat, the leather squeaks under the tight grip of her hands. "I think Renée knows something is up with my sister." She looks up at Gabriel. "And she definitely knows that you're aware of the trades I'm making."

Bailey's thin hand leaves off twisting the tracksuit jacket, clasps Gabriel's hand. "I want my brother back. How can we get him back here?"

Case's eyes widen as Gabriel pulls Bailey against him, tucks his curly head under his chin. "That's the last trade you'll make, Case. If Renée wants more fuel, then she'll have to negotiate. She'll have to come to *me*."

34 Renée

Peyton counts his way through another set of pushups. Sweat pools in the muscled ravine of his spine. Two hundred every morning. Two hundred situps. Two hundred mountain-climbers. No matter how much he drank the night before, no matter how many fights he got into during the day, he wakes at dawn to exercise. Renée used to like to watch him, it used to turn her on. She smashes a pillow between her hands, stares at the bedroom ceiling.

"Where are the two sisters you found outside the barricade with Via Bell, the girls you said would patrol with you? I've never seen them since."

He pauses mid-pushup, body taut, perfect form. "Kinda busy right now, boss."

She sits up in their bed, throws her pillow at his sweaty back. "Stop calling me boss."

"You said not to call you babe."

"Peyton, I'm *not* joking around. Where are the two girls traveling with Case's sister?"

He finishes the last three reps of his pushups. "They took off for the burbs."

"Th—? God, damn it, Peyton! And you just let them leave?"

"What was I supposed to do? Hold them prisoner? You know how to work any of the controls at the jail? Because I'm not setting foot in there. It stinks like rotting meat." Peyton stretches, bulging arms lit golden by the rising sun. He peels his boxer briefs off. He even wears black underwear. Renée wants to mock him for his whole goth wardrobe, but she feels too unsteady with him, and doesn't want to push him too far, too much. She can't risk alienating him. It would ruin everything she's built. At least he has plenty to keep him busy in the streets lately. Reverberations from the Simon kid's birthday have set them back months.

"How are Lanson and the others working out for you?"

"No problems." Peyton saunters to the bathroom.

***

The military's half of the city had no parks, no people milling in the streets. Just rubble. Semi-demolished buildings. Abandoned cars and campfires. She'd looked around, unable to hide her shock. "There's nothing here."

Peyton's club stayed sheathed on his back. "I told you shit was fucked on this side. Follow me." He led Renée and the rest of her police force—over thirty trained fighters—through a maze of crumbling infrastructure. Smoke clouded like fog at one city corner, a strange chemical smell unlike the burning pits outside the barriers. On the edge of Park Plaza district, they found Lanson standing at attention with a rag tag company of fifty soldiers. Young men and women with baggy fatigues and hungry eyes. They remained in place, facing forward, as Renée and the others approached.

Peyton gestured Renée and their own people closer. "Is this it?" he called out to Lanson. "Also, you can knock that army shit off. You're fighting for me now, not Uncle Sam, or whatever."

The men and women exchanged worried glances, but most of them relaxed, some called out greetings to Peyton like they knew him, eager to get his attention.

Renée reached out and dug her nails into the skin of Peyton's arm. "How do these soldiers know you?"

"I helped out a little over here, just to show them what they're missing." He winked at Renée, and she imagined punching him, *firing him*. But, she couldn't. The thirty fighters behind the two of them followed Peyton, not her. A thread of unease she kept buried for weeks began to uncoil.

"Reporting for duty, Mayor Dufort." Lanson dropped his rigid stance. Came forward to greet her. "I look forward to working for you."

"*See,*" Peyton gripped her wrist to release the fingernails she gouged into his skin. "He's *looking forward* to working for you."

She took a steadying breath, turned to Lanson. "You've held your half of the city with only this small company of soldiers?"

"No." Lanson sighed. His eyes looked red, irritated. The chemical smoke drifted closer to them. "I've been losing guys for weeks now. But these soldiers want to stay. They're yours."

"And what happened to the rest?"

Lanson shrugged. "They're on their own now," he said. But Peyton laughed and threw an arm around Renée's shoulders.

"Probably wanted a boring life in the burbs, right Mayor?"

It took all her willpower not to hiss at him like an angry cat.

***

When Peyton emerges from the bathroom, his skin pebbles with goosebumps. He scowls as he rubs his hair dry. "Nothing like a cold shower in the dead of winter. Fuck, man. What happened to the generator for this building?"

"The same thing that happened to the generator of all the buildings—winter rationing. Your workout didn't finish in time with the power schedule for the building, and now, you're paying the price."

Jerking his clothes on, Peyton mimics her words, *"and now you're paying the price."* The corners of his eyes wrinkle as he holds back a smile. "You sound like...." His expression drops.

"I sound like who? Like your mother? Like Case? Who are you thinking of when you get that kicked puppy look?"

Peyton turns away from her, pulls a black sweater over his head. "What's with the morning interrogation? And don't think I haven't noticed you keeping me busy during fuel drops. Like, what the fuck, you think I'm gonna let Case talk me into going back to Feathertons?" He flashes that mean smile at Renée as he tugs on his boots. "Don't tell me...you're jealous?"

"Peyton—"

He points at her. "I don't want a bunch of girlfriend bullshit from you." He shrugs into his leather jacket. "I got a big mess out there right now." He tips his chin to the window, to the barbarous world outside the penthouse, ravaged by creatures, heavy with smoke. "Meanwhile, you spend all your time picking out rugs and paint colors for your new office in the courthouse."

"I. Do. Not." Renée elbows past Peyton. "I'm coming with you." She opens her closet to scour it for jeans, a sweater, boots. And she discovers that she doesn't have to search that hard. When had she stopped wearing her designer skirts and suit jackets?

She expects to annoy Peyton with her announcement to join him, but he has that cruel smile on his face again, the one that sometimes makes her nervous, a little afraid. "Ready?" He grasps her club in one hand. Holds it out to her.

Stand with Peyton, she repeats to herself. Renée tosses her blond hair over one shoulder. "Of course."

35 Gabriel

After the lieutenants' meeting, Gabriel takes Bailey with him to do a storehouse check. At least he has decided to call it a storehouse check. In truth, he needs to show his neighborhoods that Bailey has survived the virus, that Gabriel kept him safe, helped him recover. The rumors about secret experiments in the mansion basement needs to end. But, that isn't the only reason, not even the main reason… *Admit it, you just can't stand to be parted from him.*

They head toward Quail Creek first, will then go to Pierce Heights.

"Don't think I don't know what you're doing." Bailey grins at him from the Land Rover's passenger seat. It looks strange on his face. When they'd spent time together in high school, Gabriel had gotten used to veiled hostility in Bailey's every expression. Even while Gabriel sheltered him in the mansion, that resentment still existed. But, not anymore.

"Do you?"

"Yep, I'm the walking, talking advertisement for the hospital you want to build. I remember you telling me about it before I popped." The smirk gives way to a more tender look. "I don't mind. I think you *should* try and help other people. I'm glad I can be proof that killing isn't the only way to deal with the sick."

"Hmmm… My thinking was that people will always find ways to hide, to try and save the people they love. And when they do it in secret, mistakes can happen. But, am I making the right decision? One infected person could take down a whole neighborhood. I worry that…my plan is too dangerous…arrogant." An admission like this is also new between them. Bailey might not remember everything, but Gabriel bared his soul in that basement. And now, it feels right to let Bailey in on his uncertain moments. "I might be just asking for another disaster like the camps became."

"But, now more people are immune. *I'm* immune. I could help take care of other people. Isn't that how you envisioned it?"

When he sighs, Gabriel feels it come up from that deep place he buries all his most vulnerable emotions. "It is. And I pictured you here, by my side, just like this."

Bailey's cheeks turn rosy with a blush. "We can make it work."

***

The first stop at Quail Creek goes well. Since Feathertons took over, that neighborhood hasn't caused Gabriel many problems. Even if he dislikes ruling with fear, moving Angelica's brothers into Olde Town worked as a lesson for all of her neighbors. They follow rules and don't complain. Pierce Heights will offer the first real test of Gabriel's plans to build safe houses to hold the sick.

The leader of Feathertons arrives to the sprawling Pierce Heights neighborhood in a fleet of six black vehicles. In a show of strength, Gabriel not only brought all his guards, but also all his lieutenants. And, thanks to Derek Sams' reliable love for gossip, the entire neighborhood knows that the boy Gabriel kept in his basement will also be with him. They crowd to watch as the Land Rover pulls to each of the three Pierce Heights storehouses. Bundled up in a down parka, Bailey doesn't mind smiling and showing his hands, exchanging a few words with whomever calls out to him.

"Yeah, I feel okay now," he tells a woman holding the hands of a young boy and girl. Other adults and children press closer to hear. "I'm just hungry all the time, and some of the scratches itch." He pushes the puffy coat sleeves up his thin arms to show the scabby fingernail marks. "Still, nothing too major."

When one of the kids points at his hand, Bailey holds up the left index finger missing its nail. "Okay, except this. Kinda gross, huh?" Bailey's disarming, dimpled grin has both kids smiling...as well as their mother. It's not that funny, but the cluster of onlookers laugh with relief. *Here is someone who had the virus and came through it with barely a mark on his body—or his mind.* Unlike someone returned from the camps, Bailey still has his quick wit and cheerful disposition. Unlike a creature who lived wild, he doesn't have any missing teeth, missing limbs or scars.

One of the younger runners leans in for a closer look at the finger with the missing nail. "Do you remember doing it?" The boy scrunches a freckled nose.

A teen girl beside him looks into Bailey's eyes with her own fearful ones. "Yeah, what do you remember? Do you remember popping? My sister popped, but my dad killed her right away."

"Oh..." Bailey reaches out to pat the girl's arm, must think better of touching her, so lets his hand drop. "I'm so sorry. But I can promise that your sister didn't know that was her dad. And you shouldn't blame your dad. He probably just did what he did to protect the rest of your family. But, now Feathertons is hoping to give families with sick loved ones more options." Bailey runs his fingers into his unruly curls again. "My mom popped in front of me, so I know how hard it is to just..." Bailey trails off, his face so vulnerable and open, his grief so obvious, that now the teenage girl reaches out to him, she pats his arm.

"Let's go," says Gabriel.

Back inside the Land Rover, Bailey slouches into the leather seat. "Are we headed to The Greens now?"

"We don't have to be. I can take you home." Mason Tyrone, Bailey's father, still lives in The Greens. After abandoning Peyton and Bailey to their virus-infected mother, Mason moved in with the former Neighborhood Watch President Jenny Hutton. Gabriel hates the man. If Bailey had died, Gabriel's mercy toward Mason Tyrone would have ended. He would have forced Mason out of Featherton territory with nothing. Let the creatures roaming along the roads rip him apart and eat his intestines.

"No. I want to see him."

At The Greens, word of Bailey's miraculous recovery has already spread, of course. Rico keeps losing track of the conversation as Bailey picks through a crate of apples. "Can I take one of these Cokes?"

Rico doesn't even wait for Gabriel to approve it. "Sure, man, take whatever you want. I got some Lay's potato chips in the back, too. Want some?"

"Yeah. I'm starving. Thanks." Bailey sits on a stack of soup boxes, while Rico forces potato chips, cheese crackers, and granola bars on him. When Mason appears inside the heated storehouse, he looks first toward Gabriel, and then at Bailey brushing crumbs off the front of Gabriel's bright red tracksuit jacket.

"Son! I'm so—" Mason takes a quick step backward as Bailey stands. "It's good to see you." Mason's eyes again dart to Gabriel and stay there. "Really good to see you, son."

Bailey sags back on the soup boxes. He looks tired, thin, pale. "I'm ready to go now, Gabriel."

***

"Drink another glass of milk." Back home, Gabriel follows Bailey up the wide staircase. "You've eaten nothing but junk today."

"Granola is kind of healthy. It has raisins in it." Bailey pauses in front of the guestroom he stayed in before the cage. Gabriel left it with all Bailey's posters up, his books, a stuffed giraffe that a runner brought from Bailey's childhood home. Bailey convalesced here after the dark cage, so he could spend the last stage of the virus surrounded by his own belongings. While Bailey hesitates, Gabriel's heart pounds in his chest. Then, Bailey turns away from the guestroom and enters Gabriel's bedroom.

"Lie down. I shouldn't have taken you to the neighborhoods so soon. You're exhausted."

Bailey falls back against the white comforter on Gabriel's four-poster bed. "I wanted to help. I want people to see that I survived. During the lieutenant meeting, Jadyn told me that everyone thought you were doing experiments on me or something. Like you were making creatures to use as weapons the way that Colton had."

"Did he?" Gabriel sits on the edge of the bed beside Bailey, rubs a thumb over his bottom lip to keep from making a fist. "He should have asked me before—"

"Don't get all freaky about it, okay? I'm glad *someone* tells me what's going on around here. I'm not...ugh, I keep saying 'I'm not a child,' but I still let everyone protect me like one." He tugs on the sleeve of Gabriel's shirt, grasps his arm, and pulls him down to lie across the bed with him. Gabriel lets himself get manhandled, lets Bailey twine their fingers together, and they face each other. "Whatever happens. I'm in it with you. You don't have to protect me anymore. I'm in it *with* you, know what I mean?"

"Yes."

Bailey cracks a smile at Gabriel's one-word response, but there isn't really anything else to say. Gabriel touches his lips against Bailey's. A kiss, sweet and different than the way they kissed at the Christmas party so long ago—just over a year ago—but so, so long ago. When they break apart, Bailey's ridiculously long lashes blink, his pupils have blown wide. Gabriel leans in to kiss him again, and this time the sweetness burns away. They clutch at each other, fingers seeking skin. This doesn't feel at all the way it did with Ashley or the girl at his sister's party. Bailey's touch sinks beneath Gabriel's skin into that deep well of buried sorrows, warms the block of ice where Gabriel encased his heart. *Closer… Closer…*

But, Bailey pulls away. "Oh, *my* God. Do you feel the way I do? Like this is… I don't know, like fate or something. Like fucking destiny, like Luke Skywalker levels of—" Bailey dives in for another searing kiss, their lips searching, hands clutching. Then, Bailey pushes away again, reaches under Gabriel's shirt, places his hand over Gabriel's heart, flat against his naked chest. "For so long, I thought I hated your guts. I mean, it's crazy right? You and me?"

"Can we talk about it later, Bailey? I've waited a long time for—"

Bailey surges forward, and his mouth has the same vibrant energy emanating from it as the hand on Gabriel's chest. "I'm kinda…grossly skinny right now." Bailey's words come out raspy and broken with kisses. "And…sort of banged up. I guess you've seen all that." His hand underneath Gabriel's shirt, slides down his chest. "But, I really want to get naked with you." Bailey unzips the fly to Gabriel's wool slacks, fingers creep beneath his underwear.

"Yes." He gasps when Bailey wraps a hand around him. "I want that, too."

It takes a lot of starts and stops, but clothes come off. Then an awkward moment when they both come back together without anything in the way. And Bailey is right, and it feels like fate, like destiny. Better than how Gabriel imagined love could feel.

36 Renee

Renée and Peyton meet with a group of black clad fighters, a block from the police headquarters in the Arts District. All of them wear leather and wool to stave off the icy winter air, their breath like white smoke when they talk. While Peyton seemed to want her along, Andy and the two others—Kevin and Terrance—give her irritated looks. "Mayor, you sure you want to be down here with us?" Kevin makes it sound like an apology.

"Yes, I'm sure." She turns away to see Brinda approaching, zipping up a black leather biker jacket. The black braid coiled at her neck in a bun. Renée lifts a hand to wave, and when Brinda gets closer, Renée greets her. "Hello, officer."

"Mayor."

A group of Lanson's people start to appear behind Brinda. No more fatigues, the soldiers wear denim and sweaters, leather jackets and leather gloves. Only the boots look army-issued. Peyton holds an arm up, does a loud whistle in greeting.

Renée winces. "Why weren't they at the station with the rest of you?"

Peyton swings his metal club at his side. "Because you moved them into a building all the way near the western barricade."

"I didn't."

"Well, that new asshole in Resource Management did, and that's on you, isn't it?"

Renée grits her teeth behind a laugh. *Present a unified front. Stand with Peyton.*

When the new arrivals get close, a stocky woman with a stern expression takes lead. "Colonel Lanson…Lanson decided to take a later patrol shift." She shifts the address of her report between Renée and Peyton.

"Thank you," Renée answers. "And you are?"

"First, Sar—um—*Watkins*, ma'am. Janna Watkins. I grew up here."

Renée nods, she has the sense that Peyton holds in laughter at the soldier's answer. He knows that, unlike Watkins, Renée *didn't* grow up in this city, not even in this state. Renée fishes around for the right way to answer. "Good to have you as a part of our force."

"Yes, ma'am."

Peyton rolls his eyes. "Okay. Now that we're all *friends*, let's go find some action." Without any hurry, he heads toward the northern side of Central Business, toward the heart of the latest outbreak.

Before Simon's birthday party, Renée's fighters mostly played around on these patrols. How many times had she come across Peyton tossing a football during the shifts he took walking the streets? But, as soon as they turn the first city corner, two creatures dart out from an alleyway and run for a green belt lining the city's halfway mark.

"Oh, hell, not more kids." Brinda unsnaps her club from a holster strapped to her hip. Then, she squints in the direction that the creatures ran. "Wait—did those look like kids to you?" she asks Kevin.

He knocks against Brinda's club with his own. "Those weren't kids. They were just new and charging. I think one had gray hair."

"Once they pop, it doesn't matter what they used to be." Peyton turns to the woman on Renée's left, the former soldier. "Come on, Watkins, let's see what you got." He jogs in the direction the two creatures ran, and after a startled pause Janna Watkins follows on his heels.

One of the other soldiers, a kid with an eyepatch, turns to Renée. "Should we go after them, or wait here, Mayor?"

A rush of pleasure flashes up the back of Renée's neck. "Peyton can easily handle two creatures by himself, and Watkins is there for backup. Let's keep going." She tries to gauge Brinda's reaction to her suggestion. Although Peyton claims he has no second-in-command, the other soldiers seem to do what Brinda says when he isn't around.

"Yes, ma'am… Good call."

Renée beams as she takes lead of the group. But, they don't get far. On the next street, a man huddles underneath a pickup truck, shaking and clawing at the ground. One of the soldiers slams his club against the truck bed, trying to scare it out. But the creature stays put. Brinda leans down to take a peek. "What is he eating? A mouse?"

Kevin laughs, "That's gross." But the soldier standing beside Renée, a skinny kid with an eyepatch sighs.

"Stand back, everyone." The eyepatch kid holds an arm out to block them. Pats the air with an open palm. "I'll do it. I already had the virus, so worst he can do is take a snap at me."

Brinda looks the kid up and down. "That good eye working alright? You aren't the only one with scars here, I had it, too. But come and help me anyway. I don't want any of that mouse guts on me."

The kid smiles at Brinda and joins her, squatting near the truck. "Hey, at least we'd be immune to rabies if the mouse has *that*."

Brinda slides her club under the truck. "What do you mean? I've never heard of Super Flu making you immune to rabies."

"Oh. Yeah, I think—"

"That's a bunch of bullshit," Kevin cuts in. "Like how the virus makes it so you don't get the regular flu either. You just saw that on the internet, but none of it was proved."

The eyepatch kid makes an angry huffing noise. And that finally spooks the man under the truck—he howls and thrashes his legs and arms, wanting out of his hiding spot. Eyepatch again pats at the air behind him. "Back up, back up!"

"What the hell are you guys doing?" Peyton jogs up, cheeks red, breath puffing in a cloud. He sets a hand on Renée's shoulder, but lets go to crouch down near Eyepatch and Brinda. "Ha, fucking stupid creatures. Dumbass can't figure out to slide out the other side."

Eyepatch pouts a little. "I was trying to get everyone to back up so he wouldn't be so freaked out." Peyton ignores the kid and gets down on his knees, then lies on the ground next to the truck. The kid backs away. "So, I'm guessing you had Super Flu, too," he says.

"Nope." Peyton whips the club from his back, jabs it forward, straight under the truck carriage. The man screeches and kicks. Then silence. "Okay, Brinda, get someone to scoop it out of there and drag it to the pit." Peyton examines the end of his club. "Didn't even break the skin." He tosses the club in the air, and they all watch it flip end over end until he catches it one-handed. After that, Lanson's guys have stars in their eyes when they look at Peyton. Even the pouty eyepatch kid.

"Okay, follow me." With his club pointing the way, Peyton directs them all forward. "Let's check the next couple blocks while we're out here. Simon, that little fucker, had some hardcore six-degrees-of-separation energy going on."

Jana Watkins meets them at the next barrier, covered in ash and coughing. After taking down the two creatures on the greenbelt, Peyton must have abandoned her to drag them to the burning pit. She lugs her club behind her, rubs sweat off her forehead with the sleeve of her soot-stained jacket. Renée hangs back for her while the rest of the patrol group buzzes around Peyton's animated retelling of knocking mailboxes down from a moving car. He mimes punching a baseball bat forward, the way he did under the truck to crush the panicked creature's brainstem.

Renée snatches Jana's dragging club. "Here, let me carry this. You shouldn't let Peyton ditch you with the cleanup. I've told him that I want every officer to burn their own kills."

"No, I insisted." Jana keeps hold of her club, so Renée lets go. "You should have seen him." The former soldier looks dazed to just recount the fight for Renée. "He got the old lady in one hit, and then the girl tried to charge him, and he...he ducked and got her midair. I've *never* seen someone fight like that."

Renée holds in the frustration burning in her chest. "Yes...Peyton is very talented. That's why *I* recruited him"

But, Jana doesn't hear her. "Usually, I hate it," she says. "I hate having to kill them, even though I know it needs to be done." The girl swallows against whatever emotion has stirred inside her. "But, Peyton was amazing. Just...amazing."

***

Peyton's amazingness bounces around in Renée's head while she waits for Case to bring the new tanker. As the sun goes down, the temperature does as well, another ten degrees. She waits in her Cadillac and keeps the heat running, despite the waste of precious fuel. Without a replacement for Liam, she'd had to drive herself, so she parks in the spot designated for the new mini-tanker, facing out to the street, and watches for Case. *I'll bring up the sister again. Dig for whatever lies under that strange fearful reaction.* And that brings her thoughts back to Peyton. Too busy drinking with his new admirers, he didn't ask to come to the drop-off today. Renée might not always trust Peyton to tell her everything, to tell her the truth, but she can always trust his constant desire for a good time, his selfishness.

After twenty minutes, Renée cuts the engine and sits in the cooling silence of the Cadillac. When everything first went to hell, she wanted a car that made a statement, that made her look older, that made her look important. Maybe the time has come for something more practical? Another twenty minutes pass, still no Case, no new tanker filled with fuel. And then Renée spots shadows moving behind the waiting truck. A dark hand pats at the white tank, fingers contorted into talon-like rigor mortis. A naked body with a torn shoulder, missing arm. Goopy black blood and stringy tendon.

"Jesus." Renée starts the car, the creature howls and bends, paws at the ground with its naked feet, readying to charge. Renée pounds on the horn, trying to scare it away. Finally, the creature scurries back into the dark. But now, as Renée waits, all the shadows flicker suspiciously as she feels the evening pressing in on her. She's also very aware that no one else knows where she went, that only Peyton knows about the fuel exchange spot. "Where the fuck is Case and my new tanker?"

Renée waits. And waits. *Gabriel is behind this.* She'd told Case that she knew her brother must have had a hand in their deal, and now, Gabriel cut her off. *Fuck him.* "If you won't give me the fuel I need, little brother, then I'll take it from you."

capability

37 Gabriel

The caged truck with Via Bell inside leads a slow procession through The Greens. No more secrets. No more hiding. Gabriel lets the neighborhood get a good long look at Via's bloodstained, clawed, fingers. She cowers, wild-eyed from behind her bars. Case walks beside her. Via will be the first patient in The Greens' new "medical safe house." It has a basement cage with running water, live food. The bedrooms above it furnished with recovery beds—for when the infected enter the virus' final stage.

Bailey came up with the name, medical safe house, during a lieutenant meeting. "It's a lot better than 'hospital,' or just calling it a 'cage,' right? It sounds like someplace you can trust." Bailey talked around a mouthful of peanut butter sandwich, and Gabriel pressed a glass of apple juice on him. Food at the lieutenant meetings, also an idea of Bailey's. He convinced Gabriel that it would improve the morale in the meetings. *And he'd been right.* Gabriel watched on as Bailey detailed their plans. "So, we'll staff the safe houses with people who are immune, like me. That will totally bring down the risks and still give people a chance." The wide gray eyes blinked as he nodded to each of the lieutenants. "This can work. People can survive." Gabriel had only ever known how to give orders, but Bailey had a gift for inspiring enthusiasm.

They introduce all the neighborhood safe houses with street parties, barbecues, games. Gabriel gives a speech at each opening. He ends each speech the same way. *"We need to survive. We need our friends, our siblings, our children to survive and not die at the end of a club. You want that chance don't you? Now, you have it."* After they load Via into the basement, Bailey makes the rounds again, reminding everyone of the final goal in housing—instead of outright killing—the sick.

"That's the boy he kept in his basement? But nothing's wrong with him!"

"He's not disfigured. He's not crazy."

Neighbors can't seem to resist touching him, patting Bailey's back, his arm, shaking his hand. It unnerves Gabriel a little, to let it happen. *I spent so long shielding you from them.* And selfishly, he adds, *I had you all to myself.* He can't help but remember life before Super Flu. *You hated me then…*

Bailey catches Gabriel staring and comes over to hand him a coffee. Waves a chocolate cupcake in his face. When Gabriel shakes his head, Bailey stuffs the entire thing in his own mouth.

"I know you need the calories, but you're going to choke yourself." Gabriel thumps Bailey on his back. "Are you alright?"

"So…" Bailey coughs and takes a sip of Gabriel's coffee. "Angelica and Derek Sams…didn't see that one coming. Did you?" Minus Case, the lieutenants all stand together at a long table of drinks and pastry. Case stayed behind in the safe house basement to make sure Via settled in alright.

"See *what* coming?" Derek Sams notices Gabriel's attention, points a finger gun, and winks. *He belongs on a used-car lot, maybe hosting a game show.* "I *see* that I have to keep track of every ledger coming out of Pierce Heights, or Sams will solicit bribes for whatever he can poach." Gabriel takes a long drink of the coffee, even though it burns his throat. "And I *see* Angelica telling everyone I kidnapped her younger brothers and forced them to work for me."

"Well, you did kind of do that." At Gabriel's flat look, Bailey adds, "I mean, *technically*. But that's not what I'm talking about. They're together. You know, a couple. Didn't you notice? Why did you think they were hanging around each other all the time?" A dimpled grin. "Oh wait—don't tell me—I bet you thought they were conspiring against you." Bailey has chocolate frosting on the corner of his mouth, and Gabriel imagines licking it off.

"Is something on my face?" Bailey smears the chocolate across his cheek with the back of his hand. When Gabriel laughs, the people milling around the party all turn to stare at him.

"I've never seen him laugh?" One of the runners says, a girl with spiky pink and yellow hair. She doesn't realize Gabriel can hear. "It's freaky."

Gabriel's hand jerks, and his coffee sloshes. Bailey slides his fingers over Gabriel's and takes the cup. "Here, I'll get rid of this," he whispers. "Then, we can get out of here, okay?"

"No. I'm fine. There are a lot of new people in the neighborhood, people who came off the road from the east. You need to—"

"Talk up how nice it is to be choking on cupcakes instead of getting rolled into a burning pit?" A smirk in Gabriel's direction.

"Yes, that." Gabriel watches Bailey's floppy head of hair as he makes his way back through the crowd.

Snow begins to swirl through the freezing air. Dry cold flakes that stick to Bailey's wild hair and long lashes. Peyton used to complain about Bailey's looks to Gabriel, that his younger brother needed more muscle, shorter hair, a sterner expression that would protect him from the outside world. *"Don't you protect him?"* Gabriel had asked. Peyton didn't have an answer to that. He didn't need one.

At this moment, Bailey's open, approachable quality serves Gabriel well. People ask questions about how Bailey feels, about the bite that healed and faded, about his time locked in the mansion's basement. Hope—so coveted in their new world—Bailey spreads it all behind him like a crop-dusting plane.

"Boss?" Jadyn holds his black satellite phone out for Gabriel. "This sounds important."

"Gabriel, here." The smile in his voice throws off the person at the other end of the call.

"Boss, that you?" One of the Mageo brothers asks. Gabriel can barely tell them apart in person and not at all over the phone.

He gathers his usual composure. "What happened?"

In the background of the call, someone shouts and curses. "I'm talking to him now, Felix! Get off my ass!" Hugo must cup his hand over the microphone because now Gabriel can hear the breathy quaking in his voice. "We got jacked. Military guys in a truck with guns pointed right in our faces. They took the tanker—they took the fuel!"

"Military…are you sure? Describe them. Describe every detail."

Not military. That much becomes obvious as Hugo describes the mismatched clothing, the use of first names, and the direction they took off in—south—toward the city. A staticky pause. "And, Gabriel? There's one more thing…"

***

"Why are you always picking on him?"

"Just look at him, Gabriel. He needs to toughen up, learn to protect himself from the outside world."

"Don't you protect him?"

Peyton's pained look. The answer he never gave, *"What if I'm not there."* The response Gabriel couldn't say, *"Then, he'll have me."*

***

211

All conversation dies when Gabriel approaches. He closes a hand around Bailey's thin arm. "Time to go." And thank God he doesn't need to explain anything else with all the listening ears surrounding them, Bailey can read the urgency in the strength of Gabriel's grip. A hand signal to Jadyn and all of them start for the Land Rovers. "Someone get Case. I want her in my car. We're going to the ranch."

Jadyn keeps pace with him, flicks a hand at one of his runners to gather The Greens' lieutenant from inside the safe house. "What should I do?"

"Return to Olde Town. But, send Derek and Angelica to Cushing and bring me back the kid with dyed red hair. His name is Beau." When Case arrives, Gabriel shoos her away from the driver side.

"What is it?" Bailey asks. He lets Case take the front passenger seat and leans over the middle console from the back. "Gabriel, what happened?"

Gabriel rubs at his bottom lip.

Case leans back into the seat, takes a deep breath as if to steel herself. "Something about Peyton. Isn't it?"

38 Renee

"Fuck, yeah!" The M4 Carbine pressed against Peyton's shoulder empties into the air. He stands in the back of a military truck, firing at whatever catches his eye. His laughter ignites the excitement of the others, they've shot up nearly every building since crossing back to city limits. Bullets spray an abandoned parking garage outside the eastern barrier, bursts of cement dust cloud the street.

In the passenger seat, Renée keeps a smile frozen on her face, but it feels tight, and the pain inside her head, behind her eyes, hammers with every echoing gunshot. Beside her, Lanson steers the khaki truck around an abandoned school bus as they follow the tanker.

Once they pass the school bus, he looks over his shoulder. "Get down, back there," he shouts. "You're firing too close to the tanker, and this—" The truck swipes against a rusting sedan, and Lanson has to yank the wheel to keep them on the road. "Son of a—!" He has to know he's lost control of his own soldiers. He keeps glancing at Renée for support, but she sees no benefit in siding with him over Peyton. "Yo, Sarge," Lanson hollers to the back, putting emphasis on Peyton's rank, his duty. *Does he think that Renée hasn't already tried this a million times?* "Sergeant, we don't want to waste ammo, right?"

"We aren't wasting it. This is good practice!" Peyton whoops as Andy shoots the bulb out of a street light. "Damn, son, you can shoot. You need to show me how to do that!"

Andy laps up the compliment. "Okay! Let's take these back to the station. We can set up a shooting range on the street."

Lanson's square jaw tightens. "That's not a good idea."

Peyton fires a round into the air. "Get off our backs, Lanson. You gave us guns, and we didn't even get to shoot them. I thought we'd see some real action."

"All those newly popped creatures haven't kept you busy?" Lanson's forehead wrinkles so hard that Renée wonders if he has the same tight, tense headache that she does. Peyton ignores him and fires again, shatters the windows of an empty church.

"Fuck, yeah!" he shouts again.

***

Back at the station, Brinda parks the fuel truck, a small tanker just like the ones Case Bell had delivered. Renée steps up on the running board and raps on the window. "I'll take the tanker the rest of the way."

Brinda cracks open the door. "You going outside the barricade with this? I should come."

"It's not far—"

Brinda starts the truck up again. "It's too dangerous outside the barricade."

Renée's head still pounds from the drive back to the city, the endless booming gunfire in her ears, the sick motions of the army truck as it swerved around highway debris. "It's not your place to question me, Officer. Now, get out of the truck."

Brinda shuts off the engine. "Yes, ma'am."

Renée's eyes squeeze shut. Her fingernails scratch against the hot metal of the tanker door.

"Ma'am, are you going to let me out?" Renée's eyes open to see Brinda composed and holding the tanker keys out to Renée.

I tried to put her in her place, and she's there now. Is that really what I want? Renée takes the keys and moves aside. "Thank you, Officer."

***

Night after night, a cacophony of rap and techno music blares from the police station. Alcohol and drugs get passed around. Girlfriends, boyfriends party and sleep in the officer dorms. And now that Lanson has added firearms into the mix, thundering gunshots punctuate everything. Peyton and the others act as if they feed off the chaos. Her police force has become a band of hooligans as feared as the creatures. And, the people living inside the barricaded city complain about it to Renée. *The situation has to change.* She would kick Peyton out of the city, but she needs him more than ever. The city streets still haven't fully recovered from the outbreak Simon's birthday party sparked. "Get it under control," she orders Peyton. The dramatic windows in the loft have all frosted over, like living in a room made of ice. Renée stays under the blankets in bed, watches Peyton dress.

He zippers up his jacket. "Another couple days, and it will be."

"Not just the streets—I mean get my police force contained. Clean up that station and stop—"

"Yeah, yeah…I fucking know, already." He takes a few practice swings with his club and then wiggles it into the tight leather sheath on his back.

He's already jogging down the stairs from the bedroom when she calls out to him, "I'm serious, Peyton. I'll be there this afternoon, and I better see that…" *Why do I even bother?* Renée holds a pillow to her face and screams into it.

***

Someone in the new Resource Management Office replaced Liam with an excitable girl who bites her nails. It takes her seven minutes to arrange the mirrors, the seat, the tilt of the steering wheel before she starts the Cadillac. Then, she slams the brakes at every disruption to their progress through the empty streets. "Sorry, sorry… I should have practiced more…"

Renée sighs but doesn't look up from her revised list of citizens. She's lost people, more than she'd like, but most have stayed. *Afraid to leave the barriers. Afraid to leave the nest of civilization that they know.*

From behind the Cadillac's steering wheel, her new secretary lets out a squeaky shout. "Oh! Oh, my gosh! Should I run it over?" The girl taps her finger against the windshield in case Renée might not see the bloody-mouthed creature standing in their way.

"Honk the horn." Renée shuffles her papers to focus on the list of citizen complaints she has for Peyton. *Stealing rations. Fighting. Motorcycle racing.* When she looks up, she finds her driver still dumbfounded by the creature in front of them. "Why isn't the car moving? I told you to use the horn."

"Oh, right!" The girl pounds her fist and lets loose the low train whistle sound of the Cadillac's horn. The creature staggers off to the right. But the loud horn scared two more from their hiding places. And they scurry across the street, hunched over with arms curled in, white ferocious eyes scanning around them. Renée's driver startles and rears back in her seat. "Oh, my gosh!"

Renée pinches at the bridge of her nose. "I'll have someone come clean them out, once we *finally* make it to the police station."

But, the girl doesn't listen, she unhooks her seatbelt and leans to forward to smash her face against the driver side window. "Wait... I know...I *knew* one of them. That's Kyle Nesker from the apartment across from mine!"

"Just take us to the station." Renée's words have no effect on the young girl. "I'm sure it isn't anyone you know... What are the odds that some random creature—"

"He was wearing the same clothes that Kyle had on. I stood in line next to him at grocery pickup." The girl turns toward Renée with a trembling lip and welling tears in her eyes.

"That doesn't mean you caught it. Just standing next to someone—"

"I need to check on my family. I need—!" The girl has her hand on the door handle.

"You can't just abandon the car here!"

"I...I'm sorry, Mayor. I need to see my family." The driver side door opens and the girl climbs out, then leans back in with a white face and shaking hands. "I have a little brother, and my grandmother is the only one taking care of him right now."

The creature she'd scared off with the horn hadn't gone far. It emerges from a building alcove just off the street. Skin bags off its thin arms. Blood and dirt coats its shapeless pants and shirt.

"I'll be right back," the girl tells Renée. "Just as soon as I check that—"

Renée scrambles over the center console and reaches for the door handle, ripping it from the girl's hand. "Get back in the damn—"

The creature lunges for the girl, tackles her to the ground. One of the other two creatures creep forward again, a young man—maybe Kyle Nesker.

Renée slams the door shut and hits the locks. She pounds on the gas. In the rearview mirror, she sees Liam's replacement lying in a pool of blood, Kyle Nesker licking it from the street.

"Fuck!"

At the station, she finds Peyton rinsing his club under a spigot. The guns and music from the station reverberating around him like a storm. "You look pissed off," he says. Peyton's lazy smile infuriates her.

"Can't you turn that music down?"

"Probably, but why would I?" Peyton hands his club off to Andy.

Renée knows better than to answer with, *"Because I told you to."* If Peyton wanted power, wanted to take the city from her with her own police force, he could do it. *Thank God, he only wants a good time.* And if Renée wants to hold on to her own power, she can't get in the way of that. "No reason. Have it how you like it. But, I need you to go after three creatures on 10th Street. They killed my new secretary." Her stomach gives a sickening lurch as she pictures slamming the car door, speeding off. "Dragged her from the car." Her lie doesn't make any sense, not when she stands in a clean sweater, spotless jeans, scuff-free boots. An unruffled stack of papers in her hands.

Another problem with the loud music, the gunshots—they have to talk loud enough that others can hear. Pedro, Andy, and Terrance all raise their clubs into the air. "Fucking Simon!"

Brinda crosses her arms over her chest. "It's getting worse. We get done cleaning out a building, and someone else pops and infects a bunch more people." She raises a dark eyebrow at Renée. "Maybe city life isn't such a good idea anymore."

"What are you saying, officer?"

Brinda straightens under Renée's icy gaze. "I'm not saying anything."

Renée turns away from her. "I need you to get out ahead of this, Peyton."

But Peyton ignores Renée's demands. "Do you hear that?" A loud humming fills the air, covering the sound of the music. "What is it?"

The music cuts out, and they all look up to find the source of the rumbling noise. Andy cups his hands around his eyes like imaginary binoculars. "I think it's an airplane."

It *is* an airplane. A low wing, single engine aircraft. It passes low over their heads. "The fuck?" Peyton holds up a hand to shade his eyes. "Are they trying to land it here?" The red and white plane follows the path of the streets, dipping low and climbing again, then dipping low once more. Pink and green confetti spreads out behind it. At last, it circles the police station, and the swirling papers float down over their heads. Peyton snatches one of the green sheets out of the air to look at it. A thin column of writing and photocopied pictures cover both sides of the long strip. His forehead wrinkles as he examines it. Then a slow spread of teeth, a spiteful tilt of his lips, a grin that takes pleasure at the end of a club. "It's an advertisement." He hands it to Renée. "For Featherton Territory." Peyton's cruel smile turns into a mocking, harsh laugh. "Gardens. Homes with fireplaces. Traveling nurses and teachers…" His cold eyes meet Renée's. Whatever he sees makes the laughter come harder. "I don't know, babe. Sounds pretty nice."

39 Gabriel

"All good, boss?" Hugo hunches into his jacket. The Cessna Ag-wagon blows snow and frozen prairie grass as it descends toward the rough landing strip behind the main ranch house. Gabriel inherited the plane when he captured the ranch and all the land that had once belonged to Jaxon Colton. Not only the plane, but also its pilot in Colton's nephew. At Gabriel's command, the kid, Beau, had hopped right into the cockpit, eager to show off his skills.

"All good," Gabriel drawls. He holds the satellite phone to one ear, saying the words to both Hugo standing in front of him and Shane on the other end of the call.

Shane's voice crackles with excitement for any kind of confrontation with fighters from the city. "We're ready for them."

"They'll have guns," Gabriel reminds him. Across the field, he watches Beau climb out of the little aircraft. The kid beams and gives Gabriel a thumbs up sign.

"We have guns, too," says Shane. And Gabriel can hear sliding metal, the clack of a fresh-loaded shotgun.

"They have better guns. Don't be overconfident, don't push things."

Shane makes an exaggerated sigh, but only as a joke. Not like Peyton, who would have balked at Gabriel keeping him on a leash like a dog. *How is Renée finding it trying to manage the former high school quarterback?* According to Case, his sister and Peyton appeared to have a romantic relationship. He knows his sister, can understand her thinking with taking Peyton to her bed. She hoped to make a connection, perhaps even control him that way. But it won't work.

Gabriel disconnects the call and turns his full attention to Hugo Mageo. He looks miserable contending with the icy winter wind. "It's come to my attention that some people want to permanently live on the farm," Gabriel tells him. "I want to set them up with their own land, their own income from it. There will be a tax paid to Feathertons, of course. Sharecropping."

"Makes sense." Hugo nods, blows into his hands.

"So…I'm going to need a lieutenant out here."

"Don't look at me." Stooping deeper into his parka, Hugo stomps his feet on the frozen ground like they've gone numb. "I hate the cold. I hate the heat, too. Both me and Felix want to come back to the mansion."

Yes, thank God for that. Gabriel spent enough time around the brothers to know that neither of them do well with responsibility. Much better suited to following orders than giving them. "I'm asking because you've spent the last weeks in Cushing. What is your opinion of Beau?"

"The kid?" Hugo points a thumb toward the little red and white plane. "Yeah. I think he'd probably fucking come in his pants to get a lieutenant job."

At least Hugo doesn't laugh at his own jokes. "Let's hope he can contain himself," Gabriel says. From the Land Rover, Bailey lays on the horn like an impatient child, so Gabriel waves Hugo in front of him. "I'll talk to Beau later. Now that the plane returned, we need to get to Cushing." Instead of a single long note, the horn blares in a staccato this time. Bailey stands just outside the driver's side, arm reaching into the open window. His dimpled grin spreads as Hugo and Gabriel approach, and he pounds the horn again. Gabriel flicks his eyes toward the bulky man walking beside him. "As of now, Hugo, your protection duties are back in place."

And Hugo must understand his new job because he groans. "More like babysitting, right? Does he always act like this?"

Answering that question would risk a show of emotion too embarrassing to consider. Instead, Gabriel turns his mind to business. "I'm going to need a lieutenant stationed at Cushing, too. How does Shane—?"

"He won't want it."

"Hmmm…"

"There's Denny?" Hugo offers. "Ever since Kelly—" Gabriel's satellite phone trills from his pocket, and Hugo bites off whatever he wanted to say next. The hulking boy rounds the car and pulls Bailey from the horn. "Time to go, little boss."

"Ugh, never call me that again." Bailey tries to cut Gabriel off from the driver's side door. "What's going on? Gabriel, did another—? Is Peyton—?"

Hugo drapes an arm around Bailey's shoulders, nudges his clamoring charge toward the back seat. "Let the big boss think, okay?"

"Oh, my God...*fine.*"

Gabriel slides into the driver seat and pauses with his hands gripping the steering wheel. He'd had Case taken back to The Greens, to her sister. But, the decision gnaws at him. Did he make the right call? *Yes...I won't need Case.*

Once the Land Rover pulls away from the gravel roads leading from the ranch and skids onto the blacktop, their speed picks up. In the rearview mirror, Bailey runs his fingers through his wind-tangled hair. He looks worried, sad.

When Gabriel first befriended Peyton Tyrone, he'd assumed that the two brothers had a typical sibling relationship. The mix of competition, loyalty, and love he'd seen on television and movies. But, scratch the surface of the Tyrone family's all-American veneer, and you get a nest of trouble. Peyton had bullied and lorded over Bailey all their lives, and Bailey should have hated his brother. And in some ways, Gabriel thinks that Bailey does hate Peyton. But underneath his resentment, Bailey also loves his older brother.

What if Renée and I hadn't been twins? What if she or I had a few years on the other? Maybe one of them would have stepped into the role of caretaker the way Peyton had. *Maybe that could have left a path forward for the two of us.*

40 Gabriel

"The box says, 'Level 5 For Teens and Up.' I'm only eight years old."

His father had given him a five-hundred-piece puzzle of the New York skyline. Most of the tiny pieces had a blue tint, blue sky, blue ocean, blue glass. "I expect to see this finished when I get home tomorrow night," Maurice had said and patted Gabriel on the head like a dog. Besides their color, the small cardboard shapes looked indistinguishable to Gabriel, so he'd separated the blue into piles based on their shade, blue-gray, blue-black, blue-silver. Gabriel bit at the side of his thumb, he'd worked hard to stop sucking it like a baby…like a *disgusting* baby… but this new habit had taken its place.

"It's a good exercise in problem solving. You'll thank me when you make CEO."

"I don't want—"

"Take your thumb out of your mouth," his father had snapped. "Finish the puzzle by the time I get back." But after three days, Gabriel still only had the piles. He sat on the nursery floor staring at them.

When the nursery door opened, Gabriel looked up from the tiny pieces in front of him to see Mommy drag his sister inside the nursery. Their mother's blood-red fingernails dented the tender skin of Renée's arm. "You ugly little troll." Pauline wore a long, glittery gown, had her bright red hair curled, and shiny red lips glossed. "I want you to stay in here until your father returns from his trip." She caught sight of Gabriel sitting on the floor. "Both of you!"

"What if we get hungry?" Gabriel asked. Instead of answering, their mother stomped over to his puzzle pieces, and kicked one of the piles he'd made, the blue-silver pile. The tiny pieces scattered across the floor.

"Stay out of my sight, both of you. If you leave this room, I'll throw you out into the snow and tell your father you ran away from home!" Then, she spun around. Slammed the door behind her.

Renée slumped to the ground, tears and snot smeared across her cheeks from crying. "I just wanted to watch the magazine people taking pictures of the house. I didn't try to be *in* any of them." Nanny had dressed the two of them in matching outfits, white starched shirts, green pressed slacks for Gabriel, a bloated green skirt for his sister. Renée wiped her nose on the edge of her skirt, and it left a long smeary mess on the wool. "I hate Mommy."

"Me, too. I hate both of them." On his hands and knees, Gabriel searched out the missing puzzle pieces, their minuscule tabs getting stuck between the floorboards, the blank edges grating into the wood. "You think Daddy is better, but he isn't, Renny."

"Daddy gave you a puzzle." She held a piece between her fingers. "He always gives you things." Then she put the piece into her mouth, grit between her teeth and pulled until it ripped apart. Her eyes met his in a challenge. She wanted to make him cry, to make him hurt like she hurt. But he'd gotten used to her tricks at trying to goad him into a fit.

He stuffed a piece in his own mouth, bit and ripped the little puzzle piece, and grinned around the cardboard. *I hate Daddy. I hate the word, "heir."* Gabriel jumped to his feet to grind his shoe heel into one of the blue piles.

"What are you doing?" Cardboard stuck to Renée's bottom lip, so she spit it out.

Gabriel grabbed a fistful of the puzzle pieces and threw them across the room. Turned, breathless, to find a smile battling the jealousy on his sister's face. "Come on, Renny." He bent down and took her hand, put a scoop of puzzle pieces in it. "Let's smash it up."

Renée's hand closed around the little blue shapes. Her smile gave way to something fierce, and she hurled them against the nursery window. Gabriel kicked over the little white table where they ate their meals. He broke the white wicker chairs against the wall. Renée ripped the blue silk curtains down. She tore the white eyelet bedding from the beds. Gabriel boosted Renée up on his back so she could reach the painting of the rabbit, and she dragged it down off its hook. She helped him topple the shelves with all the china figurines that Nanny never let them touch. Finally, they threw books and shoes at the antique chandelier until it crashed down, the lightbulbs shattered against the floor and all the little faceted stones spilled across the room. Wires dangled down from the ceiling like intestines, like they'd gutted it, killed the nursery where their parents and Nanny kept them prisoner. Across the mess of their destruction, they smiled at each other, panting, spent, triumphant. Gabriel had sweated into the crisp white shirt, and Renée had ripped the hem of her green wool skirt. Then, from below their feet, Gabriel heard his father call out, home from his business trip. Pauline's voice answered him, words becoming clearer as the parents neared the nursery.

"…finish the puzzle I gave him?"

"…nearly ruined my photoshoot!"

Gabriel bit at his thumb. "They're coming. They'll be mad."

Across from him, Renée's legs trembled. She started breathing hard like she did right before she cried. "You started it—you *made* me."

Then Gabriel pulled his thumb away. "I don't care. I still hate them." He balled his hands into fists.

41 Renée

"I ripped my fucking jacket. Do you see this?" Peyton holds the thick black leather under Renée's chin. "Fuck," he bellows and throws his ripped jacked across her office. It hits the embossed wallpaper with a splat, leaves behind a long muddy streak.

"I have real work to do here, you know." Renée's jaw aches with how hard she grits her teeth. "Go find another jacket. There's an entire city of jackets you can choose from."

The flimsy pink and green fliers turned to mush underneath the wet snow. And now, Peyton can't ride his motorcycle without skidding out. Well, he can't ride it *fast*. And Renée can't spare fuel to plow the streets. "Instead of racing your motorcycle, why don't you spend your time cleaning up the mess in Central Business and Arts District? People can't even leave their homes." Renée pretends to leaf through papers on her desk. She still doesn't have a new secretary assigned, or she could have avoided this meeting.

"I don't give a shit if people can't leave their homes." Peyton seethes with anger as he prowls around her office like Renée has caged him there. "Those assholes do nothing but bitch. Someone threw a fucking coffee mug at me on Reno Avenue!"

Renée feels the near constant headache pound in her temples, she rubs them with her index fingers. "They're upset. It's understandable. Once the weather turns—"

"Once the weather turns, the city will be empty." That toothy angry smile. "I hate to break it to you, babe. Those fliers Gabriel dropped had an effect."

Those fliers—all the chances she had to put an end to her brother's obnoxious, suburban gang… She could have let Dandridge arrest him…*kill* him. "What are you even talking about, Peyton?"

"I'm talking about people siphoning gas and bolting. I must have caught ten people doing it since that plane dumped all those Featherton ads. No one wants to be here when you can't even keep the buildings warm. At least in the burbs—"

"God damn it, Peyton. *Shut up!*" She slaps her hands on the desk. "I am so sick of your complaints. I hired you to clean up this city, and you let a little boy's birthday party derail everything!"

Peyton collapses into Renée's new office chair. The club on his thigh holster scratches the leather, drips water onto her rug. "You need more fuel. It's fucking cold, and no one wants to leave the station. And you need to fire up one of the street cleaning trucks." Peyton points a finger at her. "And you didn't *hire me*. What the fuck is that about?"

Deep breath. "Okay." Renée stands, her fingers still pressed against the desktop. "Let's go to Cushing then. We have the guns. We can take the refinery."

"I can guarantee that your brother has that whole place covered up with traps and people. It won't be as easy as showing up with guns and taking it."

Renée has her own mean smile. "It can be. You wanted to use your new toys, didn't you? Think of all the things you can shoot on the way there. Think of everything you can shoot to hold on to it."

He raises a blond eyebrow at her. "I'm not an idiot, you know." He strokes the hilt of his club. "They won't just be targets. They'll be Feathertons."

A knock at the door interrupts them, and Brinda appears. She has a black leather jacket under one arm. She looks at Peyton, ignores Renée. "Andy found one almost like it." She shakes the jacket out. "If you don't like it, then I think Jana and Pedro found some others."

Renée's headache thunders back, and she winces against it. "Did you send my police out to find a new jacket for you, Peyton? When the people living in this city can't even leave their homes because of the outbreak?"

"I gotta wear something. It's fucking cold, and you ration all the heating fuel." Peyton shrugs into the close-fitting, quilted black leather. "Come on, Brin. We can do a quick patrol round the courthouse." Peyton winks at Renée. "Then, the Mayor here has a new assignment for us."

Brinda finally meets Renée's eyes. "She does? What kind of assignment—jacking another tanker?"

Renée shakes her head. "I was thinking bigger—"

"She wants the whole refinery." Peyton smirks. "And she's trying to feel out if I'd have a problem killing people, not just creatures, people I know…"

"I wasn't going to ask that." Renée feels damn confident that Peyton has never cared enough for anyone to let that bother him. "I think I can count on you to do what it takes."

Peyton's joking mood drops away. "I've got nothing left to lose."

That look again. So, he'd lost someone…*of course, he had.* Everyone had. With a new jacket and a new goal, Peyton has no reason to prowl around Renée's office whining. But Brinda lingers behind, one hand on the doorknob.

"What about you?" she asks. "Peyton said that Gabriel Featherton is your brother. You would have no problem killing him, letting Peyton kill him?" Brinda doesn't wait for Renée to answer. "When I told you about my family—what I did when I was sick—you said it wasn't my fault. But, let me tell you, Ms. Mayor…that doesn't change anything about how I felt, *how I feel*, knowing what I did."

42 Renee

Her brother lunged toward her, gripped her wrist. *"Run!"* Renee's heels snapped against the uneven pavement. When she'd put on the pencil skirt that morning, she never dreamed she would have to sprint through downtown, taking three steps to every one of her brother's. But, Gabriel's lock on her arm didn't loosen, and he pulled her down the block, only stopped once they reached the neon and fluorescent lights of a 7-Eleven.

"I don't think he's following us. I think he ran off." Gabriel squinted behind them into the darkness. "From what I read, they don't—"

"Let go of me!" Renée's wrist slid free, a ring of smeared blood stained it like a cuff from her brother's torn hand.

"Go inside. Wash it off." Gabriel untucked his shirt and hid his ripped knuckles and bloody arms under the hem. He leaned back into a shadow. "I'll wait here. I'll walk you back to your car. Did you park near the club?"

She could only nod, eyes focused on the blood ringing her wrist.

Inside the store, the bright light made all the colors garish. Cellophane wrapped food. The stink of burnt coffee. Over roasted hotdogs. Tinny violin music from the store speakers. The mundane normalcy of the convenience store made her feel like a monster. *What have I done?*

Soap congealed on her wrist, and she let the water rush over it until steam clouded the mirror and her skin turned bright red. *What have I done?*

Usually, she knew exactly why people stared at her—she wore expensive clothes, even costlier shoes, had her hair done professionally three times a week. The eyes looking her way…what did they see tonight? *I tried to kill my brother.*

I did kill him.

When she found him again, in the shadows and dark, the prickling unease she'd experienced from the store's flickering florescent light abated...just a little. She fell into step beside Gabriel as they retraced their steps back toward their father's discreet club. The winter had just begun to thaw, but clumps of hardened snow still filled the gutters. Bare tree branches reached out to them like skeleton arms.

"You should have washed your hands, too. Maybe..."

"I rinsed them under a spigot." He waved back toward the 7-Eleven.

"Do you think—?"

"I don't know."

They both kept their eyes on the dark alleys, the shadows behind parked cars, under the eaves of the buildings they passed. Her eyes also went to Gabriel at times. The last time she'd seen her brother he'd been fourteen years old. *Me, too.* She'd just always felt older than him, years older, instead of the mere minutes separating them. Her *little brother,* the golden child. Daddy always loved him more. She drew her old anger around her like a blanket, tried to warm herself from the cold truth of what she'd done to him. *I killed my brother.* "What will you do?"

"I...I don't know." Gabriel's hands dropped from his shirt, still bleeding. He spotted her car before she did, a Lexus her father purchased when she first began her internship.

"How did you know this was mine?" Her fingers drew out the key fob from her jacket pocket. The headlights flashed as she pressed it.

"Because, he bought me the same car...different color, but the same."

The bitter clench in her chest. "You mean, he bought me the same car that *you* wanted. And I was an afterthought." She opened the door and got behind the wheel.

Gabriel kept his hand on the door to keep her from closing it. "You're better than this, Renny. You're better than either of them, and so am I."

"Did they teach you that in the psych ward?" She wrenched the door from him and slammed it shut.

***

By the time she leaves the courthouse, night has come, so she carries Peyton's club with her. No problem, she'd parked the Cadillac on the wide sidewalk just outside the front door. Her boot heels clack against the marble. She swings the club in an imitation of Peyton's cocky stroll. Only one other office has lights on, someone else working late. She sees them step out from the doorway.

Oh, God, it's the woman from Land Commission. How have old people like her survived this long? She stands in the doorway waiting for Renée to walk by, her bleary eyes blinking from behind the thick glasses, white hair a disheveled pile on her head. *She's going to ask about my father.* Maurice Featherton had charmed every female he encountered, whether he planned to sleep with them or not.

"Hello, Mrs. Arnold. You're staying late tonight—"

It isn't Mrs. Arnold, not anymore. Now, Renée sees the hooked fingers, the drool coating the old woman's chin. Renée drops her briefcase, holds the club in front of her. Mrs. Arnold startles as the briefcase buckle smacks against the floor. She curls down into the shadowed hallway edge, keens like an injured dog.

Renée lifts the club over her head. "I'm sorry—"

Mrs. Arnold doesn't fight back, doesn't try to run. She just pulls tighter into herself, still whining, crying.

"I'm sorry. I'm so, so sorry…" The club slips from Renée's fingers, and she scoops up the briefcase again. "I'm…" She runs for the door.

simplicity

43 Gabriel

The little bungalow in Cushing has a fireplace and wood stove. Gabriel starts fires in both. He brews them cowboy coffee on the stove, hands Bailey a cup.

"Are you sure you were never a Boy Scout?" Bailey takes a sip. He sinks into a plaid wool couch, grabs at a velvet cushion, and props it under his head. "This coffee is pretty good. I wouldn't have the first clue how to work that weird stove. More skills from when you owned the hunting cabin?"

"I still own it. Although, I doubt I'll ever see it again." Gabriel scoops Bailey's legs off the couch to sit beside him with his own mug. "I would have liked to take you there."

"Hunting? Not really my thing. I had to go to child therapy after watching *Bambi*."

Gabriel laughs, only Bailey has ever made him laugh. As good as it feels, it hurts in his chest, his heart.

"I'm totally serious, I stopped eating meat and everything. Peyton starved me for a whole day, then took me out for burgers. He said if I didn't knock it off, he wouldn't make me anything to eat for a week, and then we would go for venison. That asshole."

Gabriel threads a hand through Bailey's curly mop of hair. "Where were your parents?"

231

"My dad was on a business trip that week, and my mom had the flu…" Bailey pouts, looks down into the black depths of his coffee mug. "At least, that's what I thought at the time." He leans his head against Gabriel's shoulder. "I'm fucking stupid."

"You aren't. You just believed what you'd been told. You believed a better story." He presses a kiss to Bailey's temple. *This…* "I would have liked to take you to the hunting cabin to get away from everything else, everyone else. I want to forget every bad thing in my life and protect you from the bad things in yours…"

"It doesn't work like that. At least, I don't think it does. Those things stay with you, they stay inside you." Bailey sets his coffee mug on the floor and slides onto Gabriel's lap, he rings his arms around Gabriel's neck. "But we can put new things there. Like…the people we help. The community we build." Nonstop eating has put some more weight on Bailey's frame, and the bruises and scratches have faded. His bones don't lay right under the skin like they did. Bailey leans in until his lips brush against Gabriel's. They kiss, then kiss again. Twine together on the scratchy wool of the couch. Bailey's hands search underneath his clothes, caress his skin, the dark parts of Gabriel's past that he'd thought would always be with him. He grips Bailey tighter, as close as he can.

When he wakes, Bailey lies open-mouthed and snoring on his chest. The fire has died down to embers. A moment of confusion, then a pounding on the door has Gabriel on his feet. "Just a second!" He throws his shirt back over his shoulders, zips his pants.

Shane waits on the bungalow's front porch, a shotgun in his hands. "Someone's here."

Gabriel blinks, tries to clear his head. "My sister? She came *alone*?"

"Someone else. An army guy named Lanson. He wants to meet with you, negotiate. Says he wants to cut a deal."

***

Gabriel makes Shane wait out front while he changes into a dark suit, combs his hair.

Bailey watches him with solemn eyes. "Is it—?"

"No." Not Bailey's brother, not Gabriel's sister. "I'm actually not sure what this is."

"I *can* actually tell when you're lying, you know." Bailey narrows his eyes, but with the long curling lashes, he looks no more threatening than a kitten. Gabriel stifles his smile.

He places his hands on Bailey's shoulders. "I think someone wants to even out the odds, if it comes to that…"

"Gabriel, what the hell are you talking about? Even out the odds how?"

"I just told you that I'm not sure what—"

"Oh, my God," Bailey throws his arms up. "That's it—I'm coming with you."

***

Shane drives them back to the refinery, and Bailey agrees to wait in the Land Rover for Gabriel to question their visitor. A square-jawed man in jeans and an army parka waits under guard in the back office. He looks like he fluctuates between wanting to salute and sneer when Gabriel walks in.

Before he can introduce himself, Gabriel does it for him. "Your name is Patrick Lanson, originally from North Carolina. Older brother, father, grandfather also in the military, now presumed dead. You started at the base as a lieutenant, then worked under Dandridge since right after the outbreak. I think he called himself a general, but was still officially a colonel… I've taken in a lot of your former soldiers. I hope you aren't thinking of getting them back. They won't want to leave." Gabriel takes a seat behind the metal desk, motions to the chair facing it. "Why don't you sit down and tell me why you're here?"

"I came to Olde Town first, some kid with a purple and blue mohawk brought me here."

"Yes."

"God, you and her are both calculating bastards." Patrick Lanson falls into the seat Gabriel pointed toward. "But your sister is too much under the spell of that psycho football player. My first mistake was letting him live after he pulled that stunt sneaking in the barricade. But introducing him to your sister was a fucking disaster." Lanson wipes at his mouth. He's gotten worked up enough to start spitting his words, face bright red. "They're getting ready to move against you, take this refinery and the rest of your territory. And you won't be able to stop them."

Gabriel forces all his muscles still, his hands, his face. "Because they have guns. Artillery?"

"No," Lanson scoffs. "I destroyed all the artillery before giving the city to Renée and Peyton. He's an animal. He would have demolished everything he laid eyes on, and your sister would have just cheered him on. But, guns? Yeah, I've got guns. And I know you think you turned my guys, but…" Instead of looking smug, Lanson leans forward, meets Gabriel's eyes. "Actually, kid, in a way you did turn them. But they're still my guys."

"I see. This was always the plan."

"Get the city back for me, and I'll trade openly with you. All the pharmaceuticals you want. The barricade open to Feathertons. All I ask is that you take out Peyton and your sister. You want that, too, don't you?"

44 Renée

At the station, Renée lets Peyton shove a bottle of Stoli in her shaking hands. Now that the temperature has dropped, they keep all the liquor on a stoop outside with an armed guard on it. A waste of manpower, not that it matters anymore. "I don't think we can contain this. Can we? The city is overrun…" She takes a swig of the vodka to stop herself from babbling. She'd stomped on the gas and raced to the police station from the courthouse, determined not to encounter any more of the feral sick without Peyton at her side.

"Meh," Peyton shrugs. "The burbs were like this when I first started cracking." He takes a seat beside her on the curb outside the station. For once, she finds comfort in the loud music, the constant target practice, the strobing disco light. No creature would want to come anywhere near this cacophonous place. Peyton slides the bottle from her fingers, takes his own swig, and hands it back. "Maybe we should ditch and come back in the spring. I bet most of them will die off from exposure."

"Leave…and come…" she sputters. "What about the people here? We can't just *abandon* them."

"Why the fuck not? All they do is complain. Let them fend for themselves and then see how much they want to throw coffee mugs at me when—"

"Shut. Up." Renée throws the Stoli bottle into the street, presses her fingertips into her temples. "We need more fighters. We need fuel."

One of her officers shoots the spot where the vodka bottle crashed, rapid fire bullets turning the broken chunks to dust. Peyton laughs. Then turns a scornful look on her. "You keep saying that, but you don't do anything."

"I thought once my brother realized…" Renée pounds a fist against her denim-covered thigh. "We have *guns*. We have *soldiers*. I thought he would jump at the chance to avoid…"

Peyton shakes his head. "Gabriel's no saint. You thought he'd come crawling to trade just to avoid a fight. Man, that's not the guy

I know." He slings an arm around her shoulders. "Come on… You want the refinery, babe? Let's go get the refinery."

***

They fill the army truck, and two Hummers with the last of the gasoline. Peyton shoots into the air, gets everyone's attention. "Do not use up all the ammo before Cushing, okay?" He winks at Renée. "See? I'm doing good here. Cheer up."

But that warning to her fighters only reminds her of Lanson, of his warning the same thing after they intercepted the tanker. And the fact Lanson is missing. Peyton had passed around the news that the former army officer hadn't shown for his patrol. "His place looked clean. Locked door. But it's a walk from the western barricade, so he might have got jumped."

Brinda had agreed with him. "Now that winter is here, the sick cannot find mice or—cats, dogs. They're hungry." She'd also sighed and raised her scarred eyebrow. "But I don't think we need him. He didn't do much around here."

To Renée's shock, even the former soldiers agreed with Brinda. They shrug off Lanson's absence, all of them eager to hit the road. To fire their guns at living targets. It doesn't seem to matter to any of them that the living targets are people—healthy people.

Does it matter to her?

"You're better than this, Renny. You're better than either of them, and so am I."

She sits in the passenger side of the truck, Brinda driving. They fly down the dark highway, bouncing over cracks and debris, swerving around vehicles, bumping over dead animals. Dead *people.* Brinda opens the window to smoke, and the snowy wind howls past, making the truck cab too loud to talk. Renée steals glances at her. *Who were you before all this? Someone strong. Someone who loved your family. Someone who wouldn't get too bothered by the scars you'd wear after the virus.*

Renée closes her eyes for a moment and pictures her old face. Renée had never been ugly…just plain…ordinary. But, that hadn't been good enough for the people who should have loved her for her. She shakes her head of the melancholy thoughts.

Focus!

Brinda finishes her cigarette and closes the window. She checks the rearview mirror, acts perfectly at ease, while Renée feels like she wants to claw her own skin off. *What the hell is wrong with me?*

"I think Lanson would have sent a scout ahead…" Renée says. "Someone to look for traps, report back on manpower, that kind of thing."

Brinda just makes a noncommittal humming noise, like Renée commented on the weather instead of the battle they're driving into. Peyton's "plan" has them barreling in, guns blazing. "Shoot the place up and take over," his only instructions. And Renée has no expertise to counter that plan. No one willing to listen to alternatives. Gunfire and laughter erupt behind her. Not even Peyton can stick to his "Don't waste ammo" command. She can hear him whoop and shout, unloading his M16 into the black night. The trip feels both long and not long enough.

She killed Gabriel once. She can do it again.

"You're better than this, Renny…"

And, then what will she do? Abandon the city she fought so hard to take? Set up shop in Cushing? Live there with Peyton and the rest of his violent mob of hangers-on to drink all day, to play games, to destroy?

She'd wanted the city because it would have impressed her father. *But, Maurice is dead.* And nothing she did, *nothing*, would have ever been enough to eclipse the son he'd begged Renée's vain, selfish mother for. Pauline would advise Renée to keep attached to Peyton, someone with status, someone who could get what she wants. Her father would have washed his hands of her city long ago, he cared

237

about power and image too much to care about heating buildings and distributing food. "I'm not like them."

Brinda flicks her eyes from the path of the headlight beams to Renée. "What was that, ma'am?"

"You're better than this, Renny. You're better than either of them…" She won't abandon the people who depend on her, the city.

The lights of Cushing, of the refinery, appear on the flat horizon. "Pull over," she tells Brinda. "I'm changing the plan."

45 Gabriel

They didn't send a scout, at least not one Gabriel's people caught. But, Gabriel hadn't expected one. Gabriel did expect firepower. Peyton at the front. Gabriel had seen it brewing in Peyton before Bailey popped. And when Peyton came to deliver Via back to Case… A post-apocalyptic *suicide by cop*—where Peyton would put Gabriel in the role to deliver justice. Not for all the terrible things Peyton has done, but for what Peyton believes he *didn't* do, save his brother. *Save Bailey.*

When his sister and Peyton do show, they run two Hummers and a truck right onto the flat of spike strips surrounding the town. Feathertons spread them out like picnic blankets across every entrance to the refinery.

From outside the Land Rover, Gabriel hears Shane shout commands to surround.

"Now!"

Flood lights switch on. *There they are.* Inside a circle lit to daylight in the middle of a starless night. Three vehicles, all filled with children holding guns. Ill-fitting winter clothes, scrawny arms, runny noses. They blink against the bright lights, at the faces of teenagers just like themselves. All of them just kids trying to survive.

They aren't shooting…Why?

"I guess this is it?" Bailey shrugs out of the puffy down coat Gabriel insisted he wear.

"Let me go first." Gabriel's voice comes out as jittery as his heart, his breathing, his hands as they reach for Bailey. *Keep it together. You are in control.* But no, he is *not* in control.

"Are you kidding me? They *might* shoot me. But you?" Bailey stuffs the coat into the seat beside Gabriel. "This is why you brought me, isn't it?"

"I changed my mind." Gabriel dives forward, follows Bailey out of the car.

Hugo cracks open the driver side door. "Boss? Need me to—?" He points at Bailey.

Bailey rounds on him, open-mouthed. "Oh, my God. Get back in that car, Hugo, or I will kick your ass…or something." He points at Gabriel the way Peyton would have. "I'm doing this."

Gabriel takes hold of Bailey's arm, hauls him close. "Fine. With me, then." Shane steps out of the darkness with his shotgun. "Do not fire without my command," Gabriel tells him.

"Got it, boss."

They wind through a blockade of Featherton vans and trucks as they approach the disabled army vehicles. Renée steps out of the passenger side of the truck. "Gabriel? I came to talk." Despite the light in her eyes, she must see him, know him. Her face has turned in his direction. *She could order those kids behind her to open fire, to kill me, if she wanted. Is that her plan?*

The woman on the driver side of the truck gets out. Dark eyes squint from a scarred face. She moves toward Renée's side, pulls a black handgun from a belt holster. "I'm serious," Renée says. "I just want to talk."

Before Gabriel can answer, Peyton jumps down from the back of the truck. "What's there to talk about?" The floodlight makes a halo of his blond hair. An M16 in his hands, a sneer on his face, he looks like a furious angel come to wreak havoc on all the apocalypse.

Bailey yanks free of Gabriel's hold. "Peyton—Peyton it's me!" Bailey runs forward, and the woman beside Renée stiffens. She levels a gun at Bailey's head.

Gabriel darts from the shadows, hands out. "Stop!" He tackles Bailey to the ground just as a shot rings out. Gabriel spreads his body over Bailey's. Above them, someone screams. More shooting…yelling…

"You're okay. You're okay…" Gabriel's heart jackhammers in his chest. Panic builds inside him. "You're okay, Bailey." One of the old fits creeps under Gabriel's skin. The tunnel vision, the shaking. A storm of sound surrounds him, but it all feels muffled beyond Gabriel's awareness of Bailey's body underneath his own. "You're okay—"

"Gabriel. Get off me."

"They're shooting—"

"No one is shooting." Bailey elbows Gabriel's side, and he rolls them both up to sitting. He's right. No one is shooting. Spit fills Gabriel's mouth and he swallows it back down. *You are in—*

"Bailey?" Peyton stands over them, absolute chaos behind him. The other kids in the truck all shouting, Renée screaming at him. Peyton turns and fires his gun into the air. "Everyone shut the fuck up!" He points his gun at the woman from the driver side of the truck, her prone body face down in the dirt. "Fucking bitch pointed a gun at my brother." Peyton takes a fist of Bailey's sweater, yanks him up and behind him. "And anyone else who does the same thing is getting a bullet just like fucking Brinda."

Peyton grips Bailey's chin in his free hand. Bailey's eyes have gone wide and shocked. He tries to twist his face to see the body of the woman Peyton shot.

"Is she dead?" Bailey squeaks.

But, the girl on the ground moans before anyone can answer. Renée kneels beside her, pushes her long black braid away to check the injury. Gabriel's sister looks chalk-white, panicked. Like she's going into shock. "Peyton, you fucking piece of shit—!"

Gabriel gets back on his feet. *Bailey is safe.* He's safe with Peyton, and Gabriel can think again. He waves to a point in the dark outside the floodlights, toward the spot he knows Caroline Vu and Rhea Han wait to treat any wounded. Gabriel keeps his voice calm, soothing, like he's talking to a wild animal. "Renée, let me get help for that girl. I have medics. I can—"

Peyton ignores Gabriel, ignores everyone, shakes his brother's chin, looking into Bailey's eyes. "You cured him," he says to Gabriel. Peyton drags Bailey into his chest, a lot like Gabriel did back by the Land Rover. "You cured him," Peyton repeats. He throws his arms around his brother. Buries his face on top of Bailey's puffy curls and sobs. "You cured him… You cured him…"

Finally, the children in the truck and the Hummers lower their guns.

46 Renee

They had destroyed the nursery, every part of it wrecked.

Gabriel bit at his thumb. "They're coming. They'll be mad."

Across from him, Renée's legs trembled. She started breathing hard like she did right before she cried. "You started it—you *made* me."

Then Gabriel pulled his thumb away. "I don't care. I still hate them." He balled his hands into fists.

***

Daddy entered the nursery first, his eyes went right to Gabriel, the way they always did. Mommy looked first at the broken chandelier, torn wire, shattered glass.

"I refuse to deal with these animals, Maurice. I'm going to the Hamptons compound until this is fixed." Pauline wrapped her long thin arms around herself, as if the room's destruction had changed the temperature.

Behind her, Nanny had appeared. "I'm so sorry, Mrs. Featheron, Mr. Featherton, but it's my day off, and I thought they were playing…"

Pauline swept from the room halfway through Nanny's apologies, she'd said she refused to deal with the children, and she meant it. Daddy would have to lure her back with presents and parties.

Daddy's face turned red, his wide nostrils flared like a bull. "Your room is right next door, because we expect you to—"

"It was my day off!" Nanny insisted. She burst into tears.

That only made Daddy's face redder. He pointed at Renée. "Get her cleaned up and put her in the guest room by the library." Then Daddy turned to Gabriel. "I'm tired of you acting like this. You're not a child."

"Yes. *I am* a—"

Daddy's hand cracked across Gabriel's face, knocked him to the ground with the broken pieces of the chandelier. "I'm not raising a child, I'm raising an heir."

Then, Nanny pulled Renée from the nursery to her own room next to it. She changed Renée into pink Barbie pajamas, ran a comb through Renée's golden hair, all while crying about how it was her day off and if Renée's father fired her, that she would have to live on the streets.

But, Renée kept seeing her father's hand, wide, thick with bulging rough knuckles, hit her brother. Would Daddy also hit *her*?

The guestroom bed felt too large, she had only ever slept in a twin bed beside Gabriel, and she couldn't sleep. Every sound, the chime of the grandfather clock, the patter of rain against the window, jolted her awake. When would Daddy come? She waited for him to slap her for her part in wrecking the nursery. She imagined his hand striking her with the loud smacking noise, the way he hit Gabriel. She braced for it. But, Daddy never came.

The next day, all her clothes and toys and books moved into the guestroom, too. It became *her* room. And, Daddy moved her brother to a room near his own. With no toys.

Her child-mind only recognized that Daddy wanted Gabriel close. She forgot the slap. She forgot Maurice taking away her brother's toys. She forgot that Gabriel was not allowed to be a child.

47 Renée

"Can you hear me?" Renée touches her fingers against Brinda's temple, to feel her pulse, the warmth radiating off her skin, the proof that she still lives.

"Ma'am?" Brinda blinks as her dark eyes strain to focus on Renée."Gah, my head…" She tries to sit up in her sickbed. Looks around the room decorated with posters of half-dressed women lying across racecar hoods, beer ads, and heavy metal bands. "What the fuck is this place?"

Renée laughs, slaps a hand over her mouth when it starts to morph into something else. Her eyes fill with tears. She makes herself swallow, breathe through it.

"You okay, ma'am?" Brinda gets one boot on the floor, pushes herself up on her elbows. "Are they holding you prisoner?"

Renée shakes her head. When she has control of herself, she pulls the hand away from her face. "Why don't you just call me Renée from now on?" Her voice sounds hoarse, not like herself.

"Call you—?" The scarred lips quirk. "I might be hearing things, my head's all fuzzy."

"Then, I'll just ask you again later…when you can be sure it isn't just your fuzzy head." Renée smiles, her heart thumping inside her chest, like it jolted back to life since Brinda opened her eyes. "Oh, and we aren't prisoners. Feahtertons set up this house as a triage in case we went with Peyton's plan—guns blazing. I think this room belonged to the teenage son." Renée reaches for a water glass and pitcher on the bedside table. "You had shrapnel in your forehead. There was a lot of blood, and you passed out. I'd thought Peyton had—" She busies herself pouring water, setting the pitcher back just so. Her hands shake, and her stomach flips over, and she's not sure why.

"Peyton?" Brinda's eyes lose focus for a second. She drinks down the water Renée gives her. "Peyton… Wait, I remember—that fucker shot me!"

"He says he aimed over your head."

Brinda dabs her fingers at her bloody hairline. "Damn… I guess it's good he did all that shooting practice on the way here."

Another laugh breaks free. Laugh…sob…Renée decides not to stifle either. "Yes, it is." She lays a hand on Brinda's sternum, pushes her back down to the bloodstained pillow. "Get some rest for now. I'll be back, but I need to step outside. My crime-lord brother wants to meet with me." With her free hand, Renée gestures to the door behind her. She stands, but Brinda grabs at the hand still resting against her chest, holds Renée in place.

"Be careful...Renée," says Brinda, then releases her strong grip so Renée can pull her hand free.

Renée smiles, can feel the heat in her face. "Don't worry. I can handle Gabriel."

***

Outside the little bungalow, Renée's brother waits for her in the dark, frozen front yard. He sits on a wooden bench swing facing an empty marble birdbath. Probably a beautiful spot in the spring and summer.

"Is she going to be alright?" Gabriel turns up the collar of his dark wool coat, stuffs his hands in the pockets.

Renée makes a scoffing sound. "Those *medics* say she is."

"Good." Gabriel nods, hunches deeper into his coat. Dawn has just begun to break across the little town, and the edges of the night sky turn steel gray as the winter sun appears. Renée takes a seat beside him on the bench, and Gabriel turns to her. "I'm holding Lieutenant Lanson here. He wanted me to help him to kill Peyton...and you."

Renée grits her teeth against a scream. *Breathe. You can handle this. You can handle anything.* She'd decided to make *this* her new mantra as she watched those medics pick shrapnel out of Brinda's scalp. Fuck Granny Featherton. Fuck Pauline. Fuck Maurice. Renée never needed any of them. She takes a steadying breath. "I need fuel for the city. And I need fresh food. I know we've had our... But, people are depending on me." She looks Gabriel over. He hasn't moved, perfectly composed, unlike the volatile boy she remembers. "I can trade pharmaceuticals for them, and I have engineers, electricians, other skilled workers that I could loan you—in exchange."

Gabriel nods, thinking it over. "I can fill two tankers for you right now...and we can start trades again. *Official* trades. But..." He sighs,

245

shakes his head. "I'll need to keep Peyton. I'm certain you've noticed by now, but without his brother—"

"*Please,* keep him. I'll be glad to take back that traitor Lanson, if it means *you* keep Peyton."

"I thought you might agree. Peyton can be…" Gabriel shakes his head again, and Renée can't smother a laugh. Her brother grins back at her, a smile she remembers from their games in the nursery, impish and secret.

Who are you now?

He studies her just as intently. Like he wonders about her, too.

Renée's boots push-off against icy blades of grass to rock the garden swing. She lets them sway back and forth for a minute. "If we're going to form some kind of…alliance…I want to know what happened to him. He had the virus?"

Gabriel's eyes close and his lips tighten and release. "He was infected…by me. But he committed suicide before it…before he popped."

Oh. She knew Maurice was dead, had assumed he'd caught the virus.

"I don't know what happened to Pauline. She was gone when I woke up, and he never said." Gabriel's eyes open again, and he looks at her with a pale blue gaze that matches her own. "I'm sorry."

"I couldn't care less about Pauline. And I wasn't asking about…our father. I meant the little brother. The curly-haired boy?"

"Oh, of course…" Gabriel's alabaster skin flushes. "Bailey…I didn't *cure* him." A smile tics her brother's mouth before he sobers and falls back into the cool, controlled, gang leader—the man she doesn't know.

I haven't known him for a long time. Not since Wellspring Institute, maybe earlier, maybe since his time in that Florida dojo.

"I've constructed medical safe houses, with running water, live food. Only the immune will work inside the houses. I want to give people a chance to survive, give them hope. I can help you set up the same if you like. You can even send your people to train under my team."

Her brother pulls a hand free of his pocket to rub a thumb over his bottom lip—the gesture so reminiscent of their father that grief lances Renée's heart.

No. Maurice is gone…and he never deserved my love. "Then, I suppose this is a truce." Renée holds out her right hand for Gabriel to shake. The first bright sunlight has traveled over the little scrubby yard to touch their swing.

Instead of shaking, Gabriel winds the fingers of his own right hand in hers, tips the swing so that it goes a little higher. "Yes, Renny. This is a truce."

Renée squeezes their palms together, leans back, turns her face to the rising sun. And the two of them watch the sky brighten from a shadowed, murky gray to a cloudless, cerulean blue.

please review this book

Reviews help authors more than you may think, so if you enjoyed *Survive the City*, please consider leaving a review at Goodreads or amazon. I would greatly appreciate it.

Review now at Goodreads.

about the author

Alex Timothy writes urban science fiction and fantasy stories, YA and angst. An ex-dancer with a sugar addiction and an overactive imagination, Alex spends a lot of time drinking coffee and pacing the room while muttering. It's hard to find what matters in this chaotic world.